PRIOR TO ARMAGEDDON
DAMASCUS
MT HERMON
SYRIA
MT. CARMEL
SEA OF GALILEE
MEGIDDO
MEDITERRANEAN SEA
JERUSALEM
ISRAEL
DEAD SEA
JORDAN
NEGEV
EGYPTIAN
SINAI
RADIO ACTIVE
WASTELAND
I. KIRK
93
RED SEA

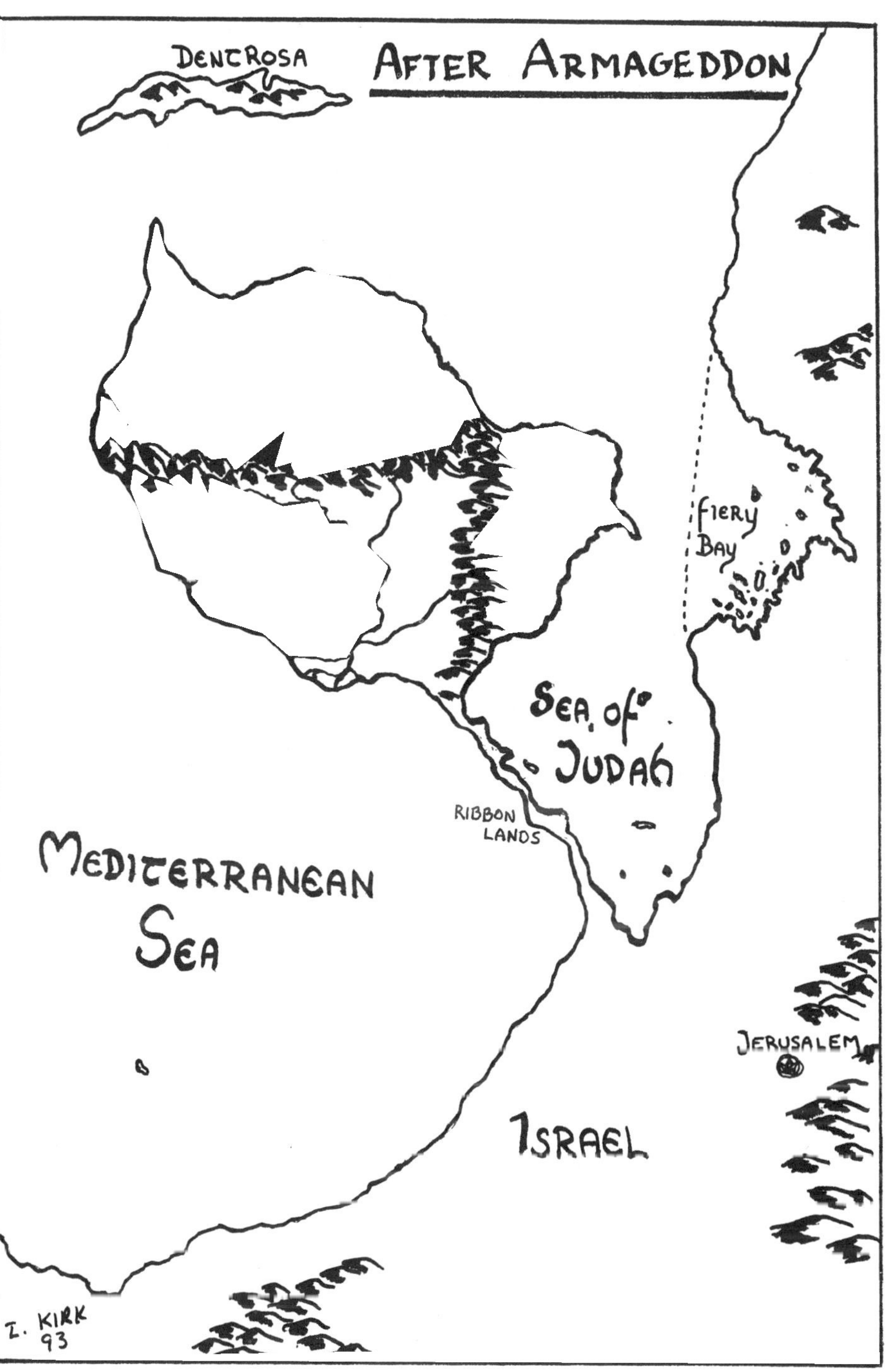
AFTER ARMAGEDDON
DENTROSA
FIERY BAY
SEA OF JUDAH
RIBBON LANDS
MEDITERRANEAN SEA
JERUSALEM
ISRAEL
I. KIRK 93

NEWLAND IN THE BEGINNING

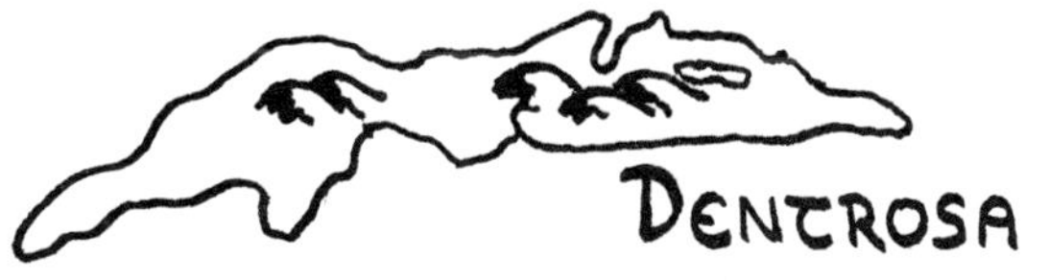

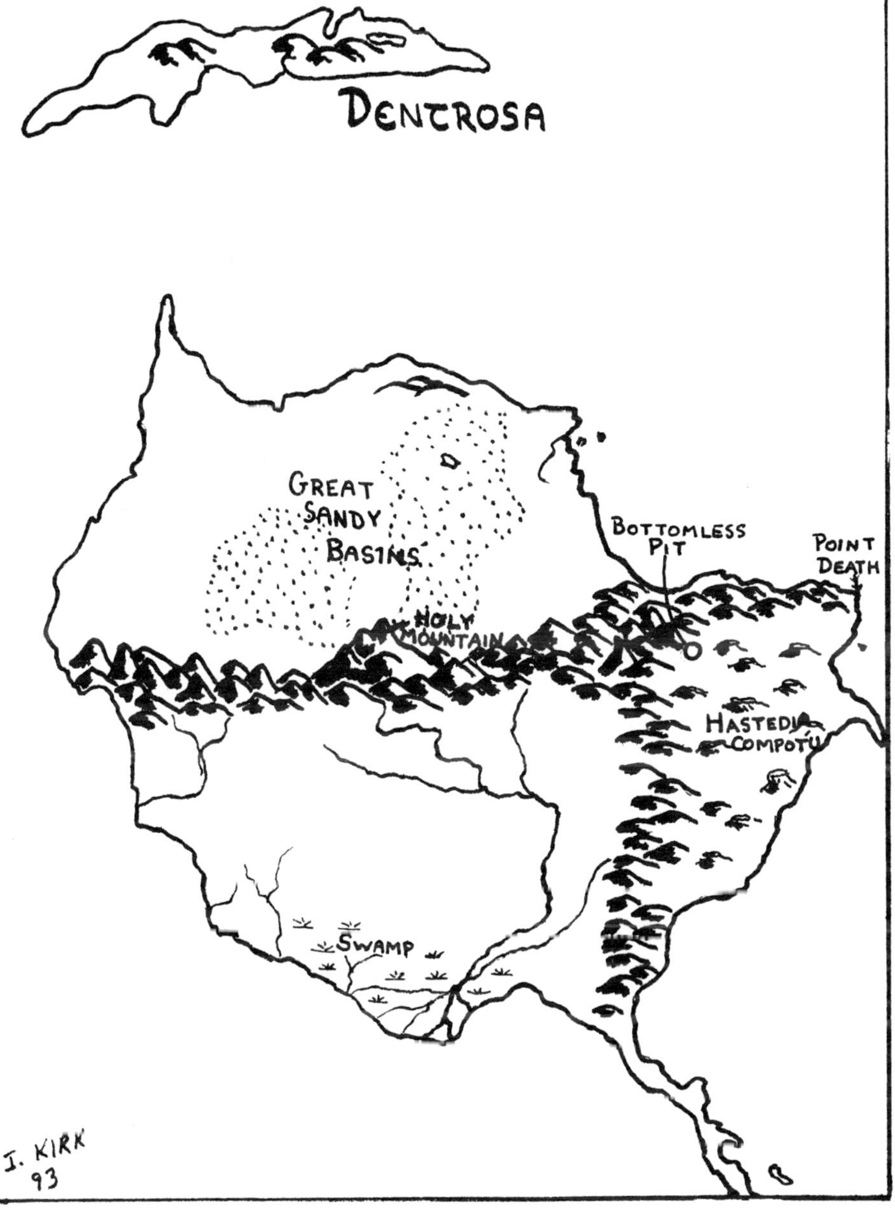
DENTROSA
GREAT
SANDY
BASINS
BOTTOMLESS
PIT
POINT
DEATH
HOLY
MOUNTAIN
HASTEDIA
COMPOTÚ
SWAMP
J. KIRK
93

Newland Near the End

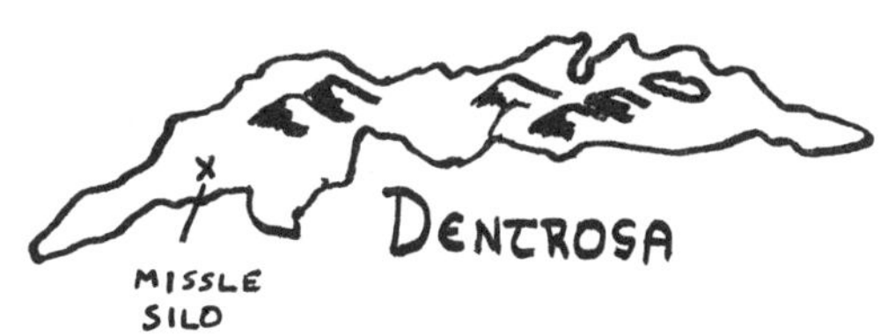

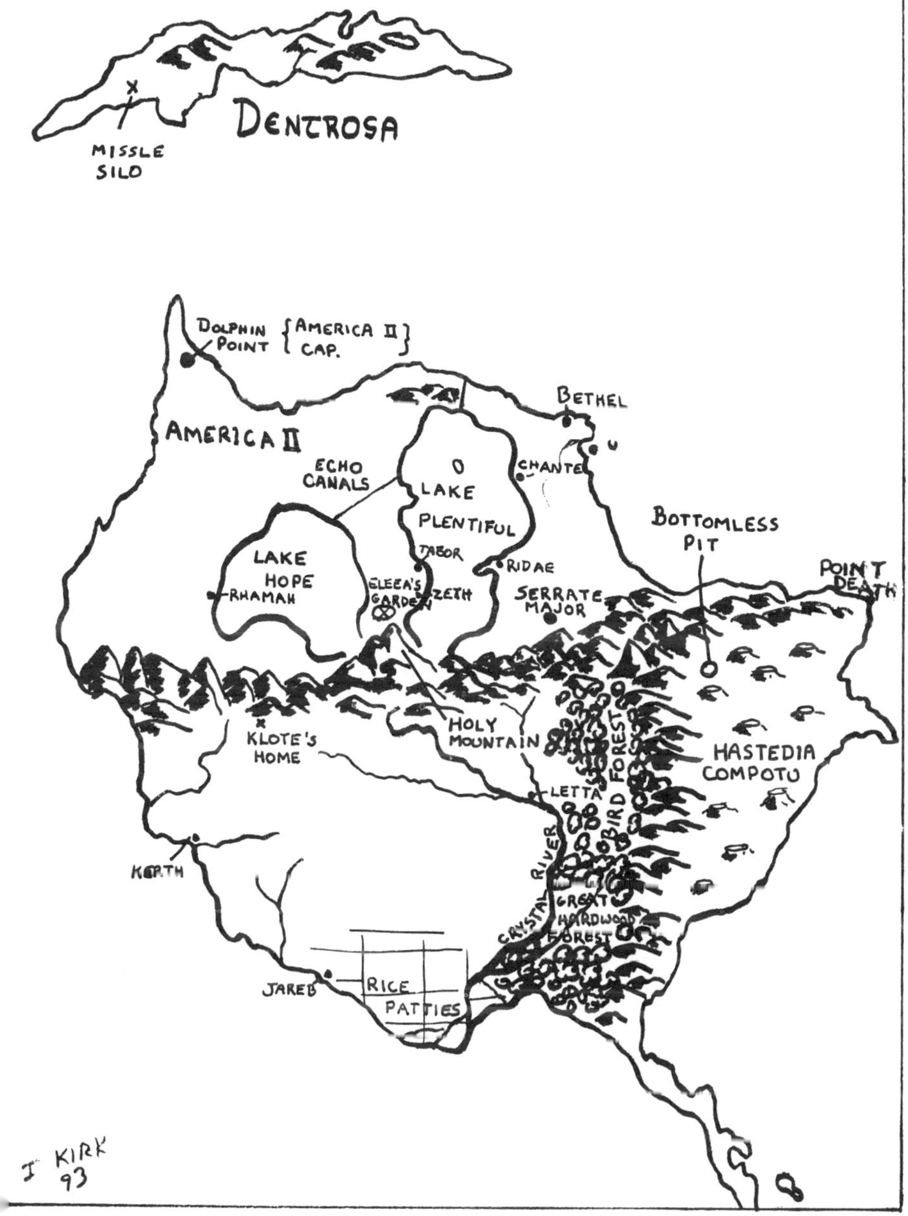
DENTROSA
MISSLE SILO
DOLPHIN POINT
{AMERICA II CAP.}
AMERICA II
BETHEL
ECHO CANALS
LAKE PLENTIFUL
CHANTE
BOTTOMLESS PIT
LAKE HOPE
RHAMAH
TABOR
RIDAE
POINT DEATH
ELEEA'S GARDEN
ZETH
SERRATE MAJOR
HOLY MOUNTAIN
KLOTE'S HOME
LETTA
BIRD FOREST
HASTEDIA COMPOTU
CRYSTAL RIVER
GREAT HARDWOOD FOREST
KERTH
JAREB
RICE PATTIES
I KIRK 93

the

LAST SHALL be FIRST

by

J.E. Kirk

APOGEE ARTS PRESS
GLENDALE, ARIZONA

 Published byApogee Arts Press, Box 238, 5126 W. Olive Ave.Glendale Az 85302

Cover artwork by Jim Kirk.
Maps by Jonah Kirk.
First printing 1993
Printed in the United States of America

Library of Congress Catalog Card Number: 93-70050
ISBN 0-9635066-7-6

This book was written with two basic goals in mind: to provide an adult audience, both male and female, with good Christian entertainment, and to honor God and His son, Jesus Christ.

THE LAST SHALL BE FIRST was written from the pre-millennial, post-tribulation viewpoint, because this is my understanding of the scriptures. However, it was never my intent for this book to be an apologetic work arguing for this viewpoint. Also, this novel was never intended to be used for doctrinal teaching of any kind.

THE LAST SHALL BE FIRST is fiction. All characters in this book are fictitious, and based only on ideas in my own mind and not on any real people, alive or dead.

I am very thankful for the creation of Apogee Arts Press which has made possible the publication of THE LAST SHALL BE FIRST.

I would like to give special thanks to my wife, Ann, and my son, Jonah, for their comments, constructive criticisms, and the many hours they both spent editing my manuscript. Both have Bachelor of Arts degrees in English.

But most of all, I am thankful for the scriptures, where many of the ideas for THE LAST SHALL BE FIRST, found their origin.

I dedicate this book to Ann, my loving wife and best friend, who somehow has managed to put up with me for over 14 years.

the LAST SHALL be FIRST

PREFACE

Two men walked quickly across the hot earth of Hastedia Compotu. One was black, and one white. The black man, shorter, had broad powerful shoulders, and was clothed in a brown robe that ended above the knees. Around his waist was a thick leather belt, and from this hung a great steel sword. His face had the look of a fierce but holy warrior.

His companion, thinner, was dressed in a long, richly embellished, purple robe. A look of worry was on his honest face. The pair were covered with the dust of the many miles they had traveled together.

Hastedia Compotu, more commonly called the Land of the Dead, was a blackened desert marred by numerous pits that sank deeply into the bowels of the planet. From these spewed a thick poisonous smoke that rose high into the air, then as it cooled, fell back to earth coating everything it touched with a sticky black resin. Deep ravines filled with boiling pitch crisscrossed the land. Dotting the country were little conical shaped hills, looking very much like giant ant hills. Some hills had caves in their sides. From a few of these flowed a stinking yellow water that collected in the depressions of the land, forming ponds where nothing would ever grow or live. As the two men approached one of the hills, the thinner of the two men reached into his pocket, and produced part of a crumpled note, and read it for the hundredth time:

PREFACE

Father, we have been followed. Please send help. We are hiding in the cave of the hill with twin peaks, almost due west of the castle, and just north of a great ravine. You will recognize the place by the pile of animal bones outside. So far all of us are...

The rest of the note had been lost.

"Look at that hill, Michael--twin peaks, and the cave. And--and over there, the ravine. And look, see the bones? This has to be the place. It just has to be."

"My king, I pray to God that this is the place, yet I beg you, please do not get your hopes up too high. We have been to so very many of these caves in this terrible land."

"I know, Michael, I know, but the bones--the other caves didn't have them. I'm going over to take a look. Stay here and keep a lookout."

"My king, it should be I who investigates. This could be a trap."

"No, Michael, I shall go," interrupted the king. "It was my idiotic idea that allowed my son and his party to go through this land of death, so it should be I who investigates. And besides, if it is a trap, remember that it was you who first taught me that I cannot die. And it was you who also taught me the foolishness of fear. And one more thing, Michael, remember that it is you who is mortal and not I."

"As you wish, my lord, but I still think that it should be I ..."

The king had already turned and started toward the cave before Michael finished speaking. He took a deep breath of the foul air, and watched King Bounteous go down into the ravine, climb the steep opposite bank effortlessly, then jog the remaining hundred yards to the cave. The king stopped outside the entrance for a moment, then disappeared into the interior of the hill.

PREFACE

The warrior seated himself on a blackened boulder, watching and listening for anything out of the ordinary. As he waited, he pulled a small leaf out of his pocket, placed it in his mouth and began chewing. Michael looked at the land all around him and remembered how it had come to be. He also remembered other things, like the day he had laid aside his authority and office as archangel to become human. So much had taken place since he first met King and Queen Bounteous. And to think that had been almost a thousand years before. Now Satan was loose again, and he, Michael, could not do a thing about it. He could not meet the demon on equal terms, archangel to archangel. Satan was far too powerful for him. But perhaps soon....

Michael's keen sense of hearing detected a soft crying coming from the cave. He was up instantly, sword in hand, and seconds later had crossed the ravine and the hundred yards to the cave. He whispered a prayer to God as he charged into the opening. The walls of the cave were lined with lighted torches made of straw and pitch that illuminated the grisly scene on the floor. They had finally found the prince and those who were with him--all laid dead in puddles of their own blood on the cold, stone floor. King Bounteous sat rocking back and forth in sorrow, holding the head of his dead son on his lap. It was obvious that the prince and those with him had been tortured before they had been slaughtered.

Michael seated himself next to his king, put his powerful arm around his monarch, then cried for the evil that had been done to these whom God had created. It was the first time that he had cried in his ten thousand years of existence.

Fifteen minutes later: "Come, my lord. It is time for us to go. There is nothing that we can do here. Come." Michael gently helped the king to his feet, then steered him toward the entrance of the cave.

"No, no, we can't go, Michael. We've got to bury them. We've got to."

"Come, my lord. I will bury them," the warrior said, helping the grief-stricken king outside the cave, then across the uneven ground. When they were a safe distance from the cave, Michael drew his sword and pointed it toward the death hill, screaming: "Estanso El comathea haute jebrad heyett," (May God bury those who belong to Him). The earth convulsed, knocking King Bounteous off his feet. When the monarch recovered and lifted his eyes toward the hill, it was no more. In its place was a heap of smoking rubble. The prince and the others had been buried, and would remain so until the Lord Himself brought them forth to live again.

The king wiped the tears from his eyes, then looked at his companion. The brown robe was gone, replaced by a gleaming white one. Michael, who had already been a huge man, was at least two feet taller. Protruding from his back were the powerful wings the angel had lost so many years before. Michael was again the powerful archangel he had been at the time of his creation.

"So, my friend, the Lord has returned your office to you."

"Yes, my king. My days as your companion and teacher are at a close, yet friends we shall be through eternity. God created me to be an archangel, a covering cherub, and a warrior. The time for me to fight the Evil One draws nigh.

"Come, I will accompany you for a little while longer, then I must begin my search for Satan." Michael's powerful hands lifted the king from the ground as if he were a small child. "Come, my lord. We must go to Jerusalem. Time itself draws quickly to a close."

PART ONE

ENDINGS

CHAPTER ONE

and the light of the sun shall be sevenfold.
Isaiah 30:26

The star that had lighted its part of the heavens for thousands of years was dying. The process started years before, and was evidenced by sunspots and gigantic solar flares of superheated gasses shooting thousands of miles into space. Just before its death it would swell to many times normal size, change from a whitish yellow color to a brilliant red, then radiate a million times as much energy as normal. Any planet held too closely in orbit around this RED GIANT would be burned to a crisp.

Then, after a very short life as a Red Giant, the star would die. As the last of its hydrogen fuel was used, the star would stop emitting light completely, begin to cool, and finally shrink to a dense black object barely a tenth its original size. It would remain in this condition until the end of time, unless God willed it otherwise.

Scientists whose jobs it was to watch the heavens seemed not to recognize the death signs of the star. It might have been that they were too preoccupied with proposing or modifying their theories dealing with the beginnings of the universe--theories that had no place for God as the Creator of it all. And because of their foolishness, God hid His truths from these men.

And so it was that these learned men would never recognize that the end of history, as man has always known it, was at hand.

But what of the other billions of humans on earth? Did none of them realize that the end was near? Unfortunately there were very few. Most were far too busy engaged in their favorite sport: WAR.

----

and they gathered them together
to the place called, in Hebrew, Armageddon.
Rev. 16:16

The stars and moon hid behind the thick clouds of springtime. The blackness of the night was pierced only by blinding spotlights aimed at thousands of narrow trenches that were being hurriedly completed. The excavations would hold the two million soldiers of the UNITED WORLD ORDER. The trenches and the men were there to stop the advancing eastern hordes. The soldiers working in the trenches were drenched with sweat. Many fainted from exhaustion, because even though it was only springtime in central Israel, it was broiling hot.

As the trenches were completed, the profane lights blinked off one by one, and the men slumped heavily to the bottoms of their diggings gasping for breath. At the bottom of one of these trenches was a soldier named Baker Dansford. As Baker sat in the darkness, he alternately tried to catch his breath and gulp the warm water from his canteen, and more than anything else on earth, he was wishing that he was at some cheap bar with an ice cold beer in his hands.

Baker and those with him were in the most eastern of the trenches. The enemy was expected to be coming from the northeast, so he and his outfit would be among the first to engage the orientals and their allies, and of course they would also be among the first to die.

Private Baker Dansford was a huge bear of a man thirty years old. Most would have simply described him as a hell raiser--always the first to laugh, the first to plan some sort of mischief, and of course the first to be involved in a "friendly" fist fight, especially if there had been too much drinking going on. And because of his size, just about anyone Baker ever met was at least a little intimidated by him.

But there was another side of Baker, a secret side. A side that was driven to kill, that relished torturing something alive. Baker loved the sight of blood, and seeing the fear in the victim's eyes just before death. But now, the tables were turned. It was Baker Dansford who was the one tasting fear, and he did not like the taste of it one bit.

Across the trench from Baker was a tiny prune of a man fairly new to the outfit, appropriately nicknamed "Little Jerry", or just "Little" for short. Little was the exact opposite of Baker. Aside from the fact that he was about half Baker's size, he was quiet and serious, and at least ten years older than most of the others in the outfit. Scuttlebutt had it that Little had once been an officer, had been busted for some reason or other, jailed, and finally released on the condition that he serve as near to the front line as they could possibly get him.

Baker hated Little, and everything he stood for. He really didn't know what Little did stand for, but it was enough that the tiny man had been to college, was quiet, and refused to participate in the drinking and sex parties Baker and some of the others loved to indulge in. But there was something even beyond even this. Something that Baker could not put his finger on. There was a basic disharmony between their spirits, though Baker would never have put it like that. And besides, Baker had a strong suspicion that Little was a Christian.

Little leaned against the side of the cool earthen trench, still breathing heavily from his exertion. His frail little body had never been designed for hard physical labor such as digging trenches; his hands were blistered, and he, like the others, was soaked with sweat. Little took his glasses off, cleaned them as best he could with the bottom of his shirt, then replaced them on his round little face, and closed his eyes.

"Hey, Little, when you gonna give us the low down on you getting busted and sent up here?" Baker said, trying to start an argument for the sake of some entertainment.

Little opened his eyes and stared at Baker through the darkness. "What do you want to know for?"

The question caught the big man off guard. Baker half expected the undersized man to just keep quiet and ignore him as he usually did. "Just--just wondering, that's all."

"Yah, Little, why don't ya tell us all about it," said one of the other guys who was a friend of Baker.

Little paid no attention to the others, but kept staring at Baker, as if he could see something the others couldn't. And even in the thick darkness at the bottom of the trench, this staring began bothering Baker Dansford.

"What ya looking at, runt? Ain't ya never seen a real man before?" Baker spit out.

Little finally took a deep breath, closed his eyes, and rested his head against the cool earth.

"Hey guys, lookie here. I think we got us a real, live hero down here. I mean he don't even know the meaning of fear, right Little?" Baker went on. "I mean here we are facing death and what does he do? He sleeps. Now ain't that something? Hey, Little, you a hero? Come on now, tell us the secret of your bravery! I mean we all want to be BIG, brave men like you. Come on, 'Little', pleeeease."

Little opened his eyes and again stared at the big man. "Baker, I'm no hero, but I can tell you what the difference is between you and me: I'm at peace with myself and with my God. I'm ready to die, but you are not. My suggestion is that you do some heavy praying and do it now." The little man paused for a second, obviously troubled, then continued. "Baker, I mean it. You will never see this time tomorrow. Use your last hours wisely."

The snickering from those nearby stopped. Baker had been in the process of lighting a cigarette; now both the cigarette and matches fell to the bottom of the trench. "You a prophet or something?" Baker growled. "You so close to the gods that you can look at a person and tell that he's gonna die?" The big man laughed, but it was a forced, phony laugh. "Or maybe you plan on doing this killing yourself. That right little man?"

"Baker, there are not gods, but God. Make peace with Him, for a messenger from the Angel of Death stands at your side waiting for permission to take you to an eternal hell."

Baker's light complexion turned a beet red, but was hidden by the darkness. "Why you little #*&%$&#. I'm gonna show you who's gonna die." Baker was on his feet in a second, grabbed Little's helmet and threw it out of the trench, then made a fist intending to smash it into the little man's face.

"Cool it, Baker, NOW! That's an order." The words came from Maddox, a tall skinny shadow ten feet away. Maddox had three stripes on his sleeve, and was the only man in the company Baker respected physically. "Baker, you started this little hubbub, now you can end it. Save your hate for the Nips; they'll be here sooner than any of us want."

The others in the trench listened as best they could but remained silent. Baker cursed the little man, spat on him, then shuffled a long way down the trench toward his buddies and away from Little. "This ain't the end of it, little man," Baker snarled as he left. "Sarge ain't always gonna be around ta change your diapers."

Baker seated himself forty feet down the trench. "That's telling him," or "way to go man," his buddies said as he seated himself among them. But a few who really knew Baker Dansford, got cold chills down their spines knowing that he would get even. He had to. Baker never made threats to anyone unless he meant to carry them out.

Little calmly watched the big man leave, then bowed his head in prayer. Sergeant Andy Maddox could barely see Little in the darkness, but heard him mumbling something with his eyes closed. "Hey, Little. Are you religious?" He said, barely loud enough for Little to hear.

Little opened his eyes and looked at the man sitting down the trench. Maddox was so thin that "bony" was more accurate than even skinny. But he was a tough, rugged type of bony. He was over six feet four inches tall, had strong callused hands, and a large beak of a nose that insisted upon getting sunburned no matter what kind of hat he wore. When he was younger, Andy Maddox had been a United States champion in judo, in his weight class. But that was in the past, in the years when there had been time for sports, and when there had been a United States of America. Back then, Andy had also gotten his black belt in karate, and that was why it was he who had trained the men under him in hand-to-hand combat. It was also the reason why Baker

Dansford knew better than to start anything with the fast moving scarecrow of a sergeant.

"Not really religious, Sarge; I'm a Christian, but sinner would be just as accurate." The sergeant scooted closer to Little, and in a voice that could barely be heard, "I figured all you Christians were dead by now. Sure killed a lot of you guys in the past seven years."

Little stared at the sergeant in much the same way he had stared at Baker only minutes before. "Sergeant Maddox, I believe that you are not far from the Kingdom of God."

"Little, what are you talking about?"

"Sarge, this is going to be hard for you to believe, but God has opened my eyes; I can see the spiritual forces of good and evil fighting all around us. And I also know that God is waiting for you to chose between HIM and Satan."

"You're NUTS, Little. Nuts, crazy, or something just as bad!"

"No sarge, I'm not 'NUTS.' Didn't you hear what I said to Baker--about him dying?"

"Well, yah, but...."

"Well, it's true, Sarge. I can see a messenger from the Angel of Death standing next to him more clearly than I can see you. Baker will be dead before tomorrow ends. But what I didn't tell him was that the rest of us will probably be dead, too, if not tomorrow then the next day or the next. Because if I'm right, this war between us and the Eastern States Confederacy, is going to be the final battle on earth. The Battle of Armageddon."

"Little, people have been saying that about every war since I don't know when. This is going to be the Battle of Armageddon, or that is going to be the Battle of Armageddon. But we're all still here, ain't we? And there hasn't been an Armageddon yet. In fact, I'd bet my next paycheck that this whole Armageddon thing is just myth--a fairy tale."

Little dug into his shirt pocket, and produced a wad of ragged dirty paper and a small pen light flashlight. The paper looked like it had once been part of a small book. Little carefully began thumbing through the pages holding the little flashlight in his mouth. When he found what he was looking for, he began reading softly to the sergeant:

> And they gathered them together to the place
> called in Hebrew, Armageddon.

"What are those papers you've got there?" Maddox asked, pointing to the wad in Little's hands.

Little turned off the little pen light and slipped it and the clump of papers back into his pocket. "You know what this is, don't you, sarge?"

"The--the Bible. But where did you get it?"

"Right, sarge, it is a Bible, or at least a small portion of one. I found it in the city dump that we crossed yesterday. Not many of these around since our one world government outlawed them."

"Well, if you know it's against the law to have one of those things, then why do you have it? I oughta confiscate that thing, and turn you in. You know that there's still a reward out for you Christians."

"Christianity is against the law, Bibles are against the law, but who's law Andy? Tell me that. And explain to me why Bibles are against the law but other so called holy books are not? Why is it that only Christians and Jews are denied their holy scriptures?"

"Well, I don't know for sure. but...."

"Andy, what did that passage mean to you?"

"I don't know. And besides, the Bible is full of nonsense. People who follow its teachings are narrow-minded, war mongers. Your religion and your Bible are old-fashioned. And that's probably why they've been outlawed--so there can be peace. Because as long as you Bible thumping Christians were around we never could have peace, or unify the world. You were always insisting that there was only one way, one truth, and of course that one way was your way."

"Well, Andy, the government has gotten rid of most of us Christians, and there sure aren't many Bibles around anymore, so where's the peace, Andy? Is this the peace that our government promised us--this war--sitting here at the bottom of a ditch waiting for millions of Chinese and Japanese and Koreans, and their allies to come pouring into this valley? But don't change the subject! What did that scripture mean to you?"

The years of brainwashing that Maddox had undergone as part of his army training had muddled his thinking. His first inclination was to defend the United World Order, destroy the arguments of the Christian sitting next to him, and then get rid of that religious "filth" in his pocket. But for some reason he really didn't want to do all that. It was as if something or SOMEONE was stopping him. And whatever, or WHOEVER it was seemed to be saying: "Quiet, Andy. Just be quiet and listen, will you?" After a long pause, Andy Maddox spoke quietly. "I don't know, Little, what does it mean?"

"Sarge, this area that we're in right now, this valley, in the Bible it's called Megiddo, and it's where the Battle of Armageddon is to take place. Two thousand years ago the Apostle John wrote the words that I read to you. He was prophesying about today sarge, about today!"

Sergeant Maddox stared at the darkness in front of him for a long time, then took a deep breath. "Little, I never told this to anybody else in our outfit--I used to be a Christian, years ago. My wife, Eleea still is, that is if she's still alive. There haven't been any churches for her to go to in a long time, but she still believes, you know, in secret. We were both baptized and everything. Only her religion seemed to stick to her a little better than it did to me."

"Andy, I thank God for your believing sister, but as for you--if you had really been a Christian, years ago, then I think you would be one now. Sarge, I don't want to hurt your feelings or anything, but I don't think you ever were a Christian, not really."

"I was a Christian. Don't tell me I wasn't!" The sergeant said this way too loudly. Then more quietly, "I was a Christian. I went to church all the time, tithed from every dollar I earned, and believe it or not, I even taught Sunday School for the kids a few times, before things started to change."

Little rested his head on his knees for a moment. "Andy, the things that you did: going to church, tithing, and so on, they don't make you a Christian. Those are just things that Christians should be doing. Andy, to be a real Christian you have to give yourself to the Lord Jesus Christ, totally. You've got to become His, and He has got to become yours."

Maddox reached over and grabbed hold of Little's skinny arm with his strong hands, and purposefully hurt the little man. "I'm telling you I was a Christian. You hear me? And you best not ever tell me I wasn't!"

CHAPTER ONE

And the number of the army of the horsemen
were two hundred million.

Twenty-five miles east northeast of the trenches, near the southern tip of the Sea of Galilee, the leader of the Eastern States Confederacy, Admiral Vo Hunhue Soo rode in the back of a refurbished American Jeep that bumped its way south. Strung out behind him for over three hundred miles was an army so vast that even Soo himself did not know its count. The hordes that followed its leader much more resembled a swarm of locusts than an army, devouring everything in its path, cities, people, crops as well as gold and weapons.

Sitting next to Admiral Soo, on his right side, was a skinny bag of yellow flesh that was crowned by a visored military hat, General First Class Kau Gion, second in command. And though it was well after dark, Gion still wore his dark MacArther style sunglasses.

Admiral Soo, soaked in sweat, spoke to his subordinate. "And now, General Gion, what do you think? Is the white fool of a World President shaking in his boots as he hears of the tens of millions who approach his precious Israel?" Admiral Vo Hunhue Soo frantically mopped his wet forehead and face with a large khaki handkerchief as he spoke.

General Gion turned and smiled at his obese superior. "That he is a fool, Admiral, is fact. But I doubt that President Earlison is afraid of us or anything we might threaten to do."

"How can you say that, my friend?" Soo laughed. "But perhaps that is why you are second in command. You still lack a full understanding of human nature. You fail to realize that the mere presence of our untold millions is enough to strike fear in the heart of ANYONE who has his senses about him. Never has such an army as MINE been assembled on the face of this or any other world. No one can defeat my millions of men in arms, and the World President surely knows this."

Gion smiled crookedly at the Admiral, trying to hide the hate that he had for Soo. "Perhaps you are right, Admiral. Perhaps." Unseen by Vo Hunhue Soo because of the darkness, Gion had quietly unsnapped the holster on his right side that held his Nambatsu 9mm pistol. Then just as quickly he snapped it shut realizing that it was not the right time to put an end to his idiot superior. He again laid his skinny right hand back on his lap.

"Of course I am right, Gion. Earlison can have no idea that we have not come to fight, especially when he sees us surround him and his puny army. No, not surround, engulf. Ha! And since he must think we have come to fight, he must surrender without a struggle knowing that he is hopelessly outmanned and can not win. Then, when our armies are in place--our millions upon millions of soldiers--we have the option to kill everything in sight or simply take over and make our enemies our slaves. Yes, our incredible presence will be enough; it will win the day for us. And when all before us is mine, I shall take the president's throne, too." The Admiral laughed loudly, and his enormous round belly bounced up and down punctuating what he had said.

"Admiral, perhaps you have forgotten that World President Earlison has a few million men of his own to dispute the capture of Israel and the takeover of the presidency. And remember, too,that it is he who has the thousands of Vampire helicopters, and the tens of thousands of tanks, not to mention the most powerful air force on earth. Admiral, he will fight to the last man. He will destroy the earth if he has to, before he concedes one inch of his Jewish nation to us."

"Ah, General Gion, now I understand you even better than before. You are a brave man and itching for a fight. But let me tell you, there will not be a fight! Not if I have anything to say about it! The loss of life. The loss of resources. It shall not be." His voice had slowly changed to an angry snarl. "There is no need for us to fight. No need for my men to die by the millions. None at all. A show of force, the use of psychology and our brains, that is what is needed. That is how we shall win our objective. And when we do win, when Earlison concedes defeat, the millions at our back will take over that damnable country, Israel, and level it to the ground, like the Romans leveled Jerusalem two thousand years ago. Then it shall become a new China, a new Japan, a new center for our peoples. And the accursed Jews will be exterminated once and for all!"

Soo suddenly realized that he was screaming, and stopped as quickly as he had begun, took a deep breath, and began again in a mellow sing song voice. "Yes, yes, that is my plan. And you, General Gion, and I will live to be old men, owning palaces, with young admiring women by our sides, and tasting the sweet spoils of victory. Then being old and full of days, we shall happily join our deceased forefathers. That is how it shall be. You will see." Soo began laughing again, and hopelessly mopping at his wet face with his already soaked handkerchief.

"Pull over, driver," Soo yelled. "This shall be our Command Post. General Gion, have the armies pitch camp, one mile between each army. This, General, is where we shall make the decisions that shall change history. And general, when you have finished, get some rest. You look tired my friend. But make sure you're in my tent at 0430 for the morning briefing. That is all!"

The skinny general nimbly leaped from the Jeep, and began barking the necessary orders. Vo Hunhue Soo watched his second in command for only a few seconds before he had made up his mind. Gion was hopeless. He was impossibly inflexible, had no imagination, and was far too dangerous a man to be second in command of such a magnificent army. Gion would have to be replaced, before the armies awoke in the morning, before they arrived at Megiddo.

"Quickly, driver, get some help. I want my tent set up in fifteen minutes, and I want some good, strong tea. And get me a weather report. It's too hot for this time of year. Way too hot."

"Yes, Sir."

The words had scarcely left the driver's mouth when the landscape exploded into a violent crimson as the moon broke through the thinning clouds.

Soo fought for breath. "It's--it's a sign," he gasped, "A terrible sign. It is a sign of men's blood." Soo slumped to his knees, pressed his trembling hands together in prayer, and began bowing repeatedly toward the ground. "Oh, my ancestors, help me. Please, help me. A moon of blood. Oh my deceased uncle, my deceased father, help me, protect me."

Little bowed his head and prayed silently before responding. "Sarge, what are the most important things in your life?"

"Well, my career, I guess--defending the United World order, and trying to make something out of myself." As he spoke, Maddox finally released his tight grip on Little's arm.

Little rubbed his arm vigorously trying to restore the blood flow. "And--and what about God, Andy? Where does He figure into your life?"

CHAPTER ONE

Andy whispered softly, moving close to Little's ear. "I believe in God. Guess I always have."

"Andy, do you know that the scriptures say that even Satan and his angels believe in God and tremble? Believing in God is not enough."

"Come on Little, both you and I know that there's no such thing as Satan."

"Satan is not a thing, Andy. He is a person as real as you and me. He has possessed World President Earlison. He, and those like him are also behind this war that's about to start. Satan is also the one behind your refusal to accept Christ."

"I believe in God. What do you want me to say?"

"Andy, do you believe that Jesus walked these lands, where we are right now, some two thousand years ago?"

"Uh, yah, I guess so."

"...and He died for our sins, and was God in the flesh?"

"God in the flesh? Nobody ever proved that to me. It's one of those things that you Bible thumpers were always saying that nobody could ever prove."

Little again pulled out the dirty wad of papers, and thumbed through them. He held his little flashlight in his mouth, as before, until he found what he was looking for, then softly read the passage to Maddox:

> I am the First and the Last. I am He who
> lives and was dead, and behold, I am alive
> forevermore
> Rev. 1:17,18

"Sarge, who is this First and Last mentioned in this verse?"

"Ah, well, God, I suppose."

"Right! There can be only one First and Last, and that One has to be God. But if this First and Last is God, then how could He have been dead? God can't die, can He?"

"I, but, but..."

"Not unless this First and Last is the same One who was crucified on the cross for our sins!"

Down the trench from Little and Maddox, Matt Kernsworth cursed under his breath as he stripped off his sweat soaked shirt. It was over five hours until sunrise, and was already well over a hundred degrees.

"Hey Baker, why the #%$@&*% do you figure it's so hot?"

Baker was still seething with anger from his encounter with "Little" and the sergeant. "Don't bug me about trivia, or I'll really make it hot for ya!"

"Hey man, I didn't mean nothin."

"Yah--yah, I know. It's that little pip-squeak, and his bodyguard. They really got to me. And what do you suppose the punk and sarge are talking about now, and reading from that wad of paper?"

"How the #@$#%#@ should I know?"

"Well, I'd bet my last buck that Little's talking religion again, and this time that jerk, Maddox is listening real good."

"Religion? So what?"

"I'm talking about Christianity, you idiot. Yah, you heard me right. Little's a Christian! I'm sure of it."

This got the attention of the men close to Baker, since everyone knew that being a Christian was a crime. Offenders could be punished by anything from fines to death, and there was still a healthy reward for turning them in to the state police.

Baker continued. "You heard what he said to me down there, about there being only one God, and getting right with Him cause I'm gonna die. And--and you Joey, didn't he talk to you about Christianity the other day?"

Joey hesitated. "Not exactly."

"What do you mean, 'not exactly,' either he did or he didn't."

"He--he, well..."

"Speak up boy! He what?"

"He talked to me about--about Jesus."

"Jesus? Well, ain't that nice? Jesus, huh. But that's the same thing as Christianity ain't it? And that proves it. And guys, there's still that reward. Hey, Joey, would you repeat what you just said to the Captain?"

Joey Haggman had never been very bright, "dull normal" they had classified him in school, and everybody in his company knew it. And because he wasn't very bright, Joey always seemed to wind up being the butt of all the jokes. Nobody ever wanted him around unless it was to make fun of him, or prove just how "stupid" he really was. Except Little. Little had always treated him with kindness and respect, and now Joey wasn't about to rat on the one person he really trusted.

"If you guys wanna talk about the sarge or Little, well, I can't stop you, but leave me out of it. I ain't got nothing to say to nobody bout Little."

"Well, lookie here. I think we got ourselves another little Christian right here. Hey, Joey, you a Christian?" Baker asked, as the others started laughing.

"Naw, he ain't got enough sense to be a Christian," one of the guys nearby said. "You gotta to be able to read the

'Good Book' to be a Christian, ain't that right Joey?" By now everyone was cracking up except Baker.

"Shut up! I was asken Joey a question."

"No--no I ain't...." the words stuck in Joey's throat. He had accepted Jesus Christ as his Lord and Savior two days before, and now in a moment of weakness and fear, he had denied his Lord.

"You better leave me alone, Baker, or the Gooks won't have ta kill ya, I'll do it myself!" Joey pulled the bolt back on his carbine, and let it slam home chambering a round, then flipped the safety off and aimed the weapon just a tad to the right of Baker's head.

Baker's eyes opened wide. "Hey man! Watch where you're pointing that thing."

After a few seconds, Joey put the safety on, then aimed the carbine at the bottom of the trench. "I'm real sorry, Baker. I didn't have no cause ta do nothin like that. It's--it's just the heat, and--and the waiting," Joey lied.

"Sure kid, sure." Baker said. But the blackness of the trench barely hid the fury in the big man's eyes.

Joey rested his head on his knees. And unseen by the others, because of the darkness, tears flowed down his dirty face as he prayed silently: Lord, I ain't even been ah Christian for two whole days, and I've already denied You. Please forgive me, Lord Jesus.

Now Baker had three enemies to deal with. His friends shivered, even in the terrible heat, as they contemplated Joey's fate, and the fates of Little and Sergeant Maddox.

But their thoughts were never completed, because in the next instant the earth and sky exploded into a surrealistic red nightmare as the moon broke through the overcast skies.

CHAPTER ONE

and the fifth angel sounded, and I saw a star
fallen from heaven unto the earth, And to him
was given the key to the Bottomless Pit. And
he opened the Bottomless Pit,
and smoke arose.
And there came out of the smoke, locusts upon the earth,
and to them was given power.
and they had as king over them: ABADDON.
Rev. 9:1, 3, 11

Fear raced through the trenches and invaded the minds of the soldiers. Not normal fear, but fear multiplied a thousand times over by the teeming numbers of evil spirits that had been released from the Bottomless Pit at the precise moment the red moon broke through the clouds.

The demons, imprisoned for six thousand years, now rebelled against their rightful master, Satan, and chose to follow another leader, the demon Abaddon. Their plan was simple: possess the minds of the United World Forces making them so insane and disorganized that they would not be able to fight the Oriental Armies. They would ruin everything that Satan and his puppet, President Earlison, had planned. They would destroy the present one world organization and substitute their own. They would create their own HELL on earth. After all, what had Satan done for them in the last six thousand years? NOTHING! Satan had reigned on earth, free, and even worshipped by some, while they had been in torments of pain, and fear, locked in their prison: the Bottomless Pit. But now they were free, and now they would have their revenge.

In a matter of minutes the disciplined soldiers of the United World Order had become maddened beasts. No longer human, the soldiers snarled and bit anyone or anything that dared come close to them. Some, staring at the blood-red moon leaped from the trenches and disappeared into the night. Gunfire was everywhere. Thousands shot by their comrades sunk to the ground and watched as their own blood drained from their bodies onto the ground. Then just before death, some still growling and snapping, tore into the fallen corpses that lay next to them, and began devouring those who had been their friends only minutes before.

Some of the more seasoned veterans, spared of the madness, tried to pull their comrades back into the trenches, tried slapping some sense into them, but it was hopeless. The madness and fear were growing plagues that had no cure.

But Baker Dansford was too full of hate to have room for the fear or madness. He slipped unnoticed down the trench toward Joey. The "dummy" was staring at the moon, trembling, and praying a childlike prayer to his God. Baker quietly pulled out his bayonet, spat on it, then drove the sharp blade deep into Joey's chest. "Got ya," Baker said, smiling.

Pain exploded through Joey's being. He tried to catch his breath, but couldn't. He grabbed at the knife handle sticking out of his chest, and with difficulty pulled the bayonet out. Blood gushed from the wound. Joey collapsed onto the bottom of the trench. As he lay dying, he remembered a story that Little had told him, about another man who had shed blood, on a cross, a Perfect Man. Joey also remembered that this other Man had not died too many miles from where he was dying right now. "Lord Jesus, help me. I think I'm a dying Lord, like you did. Forgive me of my sins, Lord. And--and I hope You'll let me come and live with You." Joey thought he heard Someone say, "Today You will be with Me in Paradise." He smiled, then lifted his head and looked at his assailant. "Baker, why? I wouldn't tah shot ya."

"Nobody threatens me and gets away with it, Nobody! Especially some no good %$#@*& Christian." Baker then calmly took out a cigarette, and lit it while he watched the "dummy" bleed to death. He inhaled deeply. "A cigarette tastes good at a time like this," he said, picking up the bloody bayonet and wiping it on Joey's dead body. Then he stepped over the corpse and crept down the trench, toward the spot where he had last seen Little and sergeant Maddox..

So many died that night that it would have been easy for Joey's death to have gone unnoticed, but Little, compelled by the Lord, moved up the trench and found the bloody remains of his brother in Christ. "Good-bye, Joey. I'll be seeing you in just a little while buddy." Then Little sat down next to Joey and wept.

Admiral Soo sat at a low table in his tent and sipped his tea. He finally had control of the fear that still was in him. Across the table from Soo was a Chinese soldier in his early forties, General Third Class Yung Fa Singh. Singh was as hard and fit physically as Soo was soft and fat. But Singh was far from the master of strategy that Soo was, nor did he have the cunning that his superior possessed. Singh's strong suit was being able to say and do the right thing at the right time to make his superiors feel brilliant and appreciated, and Singh's rapid promotions were proof that his talents were much appreciated.

"General Singh, no doubt you are wondering why I have invited you here. Well, it is quite simple. You are to be promoted. You shall be second in command of the Eastern States Confederacy, under me. The simple fact is, I need a man that I can trust, and I think that you are that man. I can trust you, can I not?" Soo stared at the younger man. "You are loyal to me and the country that put you in that uniform, are you not?" General Singh was at a loss for words, and sat in silence with his mouth open.

"Answer! Are you are loyal or not?"

"Yes--yes of course, Admiral!"

"Good, then that is settled. So what do you think of such a promotion, to General Second Class, uh--no, First Class?"

"Admiral, I am flattered. But what of General Kau Gion? What shall become of him?"

Admiral Soo had been looking at his cup of tea when Singh had spoken, but at the mention of Kau Gion's name, the older man's face hardened into such a mask of hate that chills shot down Singh's back.

"Comrade general, there is one thing that must never be mentioned in my presence again. Do you know what that is?"

"No Admiral, I--I do not," Singh replied, sitting stiffly at attention.

Vo Hunhue Soo yanked himself clumsily to his feet and in the process, knocked over the table spilling most of the hot tea onto the younger man. "It is the name of that fool, Kau Gion! Do you hear me? I never want to hear that name from your lips again. NEVER! It is he who is responsible for the sign. I'm sure of it. He and he alone."

Singh stood rigidly at attention as he had learned to do so well years before as a cadet. His uniform was a ruined mess from the hot tea. The Admiral paced back and forth in the tent staring at the dirt floor alternately cursing, praying, and threatening, seeming not to even realize that Singh was there at all. This went on for what seemed like an eternity to Sing, but finally Soo came to his senses.

CHAPTER ONE

"Ah, General Singh, you must forgive me. The pressures of command. But I am sure you understand. Just remember, never mention that name in my presence again."

"Yes, Sir!"

"Private. Get in here and clean up this pigsty. And put on some more tea!

"Relax, general, relax. Come outside with me." The two officers stepped through the tent opening into the eerie red landscape.

"And General, what do you make of this blood red moon?"

"I--I...", Singh stuttered, still shaken by Soo's loss of temper only moments before.

"Come, come general, speak freely, for I shall be asking you for many of your opinions in the future, now that you are second in command of all my armies."

Singh composed himself as best he could, then began: "Sir, the only logical explanation that comes to mind for this exceptionally rare phenomenon is atmospheric pollution."

Soo was busy mopping his dripping forehead, but stopped abruptly. "What? Atmospheric pollution? Hhummmm. I hadn't thought of that. Hadn't thought of that at all. But of course you would like to hear my opinion, would you not general?"

"Uh--yes Sir. Of course, Admiral."

"Singh, this is an evil moon, an evil omen. Yes, evil. And that is why you must kill the traitor, Kau Gion. It is he who has cast this spell, and brought down the fire from the heavens, and--and caused this damnable heat, too. It is he who wishes to spill the blood of our countrymen so that he can gain power. Kau Gion has brought forth the wrath of the gods and of our forefathers. It is they who have given us this terrible sign--to warn us before it is too late."

Soo continued: "General, we cannot let Gion live. He must be destroyed. He must pay for his transgressions. Do you understand what I am saying? Kau Gion must die!"

"I--I--yes Sir!"

"Good. Then you will do it, won't you? Kill Gion? For your old Admiral? For your country? You will kill him for the millions of men that follow us, won't you Singh?" The admiral hesitated for a moment, then: "Please."

"I will kill him, Admiral."

"You must kill him immediately--before morning. Before we reach Megiddo."

"I understand, Admiral. As soon as I find him, it will be as you desire."

This seemed to have a calming effect upon the older man. "That is good. Yes, very, very good. But I do not want to know the details. When I arise, in a few hours, after a brief sleep, I will be shocked to find that our brave General First Class Gion is dead. Killed by a spy from the UWO, no doubt. And I shall be deeply grieved. We will have a great ceremony in his memory, of course, and he shall receive many decorations. And his poor widow, she will be given a handsome retirement settlement."

Soo took a deep breath. "But for now, I must get some rest. Good night, general, and happy hunting."

Singh snapped a sharp salute, turned and disappeared into the red night. Soo entered his tent mumbling to himself: "'Atmospheric pollution'. I am surrounded by fools. But once I am World President, things will be different. Things will be very different indeed."

Soo poked his head out of the flap on his tent and yelled to a nearby officer. "Captain, on the double." The young officer had been supervising several technicians that were setting up communications. At Soo's voice, he snapped to attention, dropped his clipboard, started to pick it up, then thought better of it, and came running over to Soo, saluting and snapping to attention.

"Captain, I want this sent out immediately, to all units: General Singh has been promoted to General First-Class, and will be second in command of all personnel and operations under me. This order will be effective at 0600 tomorrow. Is that understood?"

"Yes, Sir". The captain replied, still at attention.

"Then do it, idiot!" Soo yelled. The captain saluted, turned and disappeared toward the communications trailer.

Soo then turned and barked another command, this time to his personal aide. "Lieutenant, I want a weather report, NOW! And somebody better have a good answer as to why it's so ^%$&*^#$ hot."

Unknown to the Admiral or to General Singh, was the fact that Kau Gion had been less than thirty feet away from them during their entire conversation, and had heard every single word. He had hidden himself behind some crates stacked in the back of a personnel carrier that was parked next to Soo's tent, because Kau Gion had been planning on doing a little murder of his own. When Soo went to sleep, it would be a very, very long sleep indeed. And with Soo dead, it would be a simple matter to countermand the Admiral's last orders, and have the traitor Singh hanged. Gion laughed silently as he caressed his Nambatsu pistol much as one would a pet dog. Then he screwed a six inch silencer into the gun's barrel, and carefully placed a single cartridge into the pistol's chamber. One bullet would be enough. Kau Gion was an expert in the use of his little pistol. He had executed enough men and women with this very same pistol to know precisely how to kill his fat commander quickly and silently. Kau Gion smiled at his pistol It was about the only real friend that he had. It had never let him down yet. "Yes, my little friend," he said quietly to the Nambatsu, "tonight you shall provide the means to promote this number two boy to NUMBER ONE!"

Little somehow knew that he would never see his sergeant alive again. And though he barely knew Maddox, he had already learned to love his scarecrow sergeant. And right now, he hoped more than anything else that Maddox would choose to accept Jesus Christ as Savior. During the confusion, Little had already gotten rid of his back pack, emptied his pockets of ammunition, and thrown his carbine as far away as he could. He had no intention of fighting--of killing anyone. He knew that his decision not to fight was a serious one, a violation of military law, but there was no way he was going to meet his Lord with blood on his hands. A scripture ran through his mind:

To everything there is a season,
a time for every purpose under heaven:
a time to be born and a time to die

Little knew that his time to die had come. He calmed himself, and waited expectantly to meet his Maker. His thoughts drifted to the past, to his home in Wyoming. Back then--it seemed like a hundred years ago now--he had wanted to be just an ordinary preacher in a small church. But it was never to be. He had gotten his degree in Biblical Studies, but had never been able to convince any congregation to vote him in as pastor. He just didn't seem to have what most churches wanted. His squeaky voice, average looks, at best, and lack of charisma just weren't what most churches wanted. All he had was a burning desire to preach God's truth. It was never enough in those "last days".

Then something much more important than his hopes to preach had happened: the tribulation period had begun, and it had involved him and everyone else on earth in it. Now those years in Wyoming seemed more like a dream than reality. He had to remind himself that it had been scarcely seven years since it had all begun.

Little sat down at the bottom of the trench and tilted his head back to look at God's brilliant red moon. He knew that the moon was simply reflecting the light from the dying sun. The scriptures had been right again. They always were. Little gave thanks to the God who was Creator of it all, the same God he claimed as his Father through Jesus Christ.

One moment the moon was like fire, lighting the earth with its blazing glory, and the next it became as black as darkness itself. And without the moon's reflected light, it was almost impossible to see anything. But Little was so deep in prayer that he did not even notice the change in the moon. He also did not notice the black something,on his left side, that was slowly creeping down the trench toward him. "...and Lord, if it be your will, I ask that Sergeant Maddox be saved and added to Your eternal family."

The something was very close now. Little wiped a tear from his cheek just before a pair of strong hands grabbed him. As the hands tightened around his small neck, hundreds of shooting stars streaked overhead illuminating the face of his attacker. It was the face of an enraged demon; it was the face of Baker Dansford. The huge man released his hold on Little's neck just long enough to grab his bayonet, and slice his victim's throat with it.

Searing pain ripped across Little's throat only moments before he saw the most wondrous Person he had ever seen, standing in the heavens with his hands outstretched, and Little was sure that he heard this Person say: "Come home, My good and faithful servant." A tall young man standing next to him carefully picked him up, and carried him skyward to be with his Lord.

Little's body collapsed in a bloody heap next to Baker Dansford's feet. Baker laughed at the pile of bloody meat on the ground. "Now there's only one more to go, and he can't be far away. Where are you sarge? Oh, sarge, come out, come out wherever you are. Oh, sarge...."

----

and the stars will fall from the sky
Matthew 24:29

The meteor shower that had started a few seconds before Little was killed, intensified. Never had a heavenly display such as this one been witnessed by mankind. At first the heavenly fireworks were nothing more than a spectacular show, but very quickly the show became a terror in its own right as the flaming globes got closer and closer to the earth before they burned up. As they fell from the heavens toward earth, they made a peculiar high-pitched sound as they flashed through the atmosphere at ten thousand miles per hour.

Then one hit. Somewhere toward Lebanon. Then another. And another. The last impacted only a few miles from the scattered United World Forces. The tremendous report of this last meteor's impact sent powerful shock waves through the air knocking down trees and power poles, shattering windows and the eardrums of those too near. The earth, not designed by God to withstand the shock of being struck so violently by the huge meteorite, began quaking violently, as if she were crying in agony as her mantle was pierced by the vicious chunks of fire. Deep cracks in the skin of the planet opened allowing magma to explode to the surface forming killer volcanoes.

The fear and madness that had been spread by the legions of fallen angels, were intensified by the events taking place until there was little that was human in the UWO soldiers. They had finally became the animals that biologists and psychologists insisted they were.

The soldiers began killing each other in earnest.

Two thousand miles away from Megiddo, in an abandoned building, Eleea huddled together with fifteen other believers in one of the last true churches on earth. There was no furniture in the small room where they met, no padded pews, or pulpit, or pipe organ. Each person sat on the filthy floor, and leaned against one of the walls for support, except the man in the center of the room whose name was Boris, more commonly called "the teacher".

Boris was a middle-aged man, thin and diseased from malnourishment, and like most of the others in the group, disfigured from the tortures he had endured in the jails and prisons where he had spent time for being a Christian. He wore a patch over the hole where his left eye used to be, and hid his mutilated right hand in his robe. Years before Boris had been a simple shop keeper, and in his wildest dreams had never thought about being any kind of a religious leader. But when the tribulation had begun, the real Christian leaders were the first to be put to death by the Beast. But God, being faithful to those of His children yet alive, called men like Boris to teach and to lead. Boris obeyed his God, and like the apostle Paul, had paid dearly his obedience.

The services the teacher now led were very simple, in fact much like church services had been in the very beginning. There were no complete Bibles, no commentaries, no Christian literature, and of course the singing of hymns was not done. It would have made their discovery far too easy for the authorities.

Services usually consisted of the teacher reciting scriptures from memory, then adding a short explanation of each passage and perhaps an application. From time to time, others of the group would add their own memorized verses to the services. Then there would be a time of sharing and prayer. If grape juice or wine could be obtained, and a bit of bread, the church would partake of the Lord's Supper. But tonight they had no grape juice, no wine or bread.

Boris had just finished reciting the 23rd Psalm, and was about to give the explanation when a young man entered the room through a door that should have been locked. He, like the others present, was barefooted, and dressed in old clothing. He had thick black hair that contrasted sharply with his light complexion. His face was that of a child, yet filled with the wisdom that only great age could bring. He was tall and strong and moved with the grace of an athlete. The stranger seated himself in an empty place next to a wall. Everyone present instinctively knew that there was something very different about him. Something that was not quite human.

Boris stared at the stranger with his one good eye in a piercing yet kindly manner. "Young man, who are you? And how did you get in here? I myself locked that door."

The stranger paused for a moment, taking the time to look at every person in the room, then answered. "My proper name I shall not tell, for it was given to me by God and is secret. But you may call me Troset. Like you am a servant of the living God, though my rank and calling are different from yours. Yet we, you and I, shall dwell together through eternity praising our wondrous God and His Lamb."

Fear ran up and down the spines of those present in the room as the stranger spoke. "Please do not be troubled," he said, "for I have come to bring you a message of peace from our God, and a request. Your prayers are heard and cherished by the Almighty. And now our Lord and God desires that you to pray for someone, a man who is far away--someone who must yet be saved."

The teacher nervously asked the question that was on everybody's mind. "And--and who is this man that we are to pray for? Is--is he someone important? "

The young man looked at the teacher rather strangely for a moment, smiled, then laughed. It was not a laugh that mocked or ridiculed, but one that seemed to say: you have no idea what you are asking. "Dear teacher, I can see that you do not understand who is important to God and who is not. Each of YOU is immeasurably important. More important than all the silver or gold that there is. More important than the whole of the universe, in fact. So the answer to your question is YES, this man is important, but no more important than any of you. Yet there is something a bit different about this man that demands your prayers. He is in desperate need, for he is in spiritual warfare with the Prince of Demons himself."

The teacher with quivering voice spoke again. "Young sir, are we not all struggling with the Evil One? And if so, why have you come to ask us to pray for this one, if he is not particularly important?"

The stranger looked lovingly at the seated members of the church once more before speaking. "This man, that God wishes you to pray for, will be the last human being to be saved before the end, before the Lord Himself returns to claim the throne of David, and rule the earth."

The stranger's words took a moment to sink in. "...the last human being to be saved..." Then the end was close, really close. Goose pimples covered the flesh of every believer.

The teacher spoke again, his voice trembling. "And may we know the name of this man? So that we might mention his name in our prayers."

The young man turned slowly and looked at Eleea. "This woman will tell you his name, for she knows him well. It is her husband."

Eleea fought to catch her breath. "My--my husband? He's going to be saved? He's the last man? Oh, praise God! Praise His holy name!" She bowed her head, and began to weep. "Thank you, Lord. Oh, thank you, Jesus."

"Eleea, Eleea, his name?" the teacher prodded gently. "Eleea--so we can all pray."

"Andy. My husband's name is Andy Maddox," she said, between sobs of joy.

The head of each believer bowed in prayer, and began pleading for the soul of this last man who would ever be added to the Church of Jesus Christ, asking the Holy Spirit to show Maddox the truth, and praying for the holy power he would need to fend off the enormous power of Satan.

But as for the stranger, he had departed as quietly as he had arrived.

CHAPTER TWO

Then the fourth angel poured out his vial upon the sun,
and power was given unto him to scorch men with fire,
and men were scorched with great heat,
and blasphemed the name of God
Rev. 16:8-9

Harold Earlison's official title was World President, but he liked KING a whole lot better. No one called him that yet, but they would. And after that, they would call him GOD! Because he alone ruled the world, and nobody was going to take his rule away from him. NOBODY! Not while there was still breath left in his body.

Earlison sat in his office, and mopped hopelessly at the sweat that poured down his forehead. The air conditioning system that he had paid a fortune for had given up the ghost, like most of the others, when the tremendous heat wave had hit Jerusalem several days before. Earlison sighed loudly, then with some difficulty, pulled his overweight body out of the expensive chair, given to him by Elias Peterstein, who was High priest of the newly finished Temple in Jerusalem. And though none of the public know, Earlison's office, attached to the side of the temple, had a door that connected Earlison's office and the Holy of Holies itself. Peterstein, as High Priest, was the only one supposed to enter the Holy of Holies, and then only once a year, on Yom Kippur, to offer a blood offering for the sins of the Jews. But Earlison entered the special room much more often than that--almost daily in fact. He loved to just stand there and smell the incense, and stare at the Ark of the Covenant that was over four thousand years old. The ark had been discovered the year before. And Earlison loved to stand in the small, holy room and think of himself as god. Because only God was supposed to dwell in the Holy of Holies, but it was he, Earlison, who spent the most time in there.

Surely this was close to being god, wasn't it?

The World President walked laboriously toward the wall opposite the door that led to the Holy of Holies, to a display that contained his valuable collection of black powder guns from the American Civil War. A present from Jeffery Forlow, the last American president. Above the display was a plaque that read: "Peace or these--man's choice." He stopped in front of the gift from the now dead president, and looked at the relics.

The fools. Had they really fought an entire war with these toys?

The evil spirit inside Earlison laughed remembering the tens of thousands of men and boys he had watched die a slow and agonizing death after their bodies had been pierced by one of the large, lead, minnie balls shot from the old black powder weapons now rusting in displays such as his.

Wonder what they would have done with just one of my little toys? The president chuckled at the thought.

Earlison's pudgy hand reached far behind the heavy oak cabinet and searched for the button only he knew was there. A moment later the entire Civil War display slid quietly away from the wall revealing a dull metal door hidden behind it. Earlison pulled a key from his pocket and unlocked the metal door, then stepped through.

Inside was a gasoline lantern setting atop an old wooden crate. The president carefully picked up the lantern, lifted the glass, and turned on the gas supply. The instrument hissed out an almost invisible spray of white gasoline onto its mantle. Earlison struck a match and smiled as the lantern popped into a sputtering little flame, which he brightened with the fuel adjustment. Such a little light. But there is a much greater light, and I myself am that light. Me!

Earlison carefully pulled the gun display back into place, fastened the lock, then slammed the steel door behind him. Now came the part he hated, going down all those damnable stairs. He took a deep breath, held the lantern high and began the torturous descent that wormed its way far into the earth beneath the temple mound. As he descended, the air itself, began to feel heavy, and made the president's breathing all that much harder.

In his youth, Earlison had been an Eastern European weight lifting champion. He still had the broad shoulders, thick bones, and powerful hands, but the rest of his muscles were gone. Thirty years of sedentary jobs, cigars, and the innumerable glasses of vodka had transformed one of the world's strongest men into a potbellied slob. And now, as he descended the steep stairway, he was paying the price.

The deeper Earlison went, the slower his progress became, and soon he was hanging onto the metal railing with all of his might. His knees ached and wobbled badly. His lungs were on fire within his heaving chest; small white spots began to float before his eyes. He stopped to rest before he passed out.

How much longer can my heart take this? And why didn't I have an elevator put in when I had the chance? Why?

But he could make it. He knew he could. After all, how many times had he made this very same trip? Fifty? Maybe more than that. The president paused, and waited for his racing pulse to slow, then continued.

And what's worse, sooner or later, I've got to go back up, he thought to himself. But he would not let himself think about that. Not right now at least. Finally, he was at the bottom. His chest heaved hysterically. He was dying. He was sure of it. But no, after a few moments, his head began to clear, and his legs even felt as though they might hold him up for a little while longer.

In front of him was a wooden doorway leading to his own private inner sanctum. He pulled the wet silken handkerchief from his pocket and mopped at his wet brow. But at least it was cooler down here.

Earlison's special room lacked decorations of any sort. It had been designed for one purpose, and one purpose only: to house the power supply and controls that could loose one hundred instruments of death upon the world, each one more powerful than all of the weapons used in all of the wars that mankind had ever fought since the beginning of time. And no mortal knew of this secret room but him.

It had been an interesting challenge for him to turn a huge construction project like building his room, the tunneling, the stairs, and hauling the equipment down here into a secret. But he had done it. He had ordered almost two hundred workmen killed just to shut their mouths. Then he himself had personally killed the fifteen men who had killed the two hundred.

He burst into a strange, deep laugh. A laugh that did not need the use of his vocal cords. A laugh that came from another being who shared Earlison's body and mind, the same one who had wanted to be in Earlison's position of leadership for thousands of years--in fact, ever since he had been cast to the ground and forced to crawl on his belly as a serpent by God, in the Garden of Eden. The Devil cursed as he recalled that event. Yes, he had waited long for these days of power. In the past, he had almost conquered the world so many times, but something had always deprived him of the final victory. But not this time. The demon growled.

Earlison shakily entered the room, then lit several kerosene lamps that hung from the walls. No electricity came into this unholy room from the outside world. It would have made finding his secret room too easy.

Yes, I've thought of everything this time. Everything but treason, the BEAST reminded himself. "But I'll deal with that shortly." Earlison seated himself in an old but comfortable chair, pulled out a twisted black cigar from his breast pocket, then lit it with a wooden match. He watched the fire burn up the wooden stick until it almost reached his fingers before blowing it out. The World President then sucked the thick smoke deep inside his chest before blowing the foul smelling stuff into the air.

The room was not really that large, but it contained so few items that it appeared larger than it really was. In the far corner, almost hiding in the shadows, sat a gasoline powered electrical generator. The exhaust pipe stuck up in the middle of the room, and was not vented to the outside. The generator would be used to produce the needed electricity to power the transmitter sitting next to it. Together these two machines could, at his command, propel his missiles from their secret, underground tombs, to fly toward the cities and places that Earlison had chosen as targets years before.

"And that's the genius of it all. It doesn't matter one bit if the exhaust poisons all the air in this room and kills me to boot. Because when I do have to use those missiles, it will be the end of the world anyway." Again the fat president laughed.

In front of Earlison, on a crude wooden workbench, was a metal panel containing one hundred switches lined up in ten rows of ten. On the very bottom of the panel was one large red button well separated from all the others. Imprinted on it was a single word: FIRE. Each of the hundred switches would signal the transmitter to ready a missile to be fired. The FIRE button would then send the weapon on its way.

All but one of the missiles was within a few miles of the temple. Ninety nine of the rockets had warheads that contained four separate thermonuclear devices, each rated at 5 million tons of T.N.T. A chill went down Earlison's back as he thought about the power, the death.

And then there was that one special missile. The one farther away. The Norsac IV. It was even more deadly than the others. Those responsible for building it had used a completely new technology in the making of its warhead; it contained nineteen separate thermonuclear devices, and nobody knew the yield of those. But estimates of the power of each bomb and their combined power had so horrified the world that all of the Norsacs had been dismantled and their components destroyed. Or at least the world thought that they all had been destroyed. But Earlison had managed to squirrel one of these "wonderful" machines away, and add it to his personal collection.

"One hundred beautiful missiles, and they are all mine. Enough to blow up the whole stinking world if I have a mind to. "

After the so called "Two Minute War," between the United States of America, and the Russia\Ukraine alliance, the United Nations had ordered all nuclear weapons of every type destroyed. Harold Earlison had been appointed the chairman of this committee. He and those under him had supervised the destruction of the thousands of nuclear devices from around the world. Only his committee had not quite destroyed all of the weapons. One hundred had been spared, hidden away--just in case. And now, it seems, that all of the other members of this committee, those who knew about the remaining one hundred weapons, well, they were all dead, except him. How tragic. The demon inside Earlison exploded with laughter once again as he thought about how he had used Earlison to arrange for their deaths.

The "Two Minute War" had reduced the United States and Russia and Ukraine to less importance than any of the third world nations. Mostly they were radioactive deserts, with most of the people dead. Millions had died from the initial explosions, then many more from the lingering death caused by radioactive fallout, polluted water or food. A few millions of survivors now lived the nightmare of passing along their mutated genes to their children. And the amazing thing was that all three of these countries had exchanged less than fifty missiles total. FIFTY! Earlison owned ONE HUNDRED!

In Earlison's opinion, the "Two Minute War," had been the greatest thing that had ever happened to mankind. It had eliminated three super powers from the world, and had allowed the One World Government of Earlison's to become a reality. But even now, after his government had been established, he still had enemies.

"The fools. Do they really think they can overthrow me? They've already tried once and failed. "

Earlison's hand slowly went to his forehead, and fingered the ugly depressed scar that had been made by a bullet fired by a religious fanatic who had recognized Earlison as the "Antichrist". The fool had shot him in the head and left him for dead. Had shot him hoping to postpone the so called "tribulation period". But the fool had postponed nothing!

And the idiot had paid for his mistake with his miserable life. Earlison had survived, but the traitor had died. So had the traitor's wife, and the traitor's family, and all of the traitor's friends, and everyone else they caught who dared to call themselves "Christian". The incident had given the demon inside Earlison the perfect excuse to do away with the whole troublesome Christian bunch. It had also provided excellent entertainment, watching the extinction of an entire religion.

The Jews had not fared too well the last seven years either. Earlison himself was a Jew, but had little respect for their ancient religion. It was not the religious part that made being a Jew important. It was simply the fact of being one. Since their beginnings, Jews had been genetically and mentally superior to all other races. Earlison was convinced of that.

And what was funny was the fact that for a while, he himself had been accepted as the Messiah. The Messiah. Can you believe it. But then all of his people had turned from him and just because he publicly entered the Holy of Holies. It was his right, wasn't it? As president of the entire earth? So then why did his own countrymen rebel and try to overthrow him? Why? Why couldn't they see that the rebuilt temple, their hope in God, and all the rest were foolishness? He, World President Earlison was their only hope. He, and he alone. The fools!

And the wound to his head, that was supposed to kill him, not only had failed to do that, but hadn't hurt his intellect a bit. In fact, the bullet wound actually stimulated his mind. He was smarter now than he had ever been. He was a super genius in fact. The smartest man on earth--in the universe. And that was why he was the World President. But a single fact that escaped Earlison's attention: the phenomenal intelligence that he now possessed did not belong to him at all. It belonged to another being, one so evil that only Gehenna, the eternal Hell, would be able to hold this creature's tremendous hate and violence through eternity.

Yes, the bullet had failed to stop him, and everything and everyone would fail, too, and that included Soo and his hordes, and the traitor behind it all: the demon, ABADDON. A growl came from the president as he pronounced the name. A growl that definitely was not human.

Earlison had trusted Soo, had appointed him to oversee the billions of orientals who were part of Earlison's empire, but Soo had never been content to be the world's second most powerful man. From the very beginning, the Chinaman schemed on how he could get Earlison's job.

"I'll dare you to disobey me and lead all that rabble against me and my government. But you will learn, and the price of your lesson shall be your life."

Not only had Soo rebelled against the one world government and its president, but worse than this, and without knowing it, Soo had rebelled against the PRINCE OF THE POWER OF THE AIR, Satan himself. Soo had chosen to follow Abaddon. But the demon inside World President Earlison would deal with both Soo and Abaddon, soon enough.

Earlison smiled, and reached out his hand and tenderly touched the control panel. "No, no my love," he said softly. "I cannot use you yet. Because if I do, there won't be anything left of the world for me to rule over. No, not unless everything else fails and Soo wins. Then you can have your way. Then you can put an end to this miserable planet and everything on it."

As the president finished his contemplation, the cigar slowly slipped from his hand and dropped to the floor.

Earlison's eyes rolled tightly up in his head, and he slipped from the chair onto the cold, concrete floor, twitching and kicking uncontrollably. After a few moments, the seizure ended, and the president entered into a deep sleep. Satan's spirit had left Earlison for a time.

The demon had other work to do. Work that was many miles away, and involved someone located at Megiddo--a soldier named Maddox. And after that meeting there was yet another to attend. He had to meet the second most powerful demon in the universe, face to face, his ex-general, the Angel of Death; ABADDON. He and Abaddon would then settle matters once and for all. And once Abaddon had been eliminated, the one world order could be repaired and strengthened. And then, finally, after so many thousands of years, he, Satan, would rule openly.

And Earlison's reward for services rendered? For providing his body as his evil temple? Eternal hell. The demon smiled at the thought. But for now, the president was still of some use.

Satan's polluted soul then stared coldly at the unconscious Earlison for a few moments. "I deserve so much better than that ugly body to work in. But it will have to do for now," the demon thought to himself. Then Satan loudly spat out a single word addressed to Earlison: "FOOL!", and was gone.

CHAPTER TWO

The moon shall be as the light of the sun,
and the light of the sun shall be sevenfold,
as the light of seven days.
Isaiah 30:26

The star looked to be normal only hours before, now it was clearly dying. As it used the last of its hydrogen as fuel, it swelled in size until it became a great bloated mass sending out a hundred times its normal amount of energy. What had been a life giving star of nominal size, had now became a giant, orange-red killer.

The planet nearest to the star quickly became a molten blob, then as the star swelled, and the distance between the two bodies decreased, the planet slowly spiraled into the star to forever become a part of her.

The second planet from the star had a surface temperature hot enough to melt lead even before the star had began to overheat. Now the planet became so hot that it drove its atmosphere far away into the emptiness of space leaving the small planet naked, melted, and ugly, and no longer the beautiful "Morning Star" it had been from its creation.

Nothing had ever lived on these first two planets, but on the third planet, the green one, the one with the bands of white clouds, and blue life-giving oceans, it was another story. Life did exist on this one, but perhaps only for a little while longer. For as the huge superheated monster star appeared on the horizon at sunrise, its incredible heat and death rays bombarded everything it touched on the surface, wilting, melting, scorching, and raising the temperatures towards the two hundred degree mark.

The seas, lakes, and rivers, too hot to hold the needed oxygen for their teaming life forms, became a sludge pot of the dead and the dying. And marine life that floated to the surface of the waters quickly cooked under the broiling sun.

Then, only hours later, when the giant had finished the last of its fuel, it died. It first became an impossibly beautiful alizarin crimson, then violet, dark blue, and finally a dull black that would not even reflect the light from other sources. The location of the massive, dead globe could only be deduced from the black circle it left in the heavens as it blocked out the stars behind it.

The life that had managed to survive the intense radiation and astonishing heat emitted from the red giant, now had little time left. For the earth would quickly become a frozen wasteland where nothing alive could exist. The earth in this final state, lifeless and frozen, would remain so until the end of time, unless the Lord God Himself ordered it otherwise. And the tragedy of it all was that in the entire universe, God had created biological life only on this one small planet, the third one from the sun, the one His Holy Son had once walked upon.

Yastetil read from the parchment that contained the targets for all the remaining missiles on the face of the earth, exactly one hundred of them. Most of the land masses of the United States, Russia, Ukraine, as well as Egypt, Iraq, and Iran were little more than radioactive deserts after the so-called "limited thermonuclear exchange," of a few years back. The one hundred missiles having thermonuclear warheads, could easily kill or poison the rest of the earth if they were ever loosed. Something had to be done. The cherub lifted his eyes from the paper. "Satell, have you made the assignments?"

"Yes, Sir, I have."

CHAPTER TWO

"Good. Then let us get started. There are one hundred of these things to reprogram, and not much time to do it in. Satell, if you would, please lead us in prayer?"

Satell stood, and prayed a humble prayer to God asking Him to guide each of them as they sought to serve Him. When the prayer was ended, the angels sang a hymn as old as the earth itself. Then each of the holy messengers departed.

Kau Gion dripping with sweat slipped quietly out of the troop carrier. The heat and long wait in the truck had persuaded him to abandon his uniform; he was now naked except for a large, cotton loin cloth. As he crept toward the entrance of Soo's tent, Gion carried his precious 9mm pistol carefully in his right hand, and held a flashlight, switched off, in his other.

The blazing red moon had disappeared as mysteriously as it had first appeared. But Gion did not think about this; he was just happy that it was so dark. It would make his task just that much easier.

Invisibly he crossed the short distance to Soo's tent, pushed the flap open and entered. Easy--easy, he told himself. But it was already almost too easy. Gion wanted to laugh at the excellence of his plan. But his laughter would have to wait until Soo was dead. Then he would laugh. There would be plenty of time for laughter then.

The darkness of the night was further amplified inside the tent. Gion could see nothing, but Soo was a noisy sleeper, and the admiral's snoring unerringly guided Gion toward his victim. When he stood next to his superior, Gion turned his flashlight on and pointed it at Soo's face. The admiral instantly snorted himself awake, and found himself staring into a blinding light.

"Who--who is that? Turn that &^%$@&^ light off!"

"It is I, General Gion."

"Well, you heard me, turn that thing OFF!"

Gion slammed the barrel of his pistol against the admiral's temple.

"Aaahhhhhhh. Put--put that thing down, you fool. Put it down immediately. I command you!"

"I am the one with the gun, and yet you have the audacity to call me a fool?" A barely audible squeaky laugh came from Gion's thin mouth.

"Wha--what do you want?"

"I want nothing other than your life, my fat Admiral."

Gion pulled the trigger. The silenced pistol made little more than a soft "pop" as it went off. But a moment before the gun discharged, the frightened Admiral had sprang from the bed much faster than Gion had thought possible. Soo's movement was not fast enough to make Gion's shot miss entirely, but the bullet intended for Soo's brain missed, pierced his left eye instead, hit bone, then broke into pieces, one of which passed through the Admiral's fleshy nose, another entered his mouth rupturing several small arteries. Blinded and in pain, Soo grabbed his skinny assailant and fell on top of him. As Gion fell backwards under the weight of Soo, he struck the edge of a wooden foot locker with the base of his skull, snapping his spinal cord. Soo passed out releasing his grip on the skinny general. The two semi-naked men lay on the dirt floor one atop the other, Soo face down in a quickly spreading puddle of blood, and Kau Gion on his back staring up into the darkness of the tent, with Soo draped across his legs.

CHAPTER TWO

Gion cursed to himself as he realized that his plans were ruined. But now only one thing mattered. He had to get out of there, FAST. But something was wrong. His arms and legs were not moving. They almost felt as if they were asleep. He had no choice now but to cry out for help. After it arrived, he would worry about explaining the situation.

Gion yelled, as hard as he could. But no sound came from his mouth. He yelled again. Nothing. His lips moved, but that was all. It was then that he realized he was not breathing, and he needed to badly. He made a conscious effort to suck in fresh air, to move his chest. But it didn't work. Please help me. Please. Anybody! But there was no sound inside Soo's tent, except for the labored breathing of Soo himself. Gion was now beginning to get dizzy. Mysterious white specks swam before his eyes. He was starting to lose consciousness. Then just before he died, he heard Soo groan. Soo, you stupid idiot, you have ruined everything. Simply everything.

Elitvar sat on the concrete floor in the underground missile silo, and leaned against one of the huge tail fins on the rocket he jokingly referred to as HIS. It was totally dark in the silo, but light was not needed to see by, at least not by Elitvar or others like him. He was happy. He had finished his job much sooner than even he had expected. Now he had nothing to do but wait and see if he had done it correctly. And after that, he would wait some more and see how God worked out His holy scriptures.

The Norsac IV missile that he leaned against was the only one of its kind in existence. It was the most powerful destructive device that had ever been invented and assembled by man. Atop the tall three-stage solid fuel rocket sat a warhead containing nineteen independent thermonuclear bombs, each having it's own guidance system, and each designed for one purpose: to KILL.

Elitvar shook his head in amazement thinking about all the waste of human talent, the engineering, planning, and skill that had gone into building this killing machine. He knew it was powerful, but that part did not amaze him; he had visited hundreds of stars in his many years of life. Had even flown through a couple of them just for the fun of it. So it was not the power of the weapon that amazed the cherub. Because the Norsac IV was not even a firecracker compared to even the smallest of the stars that he knew about. But the stars were different. They had never been designed with killing in mind. This thing had no purpose BUT to kill. He shook his head once again.

His rocket's computer systems had originally been programmed to deliver the nineteen bomb warhead to London and its surrounding countryside, but that was before Elitvar had worked on it. It had been a tricky and complicated job to delete all the tens of millions of individual instructions that the powerful computer held, then assign completely new ones. But he had done it. Now the rocket would be going somewhere else. It had taken him almost seventeen hours non-stop to do it, and he had accomplished his task without the use of a single piece of electronic equipment or even a simple hand tool. Elitvar had trained hard for this single task for the last six months. Now his part in the great finale was over.

As he leaned against the big Norsac, Elitvar thought of all the others, his friends, the other ninety-nine angels that were reprogramming their missiles. But they, like him, were probably finished too, and simply waiting. Waiting to watch their rockets fly out of the hidden silos, and hoping like

Elitvar, that their rockets went where their new instructions told them to go.

Elitvar had to admit that he was anxious for his powerful machine to burst into life, streak high above the earth, hurtle back to its target releasing its special packages, then moments later, become superheated atoms generating nineteen separate lights each brighter and hotter than the sun itself. He hated the fact that human beings would have to die. But then, after all the explosions would come the good part: Christ Jesus would appear in the sky, rapture those who belonged to Him, then descend to earth to assume the throne of David, to be the King of the earth as He had always deserved to be.

Yes, when his rocket flew that would mean that Christ's return was only moments away. Elitvar praised God for allowing him to have a part in bringing the most wondrous event, the second advent of Christ, just a little closer.

From the top of Mount Hermon, Abaddon could see more than two hundred miles, and all of those miles were filled with HIS armies. Two hundred million men in arms, more men than had existed on the entire globe when Christ walked the earth, and he, ABADDON, was their commander. He loved the tremendous feeling of power, even if he did have to resort to using fools like Soo and Gion to lead them.

The demon general had almost forgotten how to smile, but now for the first time in years, he did twist his mouth into an evil, ugly grin. Yes, he may have started out second in command, under Satan, but he was not number two anymore. He, ABADDON was NUMBER ONE!

Abaddon spat out the word "Satan." How he hated him. All these past thousands of years he had played second fiddle to this so called "Prince of the Power of the Air." When it should have been me who was allowed to lead the revolt against God. Me, and not Satan.

And the great Lucifer had proved his incompetence right from the start, from the very first day. He had been given chance after chance to control the world and had blown it each and every time. But things were changing now, and finally he, Abaddon, would have his chance. Because, Satan, there is no way that you can stop me from taking over Israel, or anything else that I want to take over.

What did Satan have to oppose him? Two or three million men and a pile of so called "high tech" weapons was all. That couldn't possibly stop his army. Again he stared at the incredible hordes that advanced toward him. No, Satan and his puppet Earlison would have to surrender. Yes, Xesduca, Lucifer, Satan, call him what you will, was theoretically in charge of the world, but that charge was about to be debated beginning tomorrow, at Megiddo.

Two or three million men, "Paah!" He had two hundred million. And no living being in the universe could stop him now. Not that goody, goody Archangel Michael, not Satan, not even God Himself. The Bible said that Armageddon would end the rule of evil on earth for a thousand years, but the Bible was wrong. Armageddon would not be the end of evil, but the beginning of it, under him.

"Me, Abaddon, and not Christ will be King of the World. Me, the Death Angel. ME!!!!!!!"

His wait was almost over.

CHAPTER TWO

Sergeant Maddox screamed as loudly as he could at his men, trying to get them to stop killing each other. He almost succeeded in establishing some semblance of order once, but then another meteorite smashed into the earth a few miles away and the madness renewed itself. He pulled the bolt back on his Typo 67 submachine gun, and fired it into the air. Thirty rounds blazed out of the short barrel with a deafening roar, but it made no difference at all. He ejected the spent magazine, reloaded his weapon, then sunk to the bottom of the trench, and into its darkness.

He took a deep breath, then looked up. The moon. It had been there just minutes before, blazing away in its red fury, now it was gone. What happened to the moon?

Maddox strained his eyes trying to see through the darkness, wondering at all that was taking place around him. In the trench, and on the earth above he could see a few vague shadows of the men crawling, moving about, growling, cursing, and shooting each other. Then, in a moment of time, an unnatural calmness overtook him. The growling, the gunshots, the curses, no longer seemed to be part of HIS world. It was almost as if he were watching a movie.

He took off his helmet, stretched, and lit a cigarette, inhaling deeply, anticipating the familiar narcotic effect he had experienced thousands of times before. But the cigarette tasted terrible, and the smoke stung his throat. Like it had years before, when he had first started smoking. He coughed until his chest and throat hurt.

He and his buddies had started smoking in high school, in the boys bathroom. One of them would watch out for the teachers, while a butt was quickly passed around to the participants. It was fun smoking between classes, hiding from the teachers. And after that, when he was competing in Judo tournaments, it was so hard to stop by then. His coach, Bob Steas, had told him over and over: "Stop smoking!" Bob even told him once that he could be the best fighting man on the United States team, if only he would just apply himself; if only he would just stop SMOKING. But Maddox never did stop, and he had become a champion anyway. A United States champion. Now he wondered if he could have been a World Champion, if he had just listened to his coach. But that was so long ago, and in another country, a country that didn't even exist anymore. And besides, listening had never been one of his strong suits. Like awhile ago, when Little had been talking to him.

He took another drag, then blew out the smoke. The coughing began immediately. It was as if his body were trying to get the poison out of his system, trying to tell him: "Hey, stop putting that stuff inside me." He stared at the glowing tip of his cigarette in the darkness for a moment, then crushed it out. He leaned back against the cool earth and watched the meteor shower overhead. Suddenly the earth jolted violently under him. A moment later the tremendous concussion from the impact almost shattered his eardrums. The earth swayed drunkenly under him. Now that was close, he said to himself. Still he was calm. Still it seemed to him as if he were somewhere else.

Maddox begin to feel desperately lonely. He also began wondering why he had been spared the madness that was all around him? Why him? All those disciplined men, effective fighting men only hours earlier, now they were all gone, crazy, running around, only God knows where. There was only him left. No friends, no comrades, and no wife.

His wife! He had almost forgotten about her these last hectic days. Where was she now? At this very second? Was she still alive? If she was, did she still care and think about him?

CHAPTER TWO

Then it struck him. Why was he even in the army of the UWO anyway? They had been the very ones who had been putting to death all of the Christians. One or more of the men in his own outfit could have been the very ones who put to death his own wife. What on earth was wrong with him? How could he have been deceived for so long? And why had he listened to his leaders in the first place?

So many questions. So many questions and so few answers. If only there was time to think everything through. If only there was someone he could trust and talk to. Someone like Little. Hey, where was Little anyway? Maddox was positive that Little wouldn't be up there with the rest. Not him; not running around with the others? He suddenly knew that he had to find the small soldier. But not quite yet. Not until things calmed down a little. Then he would find Little, and this time he would force himself to listen. Because it looked like Little had been right, about a lot of things: God, and--and maybe this war too. Maddox mentally began going over his last conversation with Little. And the more he thought about what was said, the more he knew that Little had been right.

So this is the end? But that would mean that there would be no tomorrow. This day, this moment right now would be all that there was. It frightened him. Not because he was afraid to die, he had dealt with that fear long ago, when he had decided to stay in the army. He felt frightened for all the others, for the world he had always known. The millions of plans that would never be completed

Before, Maddox had always been able to find comfort in the fact that when he died, things would go on, more or less, like they always had. But if this was really the end, then there would be no going on. And there would be nobody left to remember him or anybody else. There would be nobody left for anything. And this war, maybe the worst one yet, would never get into the history books. Nothing would ever be written about it.

And then what? If this was the end,what happens after the end? He answered his own question: "NOTHING!" The question and answer struck him as funny. He laughed, but it was a sad, dry little laugh.

And not only would there be nobody to remember him, but there wouldn't be anyone to bury him. His body and the bodies of millions of others would remain where they fell until--until--well, forever. Maddox began to cry for the first time in many years. He again remembered Eleea. What he would give just to see her one more time. To hold her. To smell the flower scent in her long hair. Maddox felt more alone than he ever had in his entire life.

"So you've finally accepted the fact that this might very well be the end of reality as you know it?"

The voice came from a man in uniform who stood about ten feet away, and while the darkness in the trench was thick, Maddox could see this man clearly. And what scared Maddox the most was the fact that the soldier almost looked like him. It was as if he were looking at his image in a mirror. But in this instance the image lacked the flaws of the original.

There was no insignia on the stranger's uniform, but otherwise it was identical to the ones worn by the UWO forces. It was then that Maddox realized that even though the man looked very much like himself, the stranger was both taller and heavier. In fact the man was a giant whose arms were so bulged with muscle that they threatened to rip the sleeves of the uniform he wore at any moment.

"Who are you, and what are you doing here?" Maddox demanded standing up and yanking the bolt back chambering a round in his sub-machine gun. He took careful aim at the stranger. The soldier calmly waved his hand toward the weapon, sending it mysteriously flying out of Maddox's hands onto a small pile of dirt some thirty feet down the trench.

"How--how did you do that?"

The stranger said nothing.

"I repeat: who are you? And what do you want?"

"My name is Elonote Lottan Maddox. In your language: God's Watcher over Maddox." The soldier paused for a second and watched Maddox's reaction, then: "I'm what you humans call a Guardian Angel. Maddox, I am your Guardian Angel."

"I--I don't believe you."

"I have come to offer you the choice of life or death. Not physical life, for your's is almost over. But eternal life, or eternal death."

Maddox stood up, and tensed himself, assuming a position he knew well from his martial arts training, one from which he could defend himself if he had to. Then he glanced toward his machine pistol trying to figure out how he could get to it before the stranger stopped him.

"You won't need that. I am not your enemy but your friend. I have looked after you from the moment of your conception. But now our great God has granted me a few moments to talk to you face to face."

Maddox continued glancing toward his weapon.

"I can see that you are not going to rest until you have that gun back in your hands. You always have had a one track mind Mister Maddox." Elonote waved his hand toward the gun, it lifted from the ground and flew through the air and landing gently at Maddox's feet. "Now pick it up and shoot me, if that is what you want to do," the stranger said.

. Maddox hesitated.

"Pick it up! You're wasting what little time we have together," the stranger said.

Maddox picked up the sub-machine gun, flipped off the safety and pointed it at the stranger.

"Now shoot," Elonote demanded. Maddox didn't. "Maybe it would help if I told you that I am an enemy of your President Earlison and his government. Not mad enough yet? Well, perhaps you should know that the army you serve in is evil, led by evil, and has no good reason for existing at all, and I wait with great anticipation for it's destruction. Now are you mad enough to shoot? We don't have much time left."

Maddox put the safety on and let the weapon point at the ground in front of him.

"Good! Now we can get started. Do you believe in God or do you not?"

"Yes, of course I do."

"And Jesus Christ, what do you think of Him?"

"I--I--"

"Answer! The world is coming to an end and you stand there stuttering. Do you claim Him as your Lord and Savior or not?"

"Do not be a fool and answer such a stupid question as that." The words came from another huge man dressed in a shining green robe. And whoever he was, he was the most beautiful person Maddox had ever seen, male or female. But there was a coldness about this other stranger that sent a deep chill down the sergeant's spine.

"And who are you?" Maddox demanded. "And just what's going on here anyway?"

CHAPTER TWO

Both of the huge men approached each other as if they were ready to fight, and for the moment ignored Maddox. Their eyes blazed with hatred for each other.

"So Xesduca, you have come. I have been expecting you," said the first stranger.

"And you, Elonote, trying to steal this little soul from me by using the simple magic of a flying weapon. Begone! You are no match for me."

"I have no time to quarrel with you, demon," Elonote said, then turned and addressed Maddox. "Claim the salvation that is in Christ Jesus our Lord, or die and go to the hell that was prepared for this--this Angel of Sin and those who follow him."

"Do not be a fool and listen to this liar," said the demon. "Elonote demands immediate acceptance of this Christ, a man who died thousands of years ago, and for what reason? And what do you really know of this Christ anyway? Such allegiance, should you choose to accept it, at least demands a thorough investigation. Think about it. There is plenty of time to choose whom you wish to follow, or if you wish to follow anyone at all. Consider all the points, then after a good night's rest, make your decision."

"Andy, this Spirit of Sin, this one called the Devil, and those like him have brought about this Armageddon. He knows that there is little chance of a tomorrow. That is why he counsels you to wait. But do not listen to him, Andy Maddox. Do not listen to the one who has killed the last real friend that you had in this army. Choose now! This is the only time that is guaranteed to you. And remember, the Lake of Fire and its torments awaits you if you choose other than the Lord. But you need have no fear of death or of judgement if Christ is your Redeemer. Choose Andy! Why do you wait?"

"What do you mean, he has killed my last friend?"

"He has killed Little."

"You killed Little?" Maddox reached down, released the safety on the machine-pistol, then pointed it at the demon."

"He was a nuisance," said Xesduca.

Maddox pulled the trigger emptying all thirty rounds into the devil. The bullets passed harmlessly through Satan's spiritual body. But the attack enraged the demon. He knocked the gun out of Maddox's hands as if it were a toy, then backhanded the sergeant across the face with such force that it broke his nose and knocked out several teeth. Maddox fell to the ground stunned, then spat out the broken teeth and a mouthful of blood.

"Fool, do you attack the great Lucifer?" The demon was about to kick the sergeant when the strong hand of Elonote pulled the demon away from Maddox.

"God has not given you permission to touch this human a second time!" The demon growled, but obeyed.

"Andy, this is a spiritual battle. You will not be able to harm this Author of Sin with your weapons. Yet you can dispatch him as easily as if he were a child, with the power of God. You must choose Andy: God, through the Lord Jesus Christ, or this Evil One. But now my time is gone. Andy, one more thing I say: I have loved you from the day our God proclaimed me to be your guardian, now I hope that you will humbly bow before your God, so that we need not be separated through eternity. Choose wisely, my sergeant." When Elonote finished speaking, he disappeared.

"And now my friend, you must forgive me for my eh--my loss of ah, temper. But I am a prince, and not used to being attacked, by anybody, much less a human being. But to show you that we are not enemies but friends..." Satan waved his hand, and immediately Maddox's broken nose was healed, and his broken teeth restored. Maddox gasped as he fingered the miracle.

"And now we must sit down and talk. I have much to tell you. The tale will not be short, but I promise that it will be worth your time." Satan carefully seated himself at the bottom of the trench, but not to close to the filthy Maddox.

"You killed Little, why?"

"I have told you already! He was a fool! Did he not talk to you of Christian nonsense? And did he not read to you from that pornographic book, the Bible? He was worthless! But you, on the other hand, are one of great value. Now, shall I begin my somewhat long tale?"

Maddox looked at the Evil One for a moment, then grabbed his weapon and smashed it forcefully into his mouth breaking off several of his front teeth and badly cutting his upper lip in the process. Then he took hold of the short barrel, and using his weapon like a hammer, struck his nose several times until it was broken again. Blood ran down his face, and dripped off his chin. "I will take no gift from the killer of my Christian brother. Yes, demon, I claim Christ as my own. Leave me!"

A growl more evil than any that had been uttered in a thousand years came from the demon's mouth.

Maddox threw his weapon over the side of the trench, then began to cry, for Little, for all the men he had led for so long and now knew were destined for eternal hell, and he cried for Eleea his wife, whom he missed so very much.

Maddox tried to ignore the pain as he bowed his head and prayed aloud, in front of the demon.

"Lord Jesus. I do believe in you. Guess I have for a long time, deep in my heart, no matter what the government told me over and over. I'm sorry that I never gave You the time that You deserved. Forgive me of my sins, Lord. Please."

Satan growled again, then disappeared. He had another appointment at a mountain called Hermon.

CHAPTER THREE

For they have shed the blood of saints and prophets,
and Thou hast given them blood to drink.
Rev. 16:6

Earlison awoke cursing the God he claimed did not exist. His head felt like it was splitting open. Headaches usually followed his seizures, but this one was the worst yet. He checked himself over, groaning every time he moved his head a little bit too fast. Well, at least this time there was no bitten tongue, no extensive bruises or cuts. He cursed again. The seizures were happening too frequently lately, and he was going to put a stop to them, once and for all!

Earlison had been prone to seizures ever since he had been shot in the head. The doctors, the fools that they were, had tried all of the usual medicines: phenobarbital, dilantin, and a host of others, but none of them worked well enough to stop his fits altogether. He was now having several grand mal seizures a week. And for the last month, every time he had one, he would awake to find himself in this same room, five hundred feet beneath the surface, on the concrete floor, cold, cut up, bruised, with his expensive clothing torn and ruined.

But Earlison had finally figured it all out. When his spiritual guide left him, he would have one of his spells. Then the same thing would happen when the spirit returned to use his body again. So, the Master is gone, and I am my own man again, for a while.

Earlison knew that Jedeciah (the name he had given to the spirit being) would be back all too soon. He never left Earlison alone for very long. At first the president hadn't minded this. In some ways it was like having an intimate friend always at hand. But after a while, it began to get old. There are some times a man just wants to be by himself, the president thought to himself.

But Earlison knew that it would be like this even before he had invited the spirit to share his body. And there had been rewards for letting the spirit use him--lots of them, like power, wealth, women, and everything else he had ever wanted, including the World Presidency. But he also knew that all of these things had cost him a terrible price. He no longer belonged to himself. He belonged, body, soul, and spirit to Jedeciah, and sometimes it seemed like he would never be free of this demanding spirit.

All the kingdoms of the World had been given to Earlison by Jedeciah, but somehow, the president still felt empty, and was not nearly as happy as he had wanted to be. Earlison now possessed everything that this same spirit being had once offered to Christ, in the wilderness. Christ had refused it all--Earlison had accepted.

And now, on top of everything else, someone else was trying to take what Jedeciah had given him. But Admiral Soo would never take any of it away from him. NEVER! The world belonged to him and to him only.

And what did his military advisers tell him to do about Soo? Nothing he wanted to hear. They said that Soo could not be stopped, that Soo's army was too big, too powerful. They told him that Soo's army was consuming everything in its path: cities, farms, people, all of which belonged to him. Earlison's generals advised compromise, accommodation, even surrender. Sometimes Earlison even thought that Jedeciah was afraid of Soo.

Bah! They were all cowards. It was up to him. As World President he would stop Soo, and he knew exactly how to do it. It was drastic, yes, but this was his world, and no one was ever going to sit behind his desk, in his office, and assume his title. EVER! And this time Jedeciah was not here to stop him.

The president pulled his heavy body from the floor, brushed himself off, then hurried over to the corner of the room, toward the generator. "Made in the USA," it proudly said on the tag at the side of the engine generator unit. Earlison laughed at the inscription. There was no USA, not anymore. But he had to hurry, before his spirit guide returned. "And when I get done, there's not going to be anywhere anymore." But what exactly did that mean? What would the planet be like after his one hundred toys had vaporized and radiated and blown apart their targets? It was an interesting question, but he didn't have time to contemplate it at the moment. He had other things to do right now, and he had to do them fast.

Earlison removed his suit jacket so he could work. The suit had cost him over five thousand dollars only weeks before, now he threw the jacket in the corner out of his way, and rolled up his sleeves. First he made sure the generator switch was in the OFF position. Then he opened the fuel valve, pushed a manual overflow button on the carburetor until it was filled with fuel.

Sweat poured down his face, and soaked through his shirt even though the room temperature was only sixty five degrees. He punched the start button. The engine turned over slowly, with a grinding sound that told Earlison the battery was low. He punched the button again. The engine made one complete revolution, coughed, fired once, then died. He hit the button again.

"Come on, you rotten @#%%$^# machine, START!" He hit the starter button again; it turned over one more time, then the solenoid started chattering. "No, not now." He hit the button again, but this time the engine did not even budge, and even the starter solenoid was silent. He continued hitting the start button over and over, cursing, threatening, hoping.

It isn't fair. It's my world. I can blow it up if I want to. Earlison fell to the floor, sobbing uncontrollably.

Baker Dansford moved from trench to trench looking. "Oh, Sergeant Maddox, where are you?" Baker sang softly to himself. His face had ceased to be the face of a human being. It was the face of the demon that Satan had sent to possess him. Saliva drooled down the big man's chin and fell on the ground. His eyes were wide and reddened. He was naked from the waist up, weaponless except for the bayonet in his hand. The bayonet was all that he would need.

Come on, sarge, so we can settle this once and for all, just you and me. King of the Jungle. Survival of the fittest. Come on out now. This ain't no time ta play Hide and Seek.

As Baker approached yet another trench, he could see a tall soldier sitting on the edge of the diggings, with his legs hanging down into the darkness. The soldier had three stripes on his sleeve; it had to be Maddox. His back was toward Baker Dansford. The sergeant was gently patting his mouth with a bloodstained handkerchief. And though it was pitch dark, the demon inside of Baker could see Maddox quite clearly. Baker smiled, then began to creep silently toward his victim. It was tremendously hot, yet the tall sergeant was wearing his heavy field jacket. To Baker, it made the skinny sergeant appear much heavier than he knew him to be. But his only concern was that it would be a little harder to deliver a fatal blow with his bayonet. He could do it. He would just have to make sure the blade penetrated the thick coat, then went deep enough, between the ribs, to kill his victim instantly, so the karate-jock sergeant could not retaliate.

They were now only thirty feet apart. Suddenly, several large meteorites flashed through the air lighting up the darkness. Baker cursed them for the light they produced, but his luck held, Maddox had not seen him. Now he was directly behind the sergeant, five feet away. All he had to do was be real quiet.

Two more feet and I've got you.

The sergeant still sat quietly dabbing at his mouth and nose, seemingly unaware that Baker was behind him. Baker drew the knife back, then with every bit of the strength he possessed, drove the blade through the thick coat and deep into the back of the sergeant, between the ribs. Baker quickly pulled the knife out and drove it in a second time. Maddox did not move. It was as if nothing had happened to him at all. Dansford had heard about cases like this, where shock kept someone going even though they were dying. Baker drove his bayonet into the sergeant's back again and again. Still his victim did not budge. Finally he grabbed the sergeant and turned him around. But he was not ready for what he saw. It was the face of Maddox, sort of, but with more flesh on it. And it was not the coat that made the sergeant look bigger. This Maddox WAS bigger. A lot bigger!

The man who was supposed to be Maddox sprang up, grabbed Baker, lifted him off the ground as if he were a child, then put a bear-hug on Baker so tight that he cried out: "I give up! Agh--please!"

The pseudo-Maddox dropped his victim to the ground, and watched as Baker Dansford struggled to catch his breath. But even as Baker fought for air, he was adjusting his grip on the bayonet for yet another attempt on the stranger's life.

"Shall you be a fool to the last moment of your life, Baker Dansford? Cease this nonsense and use these last few seconds to prepare yourself to meet the Lord your God."

Baker spat at the suggestion, then slowly arose from the ground, and lunged at this other Maddox trying to rip the bayonet across the stranger's face. But the intended victim moved far too quickly, grabbed Baker's right hand, the one holding the bayonet, then picked up Baker Dansford and threw him through the air as if he were a paper toy. Baker screamed as he hurtled through the air, then put both hands out in front of him to break his fall, his right hand still holding tightly to the bayonet. As he hit the ground, the force of the impact drove the blade deep into Dansford's chest. Baker groaned, then lifted his head to look at the sergeant one last time before he died. But this time the man did not look very much like Maddox at all. And whoever he was, he was now wearing a shining white robe, and his powerful wings were beginning to carry him into the air.

The two herculean demons stood facing each other on the top of Mount Hermon. Hate blazed from their eyes as they stared at one another. Lesser spirits, some loyal to one demon, some to the other, stood well back from the two, and shivered in fear. Worlds had come to an end, and billions of human beings had been destroyed physically or spiritually by each of these two spirit creations. And each was the terror of all flesh, and worthy foes for even the mightiest of the Heavenly Hosts. Now each one wanted only onc thing: to destroy the other.

"So rotten filth of a general, you commit treason against your prince, do you?" Satan spat out.

"I do not call you prince but coward! You have had six thousand years to gain victory over God and those puny humans, yet all remains as it was. Shall we wait longer still for you, 'prince', to lead us? I say, NO! Instead I shall lead the rebellion against God and his angels, and it shall be I who enslaves these pathetic humans. And unlike you, I shall not fail. I, the Angel of Death, shall be MASTER of Creation. Bow before me and I shall let you have the least placc in my kingdom.

"You fool. Do you not know that I was APPOINTED Prince of the Power of the Air, by God Himself! You can not usurp my position. No one can."

"I can and I shall. So if you are through dulling my ears with your nonsense, be gone, lest you taste the power of the Death Angel."

Satan shook with fury. His eyes had became red with the fire of hell itself. He slowly lifted both hands above his head, tilted his head back staring at the sky, and yelled out an indescribable blasphemy in the ancient Yarrore tongue. Instantly a swirling green and yellow streak of lighting exploded from the sky striking Abaddon, knocking him senseless. Thc Dcath Angcl's beautiful blue robe was blackened and singed, the demon's skin badly burned and torn. A thick pus oozed from his numerous wounds.

Abaddon's fallen angels had joined their leader at Mt. Hermon, to watch the confrontation between their leader and Satan. They had deserted the soldiers of the UWO, and with their desertion, sanity returned to their former hosts.

The soldiers looked about in astonishment, having no memory of what they had been doing. There were dead and wounded all about them. The hundreds of thousands of survivors shook their heads trying to figure it all out, but before they had, sergeants and officers were yelling out the commands that would restore order to President Earlison's army. "Get those weapons charged--Now!" Or, "Lock and Load". Others were screaming for medics to tend the wounded, and transfer them to a safer place. The dead were immediately carried to the rear, and out of sight. In a matter of a few hours, the chains of command were rebuilt, units reassembled, and the army on its way to becoming a fighting force again.

Helicopter pilots and tank commanders hurried to get ready, too. On command, thousands of engines burst into life spewing tons of unburned hydrocarbons into the hot Israeli air. In moments the death machines were ready to do their part in slaughtering the thousands of tons of human flesh that could appear at any moment. Four hours after Satan and Abaddon had met on the top of Mount Hermon, the UWO forces were as ready to fight as they would ever be.

General O'Brennan, Supreme Commander of UWO operations, was satisfied. His troops, for some inexplicable reason, had been an impossible mass of men in revolt, deserting, and even murdering their own comrades. But now they were again an organized military fighting unit. They were flesh and blood fighting machines that he could use. And though exhausted by his hurried efforts to put things back together, he was ready. With a smile on his tired face, General O'Brennan began barking out the orders that would begin the last war on earth.

"Major, get those spotter planes in the air! And I want everything we've got firing at the enemy when they are within range. And where's the air force? Get em up there! Tell them to cut the dirty #%@$%&$ to pieces. This war is ON!" Yes, both he and his troops were ready. What more could a general ask for. He smiled once again, then entered his command tent. There were still a lot of details to work out, but General O'Brennan was happier than he'd been in years.

Abaddon pulled himself off the ground. Never had he felt such intense pain before. Still shaking badly, and with some difficulty, he pulled himself up to his full height, and stared at the grinning Satan. "Borret, my sword," Abaddon ordered.

Abaddon's servant hurried to his general and handed him a huge golden sword so large and heavy that only a few beings in the universe were strong enough to wield it properly. The smile slowly disappeared from Satan's face. He hurriedly looked about him for a suitable weapon to defend himself, but he had not brought his own sword with him, and those of his underlings were toys compared to Abaddon's.

"Now do you still wish to laugh and smile at Abaddon?"

Satan's quick mind was working furiously. He had to do something , but what?

"You should have destroyed me when you had the chance." Abaddon growled, swinging the great sword in front of him, loosening up, feeling his great strength return to him. "Now it is my turn to teach you what pain is all about, puny Prince of Darkness." Abaddon continued advancing carefully toward his former superior, with his weapon poised for immediate use. Satan tried to move slowly away, tried not to show fear. For to do so would have lowered him in the eyes of all those who watched. Instead he watched and waited and hoped for an opportunity to disarm his enemy.

Abaddon inched toward his foe. He was almost close enough. He tensed his tremendous muscles, ready to strike the blow that would destroy Satan and send him prematurely to Gehenna, the eternal lake of fire. He was close enough. Satan moved to his left, stumbled, and fell. The Death Angel was upon him; he quickly drew the sword back to swing, but he could not move his weapon. A powerful brown hand held his arm in such a viselike grip that Abaddon was almost totally paralyzed.

"Eeeeeeeeiiiiiiii--," Abaddon screamed in pain. "Let me go. I command you!"

The one who held Abaddon grabbed the sword with his other hand, and crushed the huge weapon as easily as if it had been made of tinfoil, he then spun Abaddon around to face him.

"Michael? What part do you have in this affair? Begone. This is between Satan and I. You have no right to interfere in our affairs."

"Michael," Satan spat out. His worst enemy-- the one who had recently cast him out of heaven. He snarled, picked himself up off the ground, then leaped at the brown-skinned archangel with all of his might, intending to destroy him. But God had not granted Satan the power needed to harm the holy angel. The demon bounced off Michael's body as if he had struck an immovable brick wall. Satan lay on the ground growling in pain.

"I address you both, and those who have chosen to follow you. You are forbidden to continue this personal fight. Each of you has been allowed to have an army. What you do with it is up to you. But like it or not, God is your Owner, and He has decreed that neither of you shall destroy the other. Your lives and your destinies are in His hands, and His alone."

"Forbidden? Decreed? Says who, you worthless angel filth?" Satan yelled, pulling himself off the ground.

Michael said nothing, but kept a keen eye on both of his adversaries.

"I can not speak for this Satan, who is a coward and fool," snarled Abaddon, "but as for myself, I shall do whatever I like. You have no authority over me, black faced angel of God."

Michael held up his right hand. On it was a ring that was heavy and golden in color. As Satan, Abaddon, and the host of fallen demons stared at the ring, brilliant rainbow colors began to emanate from it. Then a picture began to form before their eyes, a picture of a Man nailed to a cross, an innocent Man, a Man who had conquered death, and now wore the title: King of Kings and Lord of Lords. A Man called Jesus Christ. The fallen angels fell to their knees in fear, covering their eyes, and trembling before the vision.

"LEAVE, demons," said Michael. "Go to your own, and try to destroy the world if you must. But go, at once!" The mighty archangel stared at all the evil personages on the mountain top for a moment, then disappeared.

Satan, Abaddon, and their followers picked themselves up from the dust. Then with stares of hate for their enemies, the thousands of evil spirits flew from the mountain top, some going toward one army, some toward the other. The mountain top itself was left with a putrid smell that would last a hundred years.

Maddox felt rather stupid now that his mouth and nose were throbbing. And every time he took a deep breath through his mouth, his broken front teeth sent sharp jabs of pain through his head. And to think that he had done this to himself. Had he done wrong or right? Had he pleased God or Satan with his self-inflicted injuries?

"Maybe I was stupid to do this to myself, but I just couldn't take anything from the Devil. Not anything. Not after he killed Little. I just couldn't," he mumbled to himself.

Then a still small wind seemed to whisper in his ear: "I, too, experienced pain that I did not have to bear. And I died a death that I did not have to die, for you Maddox, and others like you. And I like you, refused the gifts that Satan offered to me."

Maddox stopped, bowed his head, and thanked the Lord for His gift of eternal life to all those who believe, then he resumed walking in a southern direction. He had no particular destination in mind. He just wanted to get as far away from the craziness, the killing, yelling, and noise as he could. He wanted to find someplace quiet to think things over--to remember, and to wait for the end that he knew was close.

Overhead hundreds of airplanes ripped the sky with the noise of their jet engines as they headed toward the oriental armies, to drop their loads of death. To his left, tank after tank rolled toward the area he had just left. And now he could hear the deep rumble of the artillery that flew in both directions, killing thousands upon thousands. Maddox wondered if he knew any of those who were now dying or had already been killed. The jeeps, tanks, and other death machines that rolled toward the front drove right by him. No one seemed to pay much attention to a wounded soldier walking toward the rear.

Maddox had deserted his post, but for some reason, knew that his decision not to fight was right. The Battle of Armageddon simply did not seem to have a place in his life. Or perhaps it would have been more accurate to say that he no longer seemed to have a place in all the activities that were taking place all around him. But he remained desperately lonely.

"Mind if I walk along with you?"

The voice came from another UWO soldier. He was a big man, shorter than Maddox, but heavier. Covering his right foot was a soiled bandage stained with a mixture of blood and dirt. The soldier was swinging along on his crutches at a pretty good clip.

Maddox gave the soldier a quick once-over. He was almost tired of asking the same question over and over again, but knew he had to ask "Who are you, and where did you come from?"

"The name's Peacheck, Freddie Peacheck. I've been moving south for the better part of a week, trying to stay ahead of the orientals. They overran our position last Monday, or was it Tuesday? It's kinda hard to remember. Hey, you're hurt, too. Was it the Gooks?"

Peacheck seemed harmless enough, and Maddox was glad for the company. "You can come along if you want to. But to tell you the truth, I have no idea where I'm going. The name's Maddox."

"I've been looking for an Aid Station, but it looks like you could use some doctoring too--for your face and mouth."

Maddox knew that Peacheck probably had a lot of questions about what he was doing here, and where he came from, so right there and then, he determined that whatever came out of his mouth would be the truth, no matter what the consequences. "Look, Peacheck. A lot of strange things have happened to me in the last day or two, like--like my face. No enemy did this to me, I did this to myself. I had a good reason, or at least I thought it was a good reason at the time. And one more thing, I'm not going back. I'm not fighting or killing anybody." Maddox watched Peacheck closely to see what his reaction would be.

"Sarge, I ain't gonna turn you in. I'm kinda running away myself. By rights, I should still be up north, near Damascus, with my unit, either dead or captured." Peacheck hesitated for a moment, then continued. "Sarge, I'm gonna tell you something just as bad as you told me, then we'll have something on each other, you know, for trust. Sarge, I'm a Christian. All the men in my outfit were Christians. That's why they put us way up there in Damascus, in the way of the advancing orientals, so we would be slaughtered, for the world to see, on T.V. So Earlison would have every reason to do whatever he wanted to do to those orientals.

"A Christian?"

"Yep, that's right. Didn't figure there were any of us left, did you? But there are, a few anyway. So now you know. You could turn me in, if you wanted to. But I'm hoping that you won't."

"Peacheck, I'm not going to turn you in. I'm a Christian myself."

"You're a Christian too? Well, praise the Lord. Guess they didn't kill as many of us as they thought. The boys in my outfit thought maybe we was the last ones left, you know--in the whole world. So how long you been a Christian, Sarge?"

Maddox smiled painfully through his injured mouth. "Well, I think it's been about five or six hours now."

"Are you kidding? How did it happen?"

The smile on Maddox was slowly replaced by sadness as he remembered Little and the hard time he had given him the last time that he saw him. "Well, to make a long story short: I had a guy in my outfit called Little..."

"Little? A short, skinny, little guy with dark hair and glasses?"

"Yah. You know him?"

"Know him? Heck yes. He was the minister of our little group up at Damascus, our little church, if that's what you want to call it. There were only about ten of us, back then, that met in secret--about two years ago. Then after that...", Peacheck laughed, "he and I shared a cell at the Necturate Prison Compound. He knew more about the Bible than anyone I ever met before. But then somehow some of the officers found out that we was both believers. After our court-martials, they split us up. I never did see him after that. I just figured that Little was dead. How is he?"

Maddox looked at Peacheck sadly. "He is dead now. Somebody murdered him a few hours ago."

"Are you kidding?" But the look on Maddox's face told Peacheck that he wasn't kidding.

The two men were close to a small creek. Both men half slid, half stumbled down the shallow embankment, and finally sat themselves on the still warm, mud bank next to the water. There Maddox told Peacheck his story. When he had finished, both were silent for awhile before Peacheck spoke.

"So the little twerp beat me to the Lord. We had a little bet, kinda, just for fun, which one of us would go to be with Jesus first. So he won, huh?. Well I'll have a good friend up in heaven to meet me when I go. But I sure loved the little guy, though. I'm gonna miss him." Then Peacheck's face brightened. "Hey! It's not like we're gonna live that much longer ourselves. Cause if this IS the Battle of Armageddon that's starting, and Little kept saying that it was coming real soon, then he didn't beat me to the Lord by much."

The meteor shower had finally stopped. Both men lay on the ground and stared up at God's incredible heavens. In the background the rumbling of cannons, and bombs increased, shaking the earth beneath them. Overhead planes and helicopters roared across the skies hurting their eardrums. But the creek bed, with its embankment, shielded the two soldiers from a good part of the noise, and they were thankful for the comparative quiet they had found so close to the battlefield.

"What happens now, Peacheck, if this is Armageddon, if this is the end?"

"Boy, do I wish Little was here, cause I'm not a Bible scholar. Not by a long shot. But if I understand it right, the Lord Jesus is gonna appear anytime now, to rapture the few of us Christians that are still alive, and--and at the same time, He's gonna raise the dead too, only the good ones for right now, the saints and Christians. Then we're all gonna gather together, with Him in the air, for a while. Next we all come back to earth, with Him leading the way--his angels too. Then Lord Jesus is gonna put an end to all the evil down here and be the King of the whole world. Course we'll be ruling, too, under Him. If I'm right that is. Sure wish Little was here though."

Maddox's mouth was bleeding again, and he dabbed at it with his handkerchief. "That's all right, Peacheck. You did great. I know more than I did. I just wish Jesus would hurry up and come. My mouth's killing me."

Peacheck turned and stared at him in a peculiar manner, then started laughing at Maddox's comment. When Maddox realized what he said, he started laughing too. "Ow--ow. Stop making me laugh, Peacheck. Ow-ow--."

While the two most powerful armies that had ever existed were slaughtering each other, only miles away, the two children of God had found peace and friendship while they waited for the return of their Lord.

Earlison stood in the dimly lit corner scraping furiously at the corroded battery terminals with his pocket knife. He had already nicked himself several times. Nothing serious, but his wounds burned from the filth that had gotten into them from the battery clamps.

Keep going, he told himself. So it stings a little, it doesn't matter. What's a little pain. Faster, faster. Work a little faster.

When he finished cleaning the terminals, he put them on the battery posts, then beat them onto the terminals with a small board that he found laying nearby. Repairs would have been a lot easier if he had the proper tools, but he didn't. Earlison had already added water to the almost dry battery, and he was again ready to try starting the obstinate machine. He really wanted to pray, wanted to ask for help from someone, but who would he pray to? He had convinced himself years before that there was no God. There were only gods like him, and like Jedeciah. JEDECIAH! He had to hurry!

Earlison quickly wiped his filthy hands on his tailored shirt, then hit the start button. The engine groaned, turned over slowly, coughed. He hit the start switch again. It turned over a bit faster, belched, then caught, and started running. It picked up speed. Exhaust began spewing out the exhaust pipe on top. Nice thick black smoke. The engine kept increasing its speed until the governor took over regulating it to 2500 r.p.m.

"It's running; it's running!" Earlison danced around the roaring engine as the room began quickly filling with the poisonous exhaust. Now he really had to hurry. It would only be a few minutes before he would pass out or worse, Jedeciah could return and try to stop him.

Earlison's lungs were already protesting the black smoke--tears ran freely from his burning eyes. He flipped on the main circuit breaker on the engine panel. The needle on the volt meter jumped, oscillated for a moment, then centered in the green area. He hurried over to the transmitter, turned it on, and watched as the red light came on. Everything else was automatic; the power settings, the frequencies--everything.

The president ran back to his launch control panel and plopped down in his chair. One hundred white lights lit by the generator's electricity stared at him, and at the bottom the FIRE button glowed a cherry red. Earlison began flipping the one hundred switches as fast as he could. It was a real race now; his lungs were already beginning to convulse, crying for clean air, protesting the poisonous exhaust fumes. Hurry, hurry, he yelled inside himself.

CHAPTER THREE

He was almost done. Just a few more. In a moment he would have all of the one hundred switches set to the "on" position. Then it would easy, one punch at the red FIRE button at the bottom and his little friends would be on their way. And then the world would be no more. Earlison was flipping the switches on the last row.

"What are you doing, Fool? Get away from that panel right NOW!"

"No! I won't. I won't." Earlison managed to cough out, still flipping switches as fast as he could.

"Won't?" snarled the spirit being. "Then I shall make you." The spirit leaped through the air toward the president, and indwelled him.

General Singh was in his tent, sitting on the edge of his bed, nervously wringing his hands. He jumped every time a bomb went off nearby, or an artillery round landed close. He had promised to kill Kau Gion, and must now do what he had promised. The war was starting, and Gion had to be dead before tomorrow. No, before today. But how was he to do it? And were was Gion anyway? Singh had sent several of his men out to look for Gion, but that had been hours ago, and no one had found the tiny general yet, and time was rapidly slipping away.

Singh knew he could never face Soo unless Gion was dead. And soon, too soon, the admiral would awaken. What then? What if Gion was not dead? What could he possibly tell Soo?

"Aaaaaiiiiii...." Singh dug his long fingernails deep into his flesh on his thigh drawing blood, purposefully inflicting pain upon himself, trying to forget the greater pain caused by his fear of Soo.

"Sir. Sir--," a young lieutenant burst into Singh's tent unannounced. He was out of breath, and shaking badly.

"What is the meaning of this? You cannot just burst in here like that."

"Sir, the Admiral has been shot. He's in bad shape general. He's not dead, but he's unconscious, and has lost a lot of blood. And--and General First-Class Kau Gion is dead."

"What? How did this happen lieutenant?"

"Sir, it appears that Admiral Soo and General Gion had a fight. General Gion seems to have shot our Admiral Soo, but the Admiral somehow managed to kill the General before he passed out. And sir, the last orders from the Admiral promoted you to General First Class. Sir, you're in charge."

This was unbelievable. Kau Gion dead? Admiral Soo seriously injured? Singh shook his head, and took a deep breath before dismissing the lieutenant. So he was now in charge. The heavy burden of having to locate and kill Kau Gion, just to please the Admiral, was off his shoulders. He felt like a new man. But now he had a war on his hands, and had no idea just how to proceed. Even as a general, Singh had always been given orders. Someone had always been there to tell him what to do. But now there was no one over him. No one to direct him to make the proper decisions. And the enemy planes dropping bombs on his troops, and the artillery fire told him that he had better do something fast, and that something had better be right.

Unseen by Singh, Abaddon entered the general's tent. The evil spirit looked at the man that was taking Soo's place. Well, at least Singh's body wasn't old and fat like Soo's. In fact, he could not have chosen a better temporary vessel than Singh, not on short notice anyway. Abaddon laughed to himself. And Satan still had to use the worn out body of Earlison. Abaddon materialized in front of Singh.

"Oh--Ah.... Who, who are you."

"I am a god--your god," Abaddon lied. "I have come to help you lead this great army to victory. That is what you desire, is it not?"

Singh fell to his knees, and bowed before the evil spirit. "Oh, yes, my god. That is exactly what I want."

"Good. Then I must enter your body and mind, so the two of us can become as one. May I enter?"

"But why can't we just make plans together? I will gladly obey you."

"Fool! Do you oppose the will of your god? I have no time to sit at a table and draft lengthy plans with you or your underlings. I must combine myself with you, NOW! Will you allow yourself to be used by me or not? But beware of my wrath if you refuse my request."

"Have mercy on me..."

"I do not have time for this, fool. Will you allow me to enter or not?"

"But, but..."

"CHOOSE!"

Singh paused for only a second before speaking. After all, this was an answer to prayer. He would again have someone to tell him what to do.

"Enter, my god."

Singh fell to the floor and convulsed momentarily, but consciousness quickly returned. He slowly arose, brushed himself off, and stared into a small mirror that he used for shaving. Yes, it was still Singh's face. None of his features had changed, but now there was a coldness that distorted his appearance, an evil that twisted the mouth and changed the look of his eyes. Abaddon watched himself smile through Singh's face. He was pleased.

General First Class Singh grabbed his helmet, stepped out of his tent, and began barking the orders necessary to have his armies engage the UWO troops.

Peacheck saw Maddox staring at the black disk in the star filled sky. "Little said it would be like this just before the Lord returned. Little said the sun would first scorch the earth, then die and become black, so it couldn't be seen--just before the end."

The temperature had plummeted since the moon had become dark, and both men were beginning to shiver. A strong wind was now howling in from the Mediterranean, but it was not loud enough to drown out the tremendous explosions coming from Megiddo. The darkness of the night blinked on and off with the deadly fireworks show taking place at Megiddo, shaking the earth as the bombs and shells detonated, killing untold numbers of soldiers on both sides of the conflict.

"I wish we were in Jerusalem," Peacheck said while trying to pull himself closer to the bank, to shield himself from the cold wind.

"Why Jerusalem?"

"Cause, sarge. That's were the Lord Jesus is coming back. Let me see if I can remember the scripture:

> Men of Galilee, why do you stand gazing up into heaven?
> This same Jesus, who was taken up from you into heaven,
> will so come in like manner as you saw Him go...
> Then they returned to Jerusalem, from the mount called Olivet

CHAPTER THREE

"Wish I knew the Bible like you, Peacheck. But I guess I blew my chance when I had it," Maddox said, drooling blood and saliva.

"Aw, heck, sarge, I don't know much. I figure it's God speaking through me--helping me to remember. He knows we ain't got no Bibles to read so...." Peacheck blushed, but it was too dark for Maddox to notice.

"Can you walk on your crutches? I mean your foot, does it hurt too much for you to walk?"

"Well, all I can say is it hurts like anything. I figure I probably got gangrene by now, or the start of it. But it don't matter. I figure I'll be getting a new foot pretty soon." Peacheck smiled. Maddox tried to. "Why, sarge? Where you want to go?"

"Well, I thought we might as well head on down to Jerusalem. We haven't got anything better to do."

And the beast was taken,
and with him the false prophet
these both were cast alive
into a lake of fire burning with brimstone.
Rev. 19:20

Earlison struggled with all of his might fighting to keep the demon from taking over control of his body. He needed only a few moments, just a few, to finish his job. But incredible pain was quickly washing away his consciousness. His limbs were already beginning to twitch and jerk like they always did when he began to seizure--when the evil spirit took over. With one last desperate effort, the president forced his right hand toward the panel of switches, jabbed the red button at the bottom, then surrendered his body and mind to Satan. A bell clanged loudly indicating that the missiles had been launched, all except one that is, the Norsac IV.

"Fool! Miserable, idiotic fool," the evil spirit screamed. But Earlison could not hear him. Because a moment before Satan could indwell the president, an angel of God grabbed hold of Earlison and pulled him far into the heavens, then cast him alive into the eternal lake of fire.

The spirit continued cursing the missing Earlison for a few moments, then exited the room. He had contingency plans to make!

The two soldiers were exhausted and could go no farther. They fell to the cold ground. But at least the exercise had warmed them a little, because it was really getting cold now. They crowded close together in a shallow ditch, and tried, as much as possible, to get out of the freezing wind.

"Guess we're not going to make it to Jerusalem", Maddox mumbled.

"Guess not," Peacheck responded trying not to show the pain he was in. "But I figure the Lord knows where we are, Sarge. He ain't gonna forget us. You just wait and see. Yep, it ain't gonna be much longer now, before we're flying through the air, going up to meet the Lord. Hey, sarge, wanna race?"

The battle intensified at Megiddo. Tens of thousands died each minute as the death planes and tanks killed wave after wave of human flesh that the orientals flung at the UWO troops, until the superior technology that President Earlison had amassed simply was not enough. Lines were breached, positions overrun, and finally the last battle on earth deteriorated into a hand-to-hand free-for-all, involving the millions of men on both sides. Each soldier was intent on only one thing: to kill as many other human beings as possible before he himself was killed.

Blood drained from the dead and dying, filling the shallow gullies, then ran downhill in little streams, joining still others until a great river of blood slowly made its way toward the Mediterranean sea.

High above the slaughter, helicopters and war planes fell from the sky on fire and crashed, as the orientals fired surface to air missiles, and blanketed the skies with antiaircraft artillery. As the planes crashed, they exploded, showering the earth with fire.

Then, as Scriptures demanded, birds of prey came to Megiddo, and began dropping out of the skies and landing on the feast that consisted of the millions upon millions of dead.

The end was almost at hand.

As Maddox and Peacheck shivered uncontrollably on the ground looking up into God's heavens, they noticed the appearance of long red lines that quickly traced their way across the blackness, defacing the beauty that God had made. More and more of these red scars appeared until there were almost a hundred of them. Then they began arching down, toward Megiddo, and toward them.

The darkness disappeared. Both soldiers saw a light brighter than the sun. A light so hot that it immediately vaporized their clothing, then melted their skin and muscles off their bones. Just as the pain became almost unbearable, they heard what they were waiting for. The most beautiful sound in the universe. A trumpet so loud and sweet that they both leaped for joy--leaped high enough to fly right into the sky and join their Lord as He descended on the clouds of heaven.

God's angels had reprogrammed every rocket perfectly. They had replaced all of the previously designated targets with only one: the Valley of Megiddo, and the area immediately around it. And by doing so, they had spared the rest of the world the nightmare of blast, and burning, and radioactivity.

One by one, the ninety-nine missiles fell out of the sky, deployed their individual thermonuclear bombs, then detonated. The hundreds of these powerful devices exploding over such a small target area not only incinerated all life forms but turned the earth itself into a lake of molten elements that flowed like wax. The very mantle of the earth ruptured with an opening that was miles deep, and allowed the entire Megiddo area to slide out into the Mediterranean Sea, though still connected to its parent land mass by a thin umbilical cord of red-hot earth.

The heat and pressure from the hydrogen bombs also caused a new portion of land to surface off the coast of Israel. The new land mass rising out of the sea collided and fused together with the radioactive, burning wastes of Megiddo, and the two formed one brand new continent.

CHAPTER THREE

Henceforth, Megiddo would come to be known as Hastedia Compotu, and would continue to burn for years to come. It would be nearly ten years before a human being would walk upon any part of this new country, inhabit it, and finally call it NEWLAND.

PART TWO

NEWLAND

CHAPTER FOUR

A small percentage of the human beings on earth managed to survive the tribulation period, the last battle, and finally, the appearance of Christ Jesus as Conqueror and King. However, these few had but short time to live with their star black and dead, and only God Himself could save them.

"LET THERE BE LIGHT!"

Now the rebuilding of the planet could begin.

(And Jesus Christ) hath made us kings and priests
to His God and Father
Rev. 1:6

Maddox walked quickly across the hard soil. His short brown robe was soaked with perspiration, and though he wore a wide-brimmed hat, his large beak of a nose was well sunburned. His hair was thick and snow white. On his back, he carried a huge canvas bag that bent him over beneath its heavy weight.

The woman that followed behind was much shorter than he, and had difficulty keeping up with the man who had been her husband. Her robe too was brown, but it was hooded, and hemmed with a dingy yellow, decorative material that had once been white. She, like the man was drenched with perspiration from the broiling sun. The woman's name was Eleea.

Eleea was beautiful in a simple uncomplicated way. She had long brown hair reaching almost to her waist that usually was curly and tied with pretty ribbons. But now it hung like a stringy wet mop down her back. She carried but a single item over her shoulder, a small bag made of skin that held the last of their water.

The man and woman had set out from Jerusalem, the World Capital, almost a week before. It had been a hard and tiring journey, under a hot sun, with no shade, and little if anything interesting to look at. The country they were in was a place of sterile, rolling hills, and covered with stagnant air that carried neither sounds nor smells within it. Even the sky was empty and without a hint of clouds.

Running east and west were mountains that roughly divided the continent into two equal parts. Not that either of the parts was much different from the other. For there was nothing alive in Newland, neither plants nor animals, except for the man and woman. And the only change in weather that they had experienced in all the days of their travel was the occasional, feeble stirring of the stale air that did nothing to refresh the two lonely souls.

In the southeastern part of the continent was a large burned out region called Hastedia Compotu, a black desert that was filled with deep pits that belched out a thick, black smoke that could be seen for miles. The region had another name too: the Land of the Dead. Hastedia Compotu was an accursed land that would never be inhabited.

"Let's stop for a minute," the woman said, trying to catch her breath.

Andy Maddox dropped his heavy bag on the ground, then stretched out his aching muscles. He glanced at the woman who had been his wife some ten years before. Now she was his sister and his queen. And though the two were no longer husband and wife, they were closer than they had ever been before. Things had changed so very much since the Lord had returned. The man looked with pity on Eleea, and wished he could simply offer her a shady place to sit and rest, or maybe a tub of clean water and a bar of soap. She had always been so clean and neat. Now she looked a lot more like a beggar than the queen she was supposed to be.

"How about some water?" she asked.

He nodded, took the almost empty water skin from her, then sipped just enough to moisten his parched mouth. Andy was so thirsty that he could easily have drunk all the water they had left, and still not have been satisfied. He took another very small sip, then handed the bag to Eleea. She took only a mouthful, before carefully hanging the water bag over her shoulder.

"How much farther do you think we have to go?"

Andy looked toward the north, the direction they had been traveling, and tried to judge the distance to the mountains. "I don't know. We might be able to get there by tonight if we try, or tomorrow at the latest. Only God knows for sure," he added, under his breath.

Andy and Eleea both knew that it would take a miracle for them to reach the mountains with so little water, and under such a scorching sun, but neither spoke their doubts. Yet deep within each of them, their very souls cried out for God to help them. "We can't make it without You, Lord. Not without You."

"Fear not. You will make it to the mountains, for I have sent you."

Had it been a voice or a thought? Neither the man nor the woman knew for sure, but both knew it had been from the Lord.

"We better get started, Eleea. We're sure not going to get to Holy Mountain by standing here," Andy said.

"You're absolutely right," the woman said. "Guess I'm about as ready as I'll ever be."

But before they started walking again, Andy Maddox took a quick look toward the southeast, toward that accursed region. And though it was miles away, he could clearly see the smoke ever-rising, pouring out of the bowels of the earth. Smoke that was a memorial to the millions of human beings who had once stood, fought, and died on that very piece of blackened earth. He also remembered that he himself had been there--just before the end.

Maddox shook his head trying to clear away the memories, grabbed the heavy bag, struggled with it until it rested on just the right part of his back, then began walking north.

Eleea knew his thoughts. "Try not to think about the Land of the Dead, Andy. Try." The woman was jogging to keep up with her king. "Surely the Lord had a reason for making that place part of our kingdom. Everything will work out, you'll see."

But the man did not hear the woman. His thoughts were in the past, and miles to the southeast.

And I saw an angel come down from heaven,
having the key to the bottomless pit,
and a great chain in his hand. He laid hold of the dragon,
that old serpent, which is the Devil and Satan,
and bound him for a thousand years;
Rev. 20:1-3

CHAPTER FOUR

"Aaaaaaaaaaaaaaiiiiiiii...", the demon screamed into the terrıble darkness. No one had the right to do this to him. "Aaaaaaaaaaiiiiiii...." And with his enormous strength, he yanked at the chains that bound his wrists and ankles, but the bonds held. Satan cursed the shackles; he cursed the bottomless pit that he had been cast into, and he cursed the angel, Michael, who had put him there.

"Just give me one more chance to meet that black faced angel, face to face, and sword to sword, then we'll see. Aaaaaaaaaaaaiiiiiiiii...."

He existed, and even God would not change that. And as long as he existed, he would hate. And there wasn't anything that anybody could do about that either! He was the master of hate--had invented the word. And not only the word, but the very concept, and all of the ways that this hate could mature and flower into the foul things that were so beautiful to him, like drunkenness, prostitution, abortion, murder, and yes, even blasphemy--the worst sin of the lot.

Hate, yes....And he had a right to hate as no other created being had. After all, he had been created the highest being of them all? Higher even than that second-rate Michael. And was it not written in the holy scriptures that he had been the most beautiful of all creation, and the wisest?

Yes, he had a right to hate. And he hated God most of all. He had hated his Creator for more than six-thousand years. He would hate God through eternity. And it was this very hate that he now used as fuel, to keep him going, to keep him strong.

Look at what they had done to him, cast him out of heaven. Him! And it had been that same Michael who had done it. And for what? For wanting a little respect? And yes, perhaps more than respect: adoration. And yes, maybe even more than that. WORSHIP!

Yes, worship. And so what. Didn't God have enough servants to worship Him? Then why was this God so jealous if just a few had chosen to bow before him, Satan? The demon's lips spewed unthinkable curses as he again yanked at his chains.

"Oooohhhhhhhhh...," the pathetic creature cried out into the blackness. Tears flowed down the face that had once been beautiful. But it was beautiful no more. It had become a hideous mask of evil. A mask so grotesque that he would strike terror into the heart of anyone who beheld him.

He had to get out of this place somehow. If only he could see in the terrible darkness. But he could not. And even as the thought entered his mind, something or SOMEONE told him that he had been blind long before he had been cast into the darkness of the pit. Spiritually blind. Blind to the beauty of God and His will. The thought enraged the creature causing Xesduca to struggle with the chains once again. But they only bit deeper into his wrists.

"Just give me some light and then I'll show you. I'll show you all!"

At that moment, a memory was placed into the demon's mind reminding him of the millions he had personally lead into darkness, and had blinded, both spiritually and physically.

"So what? I'm not like them. I'm Lucifer (the light-bearer). I'm Xesduca (the great one). I was a high covering cherub! I was the Prince Of The Power Of The Air!" The beast growled into the emptiness. Yes, he was a prince or at least HAD been, but what did the human slime call him? Satan (the adversary), or Devil (the slanderer).

CHAPTER FOUR

"But I'm more than that. Much more. I'll show you. I'll show you all! Aaaaaaaaaiiiiiiiiii..."

And the unbearable heat of the pit. He ground his teeth in agony. Oh, for one drop of water to cool his tongue, just one, he would give a fortune, a kingdom. They had no right to torture him this way. No right at all!

Again Xesduca yanked at his restraints. Then an idea began to develop in his fertile mind. He began to work on it, develop it. At length, he laughed out loud. Yes, he would be free. So they thought they could hold him in a prison with a few pounds of metal for a thousand years. "Ha!", he yelled into the darkness.

Satan forced himself to relax as much as possible under the circumstances. He shut his eyes and began to concentrate his powerful mind on the task. He began to form a mental picture of the chains that held him, envisioning the very atoms and molecules the chain was made of. He began to stretch the chain, mentally, just a little at a time, slowly pulling it apart, watching the molecules separate, forcing them farther and farther apart. Slowly, very slowly. Soon they would begin to lose their hold on each other. Soon the incredibly hard metal would become weaker and weaker, in his mind. He continued the process, never hurrying. He had as much time as it would take. The chain continued to stretch in his vision, the metal became ever weaker. It would not be much longer now.

This method had worked so often before. "Positive Visual Imaging" psychologists called it. They had advocated using it for everything from trying to create good self images to envisioning for themselves the riches that God had never intended for them to have. And the humans had never suspected for a moment that the entire process had been developed by him, Xesduca, for the sole purpose of violating the very laws of physics that God had created. The fools!

But now he himself would use his own device to regain the freedom that he deserved. Mental discipline coupled with his immeasurable physical power could not fail--would not fail!

The images in his mind had became crystal clear. The molecules were ready to separate, the chains that bound him were ready to fall apart. The time he had waited for was here. He mustered all of his strength, and yanked, HARD,but the chains held.

"No. It can't be!" The evil spirit exploded into rage, screaming madly, and yelling profanities and filth into the emptiness of the pit. He yanked at the chains again and again, until the hard metal ripped the bruised flesh on his wrists, and ruptured veins and arteries. Blood erupted from his wounds and ran down his arms and legs, dripping off into the nothingness of the pit. Xesduca screamed from the shock of pain that he had never experienced before.

Then another memory was placed into the demon's mind. The memory of another Who had been bound, hands and feet to a cross, and these pierced with rusting nails. And this Other, this Holy One, had bled, and had felt the same shock of pain that Xesduca had just experienced only multiplied a thousand times over. And to think this Other had volunteered to undergo this suffering and then to die just so others could be freed from sin to live. Xesduca remembered the event well, for he himself had been the one who had tortured Christ and put him on that cross."You have no right to make me remember. No right at all."

"Aaaaaaaaaiiiiiii...", the demon screamed in pain and frustration, into the blackness of the pit, that was to be his prison for the next thousand years.

CHAPTER FOUR

"Aaaaaaaaaaiiiiiiii...."

The man and woman rested in what appeared to be a dry creek bed that ran toward the north. Eleea had her hood up, trying to shield her from the tremendous heat of the sun. She leaned against the slightly cooler embankment and was sound asleep. Maddox looked over the top of the embankment, toward the mountains north of him. They looked so close. It almost seemed like he could reach out and touch them. But Andy knew that distances were deceiving in the crystal clear desert air of Newland. And he also knew that he had to get them moving. They had drunk the last of their water hours earlier, and would both die if they just sat under the murderous sun and did nothing.

"Get up!" Something screamed inside him. He obeyed, and struggled to his feet grabbing hold of the dry embankment; it crumbled into a fine powder in his hand. Could anything ever live here ? He wondered.

"Wake up, Eleea. We've got to get going. It's our only chance. We've got to get to those mountains. There has to be water up ahead, somewhere. There just has to be."

The sound of Maddox's voice sounded unreal and far away. And besides, she knew it could not really be him. It could not be her husband. He was far away, in another land, in the army. No, it could not be Andy. She would not be fooled. Go away, go away, whoever you are. It's not time to get up, and besides, I'm too tired. Please go away. And I'm so comfortable in this soft, clean bed. Go away, go away, and come back another day. She sang the last part in her dreams from a song she had heard years before.

"Wake up, Eleea!"

She forced her eyes to open. She was not in a bed at all. She was not even at home. She was sitting on the hard earth, was filthy dirty, and her throat screamed out with thirst.

"I'm sorry, my queen, but we must get started. We've got to keep moving until we find water." Under his breath, so Eleea could not hear, he added: "SOON! Maybe on top of the mountain there will be water. Maybe."

"Yes, you're right," she forced her dry vocal cords to say. "There will be water. High King would never have sent us here if there wasn't."

Eleea had always had enough faith to sustain the both of them in times of need, and right now the man loved her more than ever for that.

"Yes, of course there will be water," Andy said more for her benefit than for any other reason. "And look, we're almost there."

"Almost there...," Eleea repeated, still not quite awake. She looked at the mountains that were their destination, but to her, they still looked very, very far away.

Andy knew what Eleea was thinking. "Maybe if we try, we can be there by tonight, or at least before sunrise. If we try. Come on, my queen, we're almost there. Almost...."

"Yes, of course," she said, forcing herself to stand, then move forward.

The man slung the heavy sack over his left shoulder, staggered, almost fell, then took a deep breath and headed north, up the dry creek bed, following Eleea.

Both the man and the woman were far too tired to notice the small tear in the bottom of the heavy canvas bag that Andy carried, or the tiny black granules that were spilling from the bag onto the hard ground behind them. But one thing they did notice; it was almost sundown, and for this they were very, very thankful.

CHAPTER FOUR

"Thank God for the coming of darkness, for the disappearance of the sun," the man said softly. Eleea heard him and added the "Amen."

The holy city was atop the tallest mountain on earth. Much of Jerusalem still lay in ruins from the times of the tribulation, except for the homes of a few skilled workers that had been repaired, and the newly completed Temple that occupied the very center of the city.

The temple building, though simple, was strikingly beautiful. It sat at one end of a marbled courtyard. Toward the center of the court was a single, earthen patch cluttered with the wreckage of another building that had once stood there. This other building had been another temple with a domed roof, to another god, and this god's false prophet. This single blemish in the temple's courtyard would remain for a thousand years to remind any who saw it of the time when some men and women chose to pledge themselves to deities other than the one true and living God, and his Son.

The walls surrounding the temple area were twelve feet thick, and thirty feet high. The west wall had no opening, for the back of the temple was common to that wall. The northern and southern walls were pierced by three domed entrances. These had strong stainless steel gates across them, and were locked except for special holidays when the single gate in the east wall was too small to handle the visiting crowds.

There was only one entrance to the temple building itself, and it faced east. No door or gate barred this entrance, but not the greatest fool on earth would have dared enter this most holy dwelling place unless bidden to do so by High King Himself.

On the western side of the temple, and incongruous with the squared features of the rest of the temple, was a tall round pinnacle that reached seven hundred feet into the sky. Atop this structure was a pointed roof covered with pure gold. So brilliant did it shine that on a bright day it could be seen for a hundred miles.

Just beneath the golden top, was a special window made of pure crystal, that wrapped itself completely around the structure, and enclosed a small, circular room. It was said that High King would often climb the many thousands of steps that wound themselves around the inside of the circular structure, then sit in this room for hours at a time talking with His Father concerning the city below, and the rest of world that He now ruled.

The main building itself had stained glass windows on its northern and southern sides. These windows were the finest and most beautiful on earth, and had been presented to High King as a present, on the day of his coronation. There were twelve of these windows on each side.

On this particular day, the ninth day of the month, Tam'muz, the sun had already been up for almost three hours. Normally there would have been the sounds of workers banging away on buildings that were either being repaired, or torn down in preparation for something new being put in its place. But this day it was quiet, for this was the Lord's Day. And while most of Jerusalem's inhabitants were still asleep or just beginning to awake and think about some breakfast, two tall men passed through the locked northern gate of the temple grounds, and crossed the vast courtyard toward the entrance. Both men were dressed exactly alike in sparkling white robes that reached just below the knee. Both were powerfully built, and stood over seven feet tall. They wore thick golden belts around their waists, and from these hung great curved swords sheathed in leather that was trimmed with silver. One of these men was white and the other black.

When they reached the entrance, each removed the belt and sword, and laid them outside the doorway. Both bowed low, then entered the building.

A long hallway connected the entrance to the center of the building. Along the walls of this hallway were hundreds of golden plaques with the names of men and women, heroes of the faith, going all the way back in time to the very beginnings of creation. Off the main hallway were other corridors, and many beautiful rooms. But the two men went straight ahead, to the most important area in the building, the throne room.

The room was furnished entirely in woods collected from all over the world. Down the center of the room were tall marble columns that supported the high unadorned ceiling. Along the northern and southern walls were the handcrafted glass windows that allowed delicately colored light to enter the room, turning the interior into a rainbow of intermingled colors. At one end of the room, on a slightly raised platform of purest blue crystal, was a heavy oaken chair that was High King's throne. Stories told by some of the older believers said that this very same chair had been made by the Lord, Himself, over two thousand years before, when he had walked the earth as a carpenter's son.

The two angels approached the empty throne and prostrated themselves before it. Instantly the room was ablaze with light. "Welcome my good and faithful servants and my friends. Arise and approach me."

The King was dressed much like the two men before Him, but also wore a woven vest of gold on his chest. On this vest there were twelve priceless jewels collected by his messengers from the twelve planets of the star Nordtome. Upon His head he wore a thin golden crown beautifully interwoven with silver, and accented with twelve glowing jewels of red. And though High King was very much smaller than the men before Him, the giants somehow looked frail and anemic in comparison to their King.

The monarch had no age. Some who had seen Him would say that He was but a young boy, though of course wise beyond His years. Yet others argued that their King was old-- very, very old, yet hearty and athletic. His face was such that seeing it could strike such terror into the hearts of His enemies that they would immediately beg for death to release them from the stare of this Greatest of all Kings. But this same face could impart such joy and peace to His friends that it would become impossible for them to control the laughter and joy that would spring up from within their hearts.

"And have the two of you an answer for your King?"

"Yes, Lord," they replied in unison. "We will go, Sir. Gladly."

"Good. And in so saying, you have made Me happy, for I would not have made such a demand upon any unless they had been willing. And though it will be strange for you to live upon the earth as humans, you will get the chance to taste all the joys that only men and women have had the privilege to enjoy. But remember, with the joy shall also come a time of sorrow."

"Yes, Lord, we understand."

"And now to you, Gabriel, My faithful and much loved messenger, I entrust to you part of my name: Alpha. For into your hands I give the authority for you to make the beginnings on the face of Newland, and in the other kingdoms of the world as well."

The white angel bowed before his Lord. "I thank You, my Lord."

"And to you, Michael, my covering cherub, and my fearless general, I entrust to you a portion of my name also: Omega. For into your hands is given all authority to end all things on earth, beginning in the land of Newland, where you will dwell."

The black angel bowed low before his King. "Thank you, my King."

Until then, the mood in the Throne Room had been one of seriousness, but now the King smiled broadly, clapped His hands, and a feeling of hilarity entered the room. A flock of birds flew into the room oblivious to the fact that they were in the holiest place on earth, and began making such a happy racket that the three immediately broke into laughter. High King arose and headed toward one of the corners of the throne room where there was a table and chairs. "Come my friends. Let us sit, talk, and enjoy one another's company for a time." The two tall men could not have thought of anything they would rather have done.

They had talked for many hours, but to Michael and Gabriel it had seemed like only moments. "And now our time together draws short, for you both have some instructing to do. Look yonder." High King motioned toward a wall. Instantly it became a tall sandy mountain, and on it were two humans, a man and a woman, struggling toward the top. Both looked to be totally exhausted. The woman was stumbling and sometimes sliding on the steep path, while the man was trying to climb the mountain, carry a huge sack on his back, and help the woman all at the same time. Neither looked as if they were going to make it to the top.

"My two beloved mountain climbers have much to learn. Go and teach them, guide them, but most of all, love them. But before you go ...."

On the small table there appeared a loaf of bread and a cup of strong wine. High King broke the bread, as he had done two thousand years before, and gave each of the angels a portion, then took a piece Himself. The three ate the bread in silence. Then High King took the cup, sipped some of the wine, and passed it to the others. Each angel drank a small portion, then bowed their heads in remembrance and worship. When they lifted their heads, the Holy One was gone.

Gabriel and Michael arose and left the temple. Outside the sun shone brightly in the western sky, but it seemed dull compared to the Light they had been with only moments before. They crossed the courtyard in strong swift strides, and entered the city. Their swords were left behind. They would not be needing them for a long while.

The man and woman had somehow made it to the top of the Holy Mountain. Eleea lay on the ground, her head next to the empty water skin, more unconscious than asleep. Andy sat on the ground next to Eleea, staring into the darkness that hid the country around him. He felt guilty more than anything else. Why hadn't he simply come alone? Then, after everything had been settled, he could have sent for Eleea. But now it was too late. She was dying and there wasn't a thing he could do about it. Andy wiped the dust from his lips with the edge of his sleeve, and saw a small trail of red on the fabric; his lips were dry, cracked and bleeding. He bowed his head in prayer.

"Lord, if it be your will, I ask that Eleea be allowed to just keep sleeping until you call her home. She looks so peaceful. Please don't let her wake up to just another day of thirst and suffering."

Andy rubbed his stinging eyes with his sleeve, then lifted his head and looked at the wondrous heavens above him. Only severe dehydration kept tears from streaking down his dirty face. He had set out for Newland with only one desire in his heart: to serve High King. Now the trip was over and had ended in disaster. He had wanted to obey and to serve, but had failed miserably instead.

Did you really fail Andy Maddox? You and Eleea are on top of Holy Mountain--your destination, are you not? Did you think that just because you were obeying your King that your task would be an easy one?

Andy was so depressed that he shoved the thought aside. He sighed, took a deep breath, then saw it. Overhead a great golden star popped up from the horizon and began to hurriedly cross the heavens. It was more beautiful than anything he had ever seen, and much closer to the earth than any natural satellite could ever be. "And what, may I ask, are you?" Andy whispered quietly.

"That, Sir, is Apartia, or if you prefer, the New Jerusalem."

The husky voice startled Andy, and he tried to jump to his feet, but his weakness tripped him and he fell in a heap on the hard ground. Standing next to him were two enormous young men, one white and the other black. Their robes were so brilliant that Andy had to squint to get a good look at the men. And whoever they were, they had not been there a few seconds earlier--he was sure of that. Then it occurred to Andy that maybe his brain had simply given up from the heat, and the lack of water. He'd seen this happen to men before, just before their deaths. He began to shake uncontrollably with fear.

"Peace. Do not be afraid," said the black man. "We have come to help you." His words were as much a command as they were a statement. Immediately Andy stopped shaking. He tried to ask them who they were, but his dry vocal cords failed to cooperate. The black man knelt next to him and gave him a drink of water from an earthen vessel. The water was fresh and cool, and had a peculiarly soothing property.

"It is from Apartia's holy river," said the black angel. Andy grabbed the vessel and began drinking way too fast.

"Slow down, Sir. There is plenty."

Andy Maddox managed to croak out a "where," before he resumed his gulping. As he drank, the white angel was busy ministering to Eleea, holding up her head, and giving her water from an identical container.

The two angels watched Andy and Eleea as they began to revive. "Thanks," Andy finally said. "We--we would have been goners if you two had not come along when you did. But who are you?"

"I am called Gabriel," said the white angel.

"And I am Michael," said the black one.

Andy seemed to be deep in thought for a moment. "Naw, it couldn't possibly be."

"What is it my lord?" asked the white angel.

"I was just wondering, but that would be impossible, for the two of you to be the same Gabriel and Michael that are mentioned in the scriptures." He immediately felt silly for having spoken his thought out loud.

CHAPTER FOUR

Michael smiled. "We are the same. Unlike members of your race, the Lord our God has no need to name any two of His creatures with the same name."

Andy's mouth dropped open, and his heartbeat increased. Then looking at Michael: "But--but you're black. I thought that angels were...." Now he really felt very foolish, and did not finish his statement.

"White? Is that what color you thought all angels were?" Michael said with a slight smile on his face. "But do not be afraid. We are but servants of the Most High, even as you and your sister are. Yes, I am black. And besides, God has angels and other holy creatures in a lot more colors than just black and white. This you shall see with your own eyes, and very soon."

"I--I think I understand," Andy said just before bowing his head in a silent prayer of thanks. Eleea too was praying. Andy finished. "Yep, we would have been goners, pretty quickly if you two had not shown up when you did. Thank you both very much."

The two angels looked at each other again with just the slightest hint of a smile on their faces.

The man continued: "I figure that Eleea wouldn't have made it through the night, and I probably would have followed her shortly thereafter."

Michael hesitated for just a moment, then spoke. "Sir, when you say: ' wouldn't have made it through the night, and I would have followed her shortly...', what exactly do you mean?"

"Why--why, we were dying of course. What do you think I meant?"

Another pause by Michael, then: "So then, you and the queen did not receive your spiritual bodies when Christ appeared?"

"Well, of course we did. I was raptured just like all the other believers. Do you think the Lord would have chosen me to rule under him if I had not received my spiritual body?"

"Then, Sir, if you have been changed, why do you think that you would have died?"

Andy Maddox wasn't thinking; his tongue followed his emotion, and not his reason. "We didn't have any water. What do you think happens to human beings when they're out in the desert for days and days, in the heat without enough water? They die, that's what!" Andy Maddox normally did not have much of a temper, but the ordeal that he and Eleea had been through put his nerves on edge. His light skin began to turn a bright red, and the veins in his neck and temples became prominent.

Eleea by now was sitting up and listening very carefully to the exchange between Maddox and the angel.

"Sir," continued the black angel, "perhaps you do not know the scripture:

> and He shall wipe away every tear
> from their eyes, and there shall no longer be death

"Of course I know the scripture. Do you think that I, a king, am a complete idiot or something?" Andy blurted out, again without thinking. Then the Lord drove home the meaning of the scripture, and Andy Maddox stopped talking.

There was silence for a few moments, then: "Are--are you saying that we would not have died?" Eleea interrupted.

The two angels looked at each other first, then at the woman. "No, Ma'am. You would not have died," said the black angel.

"But--but we felt like we were dying." Andy said. "We were so thirsty, and--and weak, disoriented...."

CHAPTER FOUR

Gabriel spoke: "Sir, you took but a little water with you, and so when the sun bore down upon you, you expected to be thirsty, and so you were. And since you had journeyed far, you expected to be weary, and so you were. Then you remembered, from before your body was changed, that humans could die from heat and lack of water, and so you...."

"And so we felt like we were dying because we thought we should feel that way?" Andy interrupted. "But this has to be a bunch of hog-wash. I'm still worn out. And look at my lips, swollen, cracked and bleeding."

Gabriel and Michael looked at each other again. This might be a little harder than they thought. Gabriel began again with the patience that only an angel of God had.

"Then banish these things, Sir, and they shall not exist. You are now master over your body, since the Great Change, and not its servant as before."

Andy was just getting his second wind, and was about to begin arguing again when Eleea interrupted. "Andy, Andy, they're right. Praise the Lord, they ARE right!"

The man turned and looked at the queen. She was no longer the woman who looked to be on death's doorstep; she was alive, vibrant, laughing, and looked like a schoolgirl that had been caught playing in the mud, for she was still very, very filthy.

"It's true," she continued. "Try it, Andy. Look at me! I feel wonderful."

"Sir, your wife is right. Feelings of fatigue or pain, or hunger shall never again have dominion over you unless you allow them to do so," Michael said.

To Andy Maddox, all of this was more than a little hard to believe. But then there was Eleea.... "O.K., O.K., I'll try it. What do I have to do, shut my eyes and concentrate or something?"

The two angels were trying very hard to keep from laughing. "Sir," said Gabriel, "if that is the way you want to do it...."

"All right, enough, enough," Andy said before he closed his eyes, clenched his fists, and prepared himself for the great effort he was sure the transformation would take. But in this he was greatly mistaken, for as soon as he closed his eyes and thought about ridding himself of his bodily ills, they were gone. "Well, I'll be...."

The angels could no longer restrain their laughs of joy. Eleea quickly joined the two, and finally even Andy saw the absurdity of the situation, and joined the other three. The laughter was good and clean, and exactly what the man and woman needed after their long trip across Newland.

Andy finally stopped laughing long enough to wipe the tears from his smiling eyes. "I have played the fool, have I not?" he said to the others.

"No," said the woman, "you and I have only been fooled. But never again," she promised. Then Eleea picked up the edge of her filthy robe. "And these? Can we simply wish these clean?"

Gabriel spoke: "No, Ma'am. I'm afraid for those, you're going to need some good old-fashioned soap and water."

The two angels arose, walked over to an immense boulder that weighed hundreds of tons, and began pushing on it with all of their strength. For a few moments nothing happened. Then there was a loud "CRACK" as the boulder broke loose from the earth, rolled across the top of the mountain, then plummeted over the side crashing down the northern side of the mountain. This was followed by rumblings deep within the mountain itself that grew steadily louder. Then the ground shook hard as an enormous geyser of water exploded from where the boulder had been, and climbed high into the sky before gravity began pulling the tens of thousands of gallons of hot water back to earth. The sun had just risen, and its bright rays met the cascading waters, producing a magnificent rainbow. "A promise from the Lord," Andy said, remembering the scriptures from Genesis. Eleea added the "Amen!"

The two grinning angels returned to the couple completely drenched from the water. Michael pointed to a large rock behind the couple that now held clean robes, towels, and the much needed soap. "We shall leave you both for a little while," he said. "Enjoy the refreshment that our God has blessed you with." Both angels looked at the man and woman for a moment, then walked toward the northern slope of the mountain, and seemed to be following a path that was there. They quickly disappeared from view.

Andy quickly stripped off his dirty robe, grabbed a bar of soap, and naked, went running toward the warm shower provided by the geyser. "Now this is more like it," bellowed the skinny king.

"But--but what if they come back?" said the woman, looking shyly around her.

"Come back or not, this is about the only place I know of where a body can take a nice warm shower. Yaaaa-Hoooo...," Andy yelled as he began attacking the caked-on dust and grime with his bar of soap.

Eleea hesitated for only a moment, then took off her robe and joined her king under the refreshing waters.

The water from the geyser was divided by the top of the mountain. Part of it flowed north and began collecting in two large sandy basins that dominated much of that part of the continent. In time these would become beautiful lakes brimming with fish.

The water that flowed down the southern side of the mountain flowed down the same gully that Andy and Eleea had traced to the foot of the holy mountain. This water would meander across the southern part of Newland and become a small but very important river in this newly born kingdom.

CHAPTER FIVE

I am Thine, save me
Psalm 119:94

Rustlipper had no idea where he had gotten his unusual name. But there were a lot of things he did not know, because the many terrors of his past had been erased from his mind by a merciful God.

The boy was short for his age, which was twelve, and wore his entire wardrobe on his back. His ragged pants, much too large for him, were held up with suspenders. Over the suspenders, Rustlipper wore several old shirts on top of one another, and covering all of these, was an old but very warm army coat that nearly hit the ground.

Rustlipper was crippled. His right leg was shorter than his left one, and completely useless. It swung about in a random fashion whenever he walked on his wooden crutches, but because of this, his hands and arms were very strong. He had no family that he knew of, and no real friends either, and these were two of the reasons that he now found himself wandering about, all alone, in a strange and deadly land.

It had started when he heard about a brand-new country, not too far from Israel, that was being opened up for colonization. No one lived there yet. Rustlipper asked a few discrete questions, then almost immediately decided to go After all, this was his big chance for wealth and adventure. And because of his memory loss, Rustlipper had no idea that he had lived through one of the greatest adventures since God had formed the universe.

Rustlipper was impetuous to a fault, so when he decided to go to this unexplored territory he saw no need to consult with anyone, or obtain advice. He had always made up his mind about everything. There was no reason that this decision should be any different. And for sure he was not going to go to Newland with one of the groups that were being formed for settlement. No way! He would go alone, get there first, and it would be he who would find the treasure, get the best land--long before any of the others arrived.

Because he had lived in and around Bethlehem all of his life and had never gone more than a few miles from his home, Rustlipper had only the vaguest sense of direction or distance. When a girl told him that Newland was "about two hundred miles over yonder" it meant about as much to Rustlipper as if she had said two thousand miles, or ten. So after panhandling enough money to buy a few small loaves of bread and some cheese, he filled a large plastic jug with water and started off in the direction that the girl had indicated. There had never been the least doubt in his mind that he would make it.

But now, Rustlipper's feelings of confidence were long gone. They had slowly died in the long, hot days, and in the many miles of his journey. And worse yet, he was not only out of food and water, but was terribly lost.

Though Rustlipper did not know it, he had indeed made it to Newland. However, after traveling up the long, narrow land bridge that connected the mainland with Newland, he had veered to the east instead of going a bit to the west. So instead of finding himself in the main part of Newland, he found himself in a land of blackened earth and smoking pits. And Rustlipper instinctively knew that death was all around him. So far, he had managed to force himself to keep moving hour after hour, but now he stopped. He could go no farther. His hands were covered with blisters, some of which had already broken open and were on their way to becoming infected. And he was overwhelmed with a strange fatigue that was more than just a physical tiredness. He sat down heavily on the burnt earth. His plastic water jug was slung around his neck with a heavy cord. He pulled it off and tried to coax another couple of drops of water out of the container and into his mouth, but it was bone dry. He cursed, then threw the empty jug into a nearby hole that weakly puffed out a stinking, black smoke. Flames momentarily leaped out of the hole as the jug caught fire. "Serves it right, the worthless thing."

Rustlipper had been so busy trying to cover as many miles as he could, that until this very moment, he had not taken time to have a good look at the land he was in. Now for the first time he really saw it. Both fear and despair settled upon him. It was as ugly as Rustlipper could have ever imagined. No, uglier. And as far as his eyes could see, there was nothing alive--insects, trees, birds--nothing. It was a land of ashes. A land where everything that had ever been beautiful had been purposefully burned up. A monument to death itself. Rustlipper laid down on his stomach, lonely, and cried himself to sleep.

As Rustlipper slept, the poisonous gasses hissed into the air from the pits that were all around him, polluting the air that he breathed. They had already accomplished their deadly purpose upon his body, for he had breathed in far too much of the poison to live for very long. But there was even more than just poisonous gasses in this land that hated life. The charred earth itself gave forth invisible beams of deadly radiation that penetrated the boy's flesh, and began their own program of destruction in his body. In fact, everything in this land was the very antithesis of life. Anything or anyone who dared to violate the land's damnable borders had to die. The land itself demanded it. For the very soil covering the land had been formed from death, from the flesh and bones of over two hundred million human beings.

The boy continued to sleep, but it was not a sleep that gave him rest. He began to dream:

The blackened smoke from the pits all around him rose high into the sky. But this smoke was different than any Rustlipper had ever seen before. It was alive. At first, the smoke did not seem to notice him, but then it sensed that there was something in its territory that was alive. The black cloud began its search for this living thing. It bent low, sniffing the ground, investigating every nook and cranny. It came closer to him. There was nowhere he could hide. He wanted to scream, but knew that the sound of his voice would simply attract the snooping terror. It was just a matter of time before the smoke found him. Then it did.

The deadly black soot now directly above him began to slowly curl toward the earth. It touched his chest, seemed to caress him with its death. Then it engulfed him. He could not see--could not breathe. The whole earth was smoke. He held his breath as long as he could, but finally he had to inhale. The smoke entered his mouth and nose, rushed into his lungs, and devoured them. He wanted to scream from pain, but his lungs were already gone. He had no air with which to scream. He fought to arise, to run from the smoke, but when he grabbed his crutches, they crumbled into dust.

The blood in Rustlipper's head, deprived of the needed oxygen, began pounding harder and harder, building up so much pressure that the skin on his head split open revealing the raw bone under it. By now the smoke had eaten holes in his skull. His brain began to spill out onto the thirsty soil. "No! I can't just let it be soaked up like that." He tried to scoop his brains up with his hands, to shove them back into his skull, but his hands wouldn't work. How could they? There were no brains left to control them.

Rustlipper awoke trembling and drenched with sweat. He had to get out of whatever place he was in. He forced himself to get up with great difficulty. He was lightheaded and queasy as he grabbed his crutches. He was having trouble balancing himself. He was almost up. Almost. Then the left crutch slipped out of his weakened hand. He fell heavily to the ground striking his head on a large rock, knocking himself unconscious.

The dream changed. The ground was sending out long, thin ribbons of radioactive flesh that looked like worms. Like the smoke, the worms at first seemed not to notice him. But then the air began to grow cold. The skinny, wiggling creatures needed heat to survive. Rustlipper hoped that they would just shrivel up and die from the cold. And at first it seemed that his hopes would be realized, because he could see that some of the worms had stopped wiggling, had stopped their struggling. Then a few sensed that something warm was nearby. They slowly wiggled closer to investigate.

"No!" he yelled in his dream. "Get out of here!" The worms paid no attention. "Shoooo, shoooo..." Still they came. Rustlipper grabbed one of his crutches and began swinging it at the creatures, smashing them. They were easy to kill, soft and thin skinned. He was winning. But the more he killed, the more that seemed to come. Dead masses of slimy flesh were piled all around him, and still they came. Thousands of them, tens of thousands. He was tiring. He could not keep beating them off forever. His muscles burned from fatigue, his lungs cried out for more oxygen. He stopped to rest, panting for breath. But the worms needed no rest. As Rustlipper fought to fill his lungs with air, he could feel them touching his hands, legs, crawling onto his sweaty hair. They covered him. He tried to get up. To run away. But there were too many of them upon him; they pressed Rustlipper to the ground with their combined weight. He opened his mouth to scream, but the worms quickly filled his open mouth and choked him before he could utter a sound. He could feel them boring into his body with their sharp teeth. The worms were hungry. They were cold. Rustlipper quit resisting them, for he was dead.

He screamed himself awake. It was just another nightmare. He was not dead. He was alive. But now weaker than before. I've got to get out of here. Somehow. But how? He couldn't even stand up by himself. Maybe he could crawl out. Rustlipper managed to choke out a laugh at the absurd idea. His brain was spinning, and his lungs burned terribly. With as much effort as he could muster, Rustlipper rolled over on his back, and stared at the dark sky above him. Except for the smoke, the sky was clear, and filled with billions of little sparkling stars. "Why can't you help me?" he whispered out loud. "Why?"

As he stared at the sky, his eyelids began to close again, but before they did, Rustlipper saw a beautiful, golden star come into view and begin crossing the heavens. It had to be the beginning of another dream, because nothing could be that beautiful. "Oh, God," he whispered. "If you really do exist, please help me." It was the first prayer Rustlipper had ever said. Then just before Rustlipper drifted into yet another dream, he heard Someone say: "I do exist, Rustlipper. You know that I do."

----

and the leaves of the tree
were for the healing of the nations.
Rev. 22:2

The being was so brilliant that he was hard to look at. His powerful wings beat so rapidly that they were a blur. He had just taken off and was circling smoothly to gain altitude. When he was high enough to see the entire orchard, covering thousands of acres, he hovered and surveyed the countless rows of special trees below him. He had planted each and every one of them with his own hands. The Lord had also allowed the being to name each individual tree. The being was happy. He considered himself to be the most blessed of all God's servants, to have been given the job that he had, the job of gardener and caretaker of the holy trees.

The trees ranged in size from the huge old giants laden with fruit, to the just sprouted seedlings. In the very center of the orchard, was the very oldest and largest of the trees. It was so huge that some of its branches had to be held up with metal supports that were sunk deep into the ground. It had originally been planted on the earth, in a garden called Eden, at the very beginning of time. It was there, in that same garden, that a man and woman had sinned against God, and as a result, had been forbidden to partake of the fruit of this tree. All of the other trees in his orchard owed their existence to this one original and holy tree.

When he was satisfied with his inspection, he looked toward the distant south, toward the source of all the light in the city. In the very center of this light was a castle so tall that its top was hidden in the clouds. He turned and began flying toward the magnificent structure. As the cherub approached the castle, his own brightness became less, but that was to be expected, for everything in the universe was dark compared to the light that emanated from the Creator Himself, or even the Creator's dwelling place.

The cherub's name was Polat-Shar-Alt.

The castle, atop Most Holy Mountain, towered many thousands of feet above the beautiful valleys below. And flowing from the castle was the River of the Water of Life, that came from the very throne of God, and flowed through the villages of the Saints. On either side of the river were planted more of his trees, Trees of Life, that bore fruit twelve times a year. At most other times Polat-Shar-Alt would have flown slowly over the valleys taking in the wondrous sights of the mansions and gardens below him. But on this particular day, he had a very important appointment to make. An appointment with the Lord God Himself.

Polat-Shar-Alt flew higher now, circling to gain the needed altitude. He approached the castle high above the clouds, aimed for an open doorway in the very top of the structure, and flew inside. His heart was beating wildly, as much from the anticipation of meeting the King of all Kings, as it was from the tremendous effort it had taken for him to fly so very high. And to think that he, a lowly cherub, was going to have a private meeting with the Lord. He began to wonder why.

An hour later, the cherub flew out of the same high opening that he had entered, and spiraled down through the damp clouds to the valley below. Now he knew why God had called him to the especial meeting. God had given him a strange mission to complete. He would be leaving Apartia, the only home he had ever known, and journeying to earth, a place he had only been to once before. On earth, he would serve a human king and queen.

The orders had at first shocked him. But he dared not question his Lord, for he knew nothing of disobedience. And in his heart, he knew that God was right. For there was no one else who could do his job. For in the entire universe, he alone was Keeper of the Trees of Life.

The angel flew north toward the orchard he would not see again for a thousand years. True, he would miss his trees and the peace and beauty of Apartia, but even these treasures could not replace the joy he had that came from serving his God, from doing his will. And there was another nice thing about his mission, too. He would get to see his good friend Michael again, and he would finally meet Gabriel, the special messenger of God.

As Polat-Shar-Alt flew farther from the great castle, his brightness increased until he lit up the ground a thousand feet below him. Yes, he loved being alive, loved serving his Master. Surely, he, Polat-Shar-Alt, was the most blessed of all God's creatures. The angel did a cartwheel in the air leaving a red trail of light in the sky behind him.

And there was another thing that made him happy, too. He would get to give the earthly king and queen a present, a small seedling that would grow up to be a beautiful Tree of Life. It would produce a new crop of fruit each and every month, and its leaves would be used for the healing of nations.

But it would be strange to be human.

Rustlipper watched the brilliant golden star inch its way across the heavens for a few moments, then allowed his heavy eyes to close. In his past, he had seen hundreds of people die exactly like he was dying right now, from the poisons and radiation resulting from the Battle of Armageddon. And though he did not remember, Rustlipper knew in his heart that his eyes would probably never open again.

Dying? Was he really dying? But if he was, what happened after he died? Would his soul really leave his body like some people said? And was there really a heaven and hell like the Boeterqe taught? But in any case, it was too late to worry about now. And yes, in a way he wanted to die. Wanted it all to end. But even as he was wishing for death, he was also hoping that there was no hell. For as surely as he now lay all alone, in a strange land, if there was a hell, he knew that he would go there.

"Please, if anybody can hear me, don't let me go there. Please."

Rustlipper slipped into his world of dreams once again. This time, he found himself tied down with ropes and stakes in the middle of a burning desert. The sun, directly over him, was slowly destroying the flesh on his body. And not only could he not move, but he could not speak either. But even if he could have spoken, there was no one around to hear him. No one to listen. But this part of the dream was no different from his real life. There never had been anyone who really wanted to listen to him as long as he could remember. There had never been anyone who really cared.

He wanted to cry, but the tears would not come. He was too dehydrated. He looked up at the sun, and saw it slowly began to spill some of its fire upon the earth. The liquid fire splashed as it hit the blackened earth. Hissed. Then, inch by inch the fire slid along the ground toward him. It paused inches away, then engulfed him. He knew that if he breathed in the liquid fire it would burn out his insides. He kept his mouth and eyes closed, held his breath as long as he could, until his lungs threatened to burst, then he took a breath. The fire rushed into his lungs and incinerated them. He could not believe the pain. Then the fire began to devour his entire being.

But this was not the end of the dream. Rustlipper then saw a man who looked like he was made out of fire. He had powerful wings that carried him through the sun's fire. He was even brighter than the sun itself. The creature landed next to him, and with his rapidly beating wings drove the sun's fire away, cooling Rustlipper in the process. Then the man, if that was what he was, knelt next to Rustlipper, held up his head, and poured a little water into his mouth from a plump bag that hung over his shoulder. The water was deliciously cool and sweet. Very different from the stale water he had carried with him in the plastic jug. This Man of Fire pulled a single leaf from a small plant that he was carrying, and forced it into Rustlipper's mouth. The leaf's taste was strong and fresh. At first it stung Rustlipper's mouth, but in the next moment, the sting was replaced by a tingle, then a sweet minty flavor. It made Rustlipper smile. He chewed the leaf and swallowed it. The tingling traveled down his throat, into his stomach, then began to spread to his arms, head, and down his body. The burning in his lungs disappeared. Surely he had to be dead. Surely.

Dead? The thought jarred him awake. No, he wasn't dead. He was alive. Very much alive. The sun's fire was gone, the Man of Fire was gone. The being had probably been just part of another dream. But one thing was for sure, he was still in the same grotesque land of smoke and death, and he was still lost. But at least his strength had returned.

And the terrible burning in his chest was gone, too. Then Rustlipper remembered his prayer. Was there really a God? And had it been God who had saved him?

Rustlipper yawned, and stretched his arms above his head, as if he were awakening from the most restful of sleeps. As his head tilted back, his eyes fastened onto the beautiful object still in the black sky. It was the golden star he had seen before. The one he had thought to be part of his dream. It was just disappearing over the horizon. So, that part had been real

The crippled boy quickly found his crutches and mounted them without difficulty. The dreams had to have been a warning. He would get out of this place as fast as he could. But which way? Maybe distance was all that mattered. Distance and plenty of it. One way was probably as good as another. Right?

He would head northeast, the way that he had been traveling to begin with. Surely it couldn't be much farther before he was out of this area. Surely! Then he spotted two items lying on the ground, in the shadows: a water bag, like the one the Man of Fire had carried, and next to it, a small cloth bag. He hobbled over, lifted the water bag up to his mouth, and pulled the cork out with his teeth. A bit of the water splashed on his face and shocked the boy with its cool refreshment. Rustlipper took a small mouthful of the water. It was delicious, and seemed to soak into his bone dry body. This time he would ration the water better than he had before. He corked the bag and slung it over his shoulder.

Next he carefully picked up the little cloth bag and opened it. Inside was a light flaky material, yellow white in color. Rustlipper tasted a bit of the food cautiously. It had a deep nutty flavor, and was sweet as honey. He ate just a little of it, then carefully folded the cloth top over the grain so it would not spill out. On the side of the bag was written a single word, but Rustlipper had never learned to read. "Maybe it's the name of the guy who gave it to me," he thought out loud. He carefully tucked the small bag of food deep into one of the cavernous pockets in his old coat.

Rustlipper knew very little about God, but thanks welled up inside his heart, and demanded expression. He wiped a tear of joy from his dirty face: "Thanks God, for helping me. Now if you could just get me out of this stinking place, I sure would appreciate it."

Rustlipper stood there, readying himself mentally for the rest of his trip, when something else caught his eye. Next to where he had found the two items was a deep arrow dug into the earth. It pointed forty five degrees from the direction he had chosen to take. The boy looked in the direction that the arrow pointed, but it was still too dark to see much. Bet it was made by that Man of Fire, he thought to himself. Well, there was only one way to find out. Maybe it's time I started trusting in somebody besides myself anyway. Rustlipper took a deep breath, then began hobbling northwest, in the exact direction that the arrow had indicated.

He felt great. He smiled for the first time in many days. But he did have one small concern. His crippled right leg and foot, the one that had been numb all of his life, had begun to tingle and itch.

"Come on, child. We ain't never gonna get there by just a standing here," Windella said as she wiped the little girl's dripping chin, and put the jar of water back into the old toy wagon that held all of her worldly possessions plus what was left of the food and water.

Windella was a skinny, humped old lady who had lost the last of her teeth years before. But other than that, she was as healthy as a horse. In fact, Windella had never really been sick a day in her whole life. And because of this, the old woman was convinced that most sick people were usually a lot less sick than they wanted others to believe. Most simply used their illnesses to get out of work, or to get other people to feel sorry for them. "Lazy bums," she would sometimes say. "Why don't they get up and work for a living, like the good Lord intended?"

Windella had worked hard all of her life, and yet had sampled few of the better things in life. Overtly, this made her a hard and independent cuss, but inside, she had a heart of gold. She would never have admitted this to anyone, of course.

She had been married once, when she was young, but that had been so long ago that Windella's memories of being a wife were but treasured shadows. Her husband had been a good man, poor as a church mouse, and impractical to boot. When he died, he had left Windella penniless, and she had made her own way in the world ever since.

The little girl that tagged along with her was one of the many orphans that seemed to be almost everywhere nowadays. And if she had a name, Windella did not know it, for the little girl had not uttered a single word since she had hitched up with the old woman.

Windella had heard about Newland, and how it would soon be open for settlement. She had not waited, but had packed up her meager belongings, loaded them onto an old wagon she found in a dump, and headed out for the new country. On the second day of her trip, she glanced behind her and saw the little girl, half dead from hunger and thirst, following behind her. The old woman had taken care of her ever since.

Windella had never admitted to feeling sorry for anyone in her entire life, and she would not have admitted that she felt sorry for the little girl now, if anyone had asked. If a person had a rough life, or did not get the breaks that another got, well that was just the way things were. "And crying in your milk ain't gonna change nothing," she would say. "Ya gotta take what the good Lord gives ya and make the best of it." She had said these words so often that she almost believed them herself. Yet it was always Windella who was the first to share what little she had with another human being, the first to try to help.

In the few days the woman and child had been together, Windella had already grown very attached to the girl, but if they met anyone on the road, she intended to tell them: "Just watching over her. She's lost, you know." Or she could say something like: "It's fer the company. On uh long trip like this, a body can certainly stand to have some company." She had practiced these little speeches in her head over and over, so she wouldn't stutter or forget them when the right time came to explain.

"And now little girl, iffin we have any luck at all, maybe, just maybe, the two of us might find us a good place ta stay, en uh little plot of ground ta call our own. You'd like that, wouldn't ya?" But the girl did not speak, nor indicate in any way that she understood the question. Windella continued. "Yep, uh little plot of ground for our very own. A body can't ask fer more'n that."

But the farther Windella and the little girl traveled across the barren land, the more doubts the old lady had. "Don't seem ta be nothing here," she would whisper to herself. "I never did see uh place like this. I was uh hope'n to find some good land. Uh land of opportunity. But this is, well..." Then louder: "Come on, child. You're a poking along so slow it's gonna be next year afore we get to that there king they was telling me about. We gotta get movin, or all the good places is gonna be gone." Windella hoped with all her heart that there were some good places in this land, somewhere.

The little girl could have been pretty if she were clean, and wore a pretty dress, but she wasn't pretty now. She wore a pair of worn-out blue denim overalls that were too big for her, and it had been months since she had been properly bathed. But the girl didn't mind looking like a vagabond at all. Being pretty had never gotten her a thing. Food and other handouts came much easier to a little ragtag girl, so she was content to be as ragtag as she could possibly be.

There had even been a time when she could talk. But since then she had watched so many people die, and had watched so many graves being filled with the putrefied remains of human beings that, well--there just didn't seem to be much to say anymore. And besides, it was much easier for people to feel sorry for a little girl who couldn't talk. She always seemed to get just a little bit more than the other kids that begged. So if she had her way, she might just stay mute the rest of her life. If that's what it took to survive.

"Come on, girl. I never did see uh body as slow as you," Windella said as she yanked her wagon out of a rut. "Come on now. We got lots uh miles yet ta go," she said heading toward the tallest mountain in Newland.

Xesduca had quit pulling on his restraints. It was apparent that they were not going to break. But it didn't matter; he had another plan, and this one WOULD work. Then everyone who dwelt upon the earth would feel his wrath. And Michael would be destroyed.

Another idea entered his mind. Wouldn't it be perfect revenge if the great Michael were chained in this damnable place instead of him? What would the great cherub do then? The spirit gargled a laugh that filled the black emptiness.

Then he began. He shut his eyes lightly, and began to empty his mind of its many thoughts. All sensations must be ignored. His mind had to become as void as the space that was all around him. He began to chant, meaningless and monotonous pseudo words that he had invented centuries ago. Words he had taught to millions of people caught up in their false religions. The words had no particular power. It was the monotony of the sounds, the repeated resonances, over and over, that dulled the senses, then slowly began to sever the connections between the nonmaterial soul or mind, and its physical containment, the body.

For hours Xesduca chanted. The aches and pains in his arms, wrists, and ankles slowly began to fade away. All of these things were becoming less and less a part of him. The pain, the imprisonment, all that belonged to his flesh. They were not a part of the real him.

He continued to chant.

He was slowly becoming only mind, pure intelligence, the greatest intelligence that had ever been created. He continued the monotonous words, hour after hour until it was no longer he who chanted but only his body, the one that used to contain his essence. The impenetrable blackness around him began to dissolve. He could see!

Xesduca's essence began to separate from his body, pulling away from the prison that had been him. Finally, the last of the bonds separated, and the eternal soul of Satan floated free. He had done it. He stared at the pathetic body that was still chained, the one that continued to chant. He felt sorry for it. He would be separated from his own flesh maybe forever; he didn't know. But the world would pay for this separation! And God would pay the most of all! He would find his way out of this blackened pit, and then somewhere, he would find another body. Like he had before when he had possessed Earlison. But this time, the body would be better, younger... There were always fools around who were willing to let him enter in and possess them. There always would be. He and his followers had been in the business of possessing humans almost from the beginning.

And now that he was no longer restrained by his body, not only could he see, but he could hear. The total silence of the Bottomless Pit had been a large part of the agony he had had to endure. Now it was over. He listened to the sounds that were all around him. Faint sounds that now tickled his senses. Cries coming from somewhere. Thousands of cries --screams of agony, much like those he had uttered only hours before. Then he knew. He understood. They were the cries of the DAMNED. Those who had followed him all the days of their lives. They were the cries of souls that were in torment, stuck in Hades awaiting their final judgement from God. "Not if I have anything to say about it," he yelled into the abyss.

But what could he really do about it? Could he really free his followers once he got out? And where exactly was Hades anyway? He knew it was hidden away somewhere in the dark bowels of the earth, but where? He would find out. He had to. After all, he had to have followers, didn't he? Then the anger welled up inside of him. The fools, why didn't they use the intelligence that God had given them, like he had just done. Why didn't they practice the black arts that he had taught them, and separate from their bodies?

CHAPTER FIVE

At that moment, Xesduca hated his followers for their stupidity. No wonder he and they had been defeated. Maybe he should leave them where they were, for failing him in the past. Yes, he would have happily let them stay in flames and torments forever if he didn't need them. But he did. He would have to free them somehow. The idiots!

The evil spirit willed his essence to begin the long journey up the seemingly endless tunnel called the Abyss. Satan's soul looked much like a dark wisp of blackened smoke as it drifted toward the surface of the planet seeking a way out. There would be an opening up there somewhere on the surface. It would be sealed, of course, but such a seal could never keep his nonmaterial soul from passing through it. Xesduca sneered.

And even now, after he had freed himself from the chains that had bound his bruised and cut body, even now in his victory, the demon was not happy. For it was impossible that he should ever know the full meaning of the word. For true happiness came from God, and Satan wanted nothing from God. No, nothing at all.

As he drifted down the long corridor, he cursed and blasphemed God, knowing that the Lord had been behind his many defeats. And then there was Michael. He would almost be willing to go into the eternal torture of hell if he could somehow drag that black, angelic general with him. There was no one in the universe that Xesduca hated more than Michael, except God of course.

He and Michael were exact opposites. Only in strength, skill, and intelligence were they equals. But each angelic being had chosen to use the gifts God had given to him in different ways. Michael had submitted himself to God; Xesduca had submitted himself to no one. And even now, after all that had happened to him, the demon was convinced that he had made the perfect choice.

The disembodied spirit floated slowly toward the surface of the earth that was some fifteen hundred miles away. So slowly did this wicked essence travel that it would be months before he would break free of his prison.

Its streams thereof shall be turned into burning
pitch, and its dust thereof into brimstone;
It shall not be quenched night or day;
the smoke thereof shall ascend forever.
From generation to generation it shall lie waste;
and none shall pass through it
Isaiah 34:9-10

The eastern part of Newland was dominated by the LAND OF THE DEAD. Nothing beautiful could be seen in this land of melted hills, and deep smoking pits. However, there was at least one interesting feature in this unholy land, in the northern part. There was a large mound of dirt that was not charred and blackened like the earth around it, and on top of this mound sat a thick metal lid weighing many hundreds of tons. On this lid was inscribed in silver: Entrance to the Abyss.

CHAPTER SIX

With Hastedia Compotu far behind him, Rustlipper climbed down into a shallow ravine, and sat next to the earthen bank to rest. He drank a little of his precious water. Though the liquid was no longer cool, it still possessed the strange, refreshing qualities it had when he had first tasted it. And now for the first time, he noticed how little it took to completely quench his thirst.

But his one problem persisted: the itching in his leg and foot. Rustlipper began to wonder if something might be seriously wrong. Had the smoke in the terrible land gotten inside him and poisoned his atrophied limb? Or was it simply that after all these years, the worthless thing was finally going to just rot off? The thoughts scared him. Rustlipper took off his shoe, and began massaging his crippled leg and foot.

As long as he could remember, this appendage had dangled uselessly from his body, dead to all sensation. Now, Rustlipper was sure he was feeling something. He could feel himself rubbing his foot and leg, at least he thought he could. And the itching

But this was crazy! He couldn't feel anything. It was impossible. All the doctors agreed: his leg would always be paralyzed, would always hang useless and numb. The nerves leading from his spine to his leg and foot had been severed by a stray bullet when Rustlipper was a baby, before he had even taken his first step. And even before his mommy and daddy had been killed. But Rustlipper had no memory of those times, when he had had parents. As far as he knew, he had always been a cripple, had always been an orphan, too.

No, there was no hope--never had been really. He looked at his leg and foot. So soft and skinny, and flabby. But didn't it feel just a little firmer now? Just a little? Almost like there was some real muscle in there somewhere.

"Oh, if only I could really get well. If only I could walk like all the other kids my age." But as soon as he spoke these words out loud, he stopped, angry with himself for beginning to hope once again. How many times before had he hoped and wished this very same but impossible wish? Too many times! His broken heart could stand to hope no more. So he had vowed, years ago, that he would accept the fact of his handicap, that he would never run or jump like the other boys his age. He had also vowed that he would stop hoping. Hope only made being a cripple that much harder. But even harder to accept than being a cripple was the fact that he would be married to his two damnable wooden crutches until the day he died.

Rustlipper hit the ground repeatedly with his fist, cursing himself and everything else he could think of. He cried, lonely and frustrated. Then, after some moments, when his anger and frustration had vented themselves, he dried his eyes, and took a deep breath. He would forget the entire incident. But the tingling and itching in his leg would not quite let him do that.

Rustlipper replaced his filthy sock, and old shoe, then arose from the gully, and mounted his crutches. From where he stood, all of Newland looked pretty much the same: endless miles of flat, barren desert, except for the smoky land behind him, and the mountains to the north. But surely there was more to Newland than that. After all, all those people were signing up to come here to settle and begin their lives all over again. Maybe over the mountains, on the other side, the land would be different. He began hobbling in the direction of the tallest peak.

Once Rustlipper had put the thoughts of healing out of his mind, he again realized that he felt great. Even the blisters on his hands were gone. He began to wonder about that. How could blisters just disappear? But he was not in the mood to do any deep thinking at the present. His three immediate goals were simple: get to the mountain in front of him, get over the thing to the good land he hoped was on the other side, and then get his life started again. Only better this time, owning land, and maybe finding some treasure, too.

He covered the ground quickly and smoothly on his crutches, and marveled at just how fast he could really go with only one good leg, and a pair of ugly wooden sticks. In fact, he could go just about as fast as a normal person--no, faster than that. And on top of that, Rustlipper was quite proud of the bulging muscles in his arms and shoulders that came from having to use the crutches to walk.

"See! I don't need two legs. I can do anything I want to just the way I am," he yelled with the tears again beginning to stream down his dirty face. "See! I'm just as good as anybody else, even if I am a cripple."

He would make his own way in this world, and show them all. He didn't need anybody but himself, "and--and You, of course, God," he added, remembering his deliverance from the terrible land behind him.

Rustlipper forced himself to go faster. He began concentrating on the ground in front of him, looking out for rocks and holes that could cause him to lose his balance. He pushed himself harder and harder. He was flying over the dry earth. Even normal runners, the best in the world, could not keep up with him for long, not at this speed. His chest heaved; the muscles in his arms and leg burned as they were pushed to their absolute limit. Finally, panting for breath, and with sweat soaking through his clothing, he stopped, with a huge smile on his face. Yep, there wasn't anybody even with two good legs that could have done any better than that. NOBODY! He laughed out loud, then he lifted his eyes from the ground to see where his incredible flight had taken him.

No! It couldn't be true. He had been so busy going fast, concentrating on the ground in front of him, that he had not noticed the two people just a short distance away. And they had seen him--an old lady pulling a toy wagon, and a little girl trailing along behind. Rustlipper's first thought was to get out of there as fast as possible, or better yet, hide. But where? There was nothing close by to get behind, or under. And anyway, it was already too late.

"Hey, boy! Hey, over here. Right now, boy!"

Rustlipper cursed under his breath. He almost decided to disobey the old woman, and take off on his own, but something inside him compelled him to slowly make his way toward the bent old lady.

"Come on, boy. I ain't bit nobody in a coon's age. Fact is, I can't bite. Ain't got no teeth to do it with, " she laughed. Then, when he got closer: "Crippled, are ye? Well, crippled or not, you sure know how ta move fast, and use them sticks, don't ya, boy?"

"Yes, ma'am," Rustlipper puffed, still out of breath and with sweat running down his face.

"Well, even if you are crippled, it ain't no mind. Guess we're all a little crippled in one way or atuther. But where ya going in such a doggone hurry?"

"I--I don't know, exactly. I'm just trying to find a place to make a new start for myself, and maybe look for some..."

He almost said treasure, but decided not to tell the old woman this, "...some good land or something. You know, before all the others get here."

"Where's your folks at?"

"I ain't got none, ma'am. I'm an orphan."

"An orphan, and all by your lonesome? And way out here in the desert, too. And on top a that, you're just a pup. Well, one things for sure, ya can't be a wandering around in this God forsaken place by yourself. Excuse me, Lord," the old lady said, glancing toward heaven for a moment before continuing. "Uh soul could die out here. You'd better hitch up with us till we find that there king, who owns this place. He'll know what ta do with ya. He'll put everything right. You can bet your bottom dollar on that."

"Oh, no! I mean, no ma'am. I don't mean no disrespect, but I'll be alright by myself. I'm used to being on my own. And, and I don't want to be no bother to..."

"Bother? Why boy, I can't just let you wonder around this here place by yourself, and die, as likely as not. And bother or not. You're uh coming with us. Lands ta Goshen, ain't no telling what I'm agonna meet up with next. First I found me a girl child that can't talk, and now I got me a lame boy."

"But ma'am, I'd just rather be on my own way. If you don't mind, that is."

"Well, I do mind. Now lookey here, boy. We all gotta meet up with that there king who's in charge a this place, so we gotta go the same way anyhow. And since we do, I don't want ta hear no more about you a goin your own way, and us a goin ourn. Cause I ain't too old ta switch ya iffin I have to."

Rustlipper started to argue with the old lady, but she read the look of defiance in his face, and started digging around in her wagon looking for something to spank him with.

"O.K., O.K., I'll go with you," then under his breath, "for a little while." Then he changed the subject. "But what about this king you was talking about?"

"Ya mean ya ain't heard? Why, this is his land, his and the Queen's, that is--every acre. And everybody that comes inta this land has gotta report ta him, and receive his blessing, and find out where he wants a body ta go, and all that. And iffen he has a mind to, he just might give a body a hunk of land ta call her own."

To Rustlipper, the news couldn't have been worse. Not only was he going to have to travel in the company of the old lady and a little girl, but now he had to report to some king who might or might not let him come and go as he chose. He had to get away. Maybe when it was night.

"I can read your mind boy, plain as the nose on your face. So you better stop uh thinking about running off. I don't like this situation any better then you, but we'll stay together until we find his highness. After all, that's what us grownups is for, right? To protect youngins like you and this little girl. So ya hear?"

"Yes, ma'am, I hear," Rustlipper said with more than a trace of sarcasm in his voice.

"Now then, what ya got in that there pocket, boy?" Windella pointed to the bulge in the old coat. "Something ta eat, I'm uh hoping. All the girl and I has had to eat for the last three or four days is some stale bread, and these here apples, more cooked than raw. Course you're welcome ta help yourself to em iffen ya have a mind to."

"I've got some kinda flakes," Rustlipper said, reaching for the small bag in his pocket. "Kinda sweet. I've just got a little. I was hoping to make them last. But I got so hungry this morning that I ate almost all of em up." Rustlipper looked at his little bag that had been almost empty only hours before. Now it was as plump as when he had first found it. He opened the bag with his mouth hanging open with surprise.

"Let me see that. I never did see nothin like that."

"Go ahead, help yourself," he said, handing Windella the little bag.

"Thank ya, boy. Don't mind if I do." She took a small pinch of the flakes and tasted them. "Why, they're good, ain't they boy? Real good. I ken tell that this here stuff would put some meat on your bone if ya had a need ta. Come here, girl." The old lady put a pinch of Rustlipper's food into the little girl's mouth. "What's this here stuff made out of anyway?"

"I--I don't know, ma'am."

"Well, it's your sack. Where's ya get it?"

"Please, don't ask. You wouldn't believe me."

Windella looked at Rustlipper for a moment. "Well, I suppose everbody's got a right ta some little secrets. But what are these leaves in here for?"

Rustlipper looked into the bag. He hadn't noticed any leaves in the bag before, but they were there now. Then he remembered his dream, in the blackened country, and the Man of Fire, and how he had put a single leaf just like the ones in the bag into his mouth. "I--I don't know, ma'am," he said, somewhat frightened.

Windella picked one of the leaves out of the sack, smelled it, then cautiously bit just the tip off for a taste. "Woo--bitter, they are." Then after a few moments. "But they leave the nicest flavor in your mouth, after."

"You--you can have them, if you want." Rustlipper said, trying to be nice.

"Well, thank ye; don't mind if I do. Something nice ta chew on, that'll be a treat." The old lady stuck a leaf into her mouth and began gumming it like she would have if it had been chewing gum. "Woo--woo. Fresh." Then she spotted the word written on the side of the bag, and caught her breath in surprise. "Who--who are ya, son?" she said trembling.

"Rustlipper, Ma'am."

"And--and are ya uh real boy, or are ya somethin else. Cause I want ya ta know, that I never did mean no disrespectfullness, or nothing like that, iffen ya are what I think ya might be."

Rustlipper could see that the old woman was frightened. "Of course, I'm a real boy. What else would I be. I'm just an ordinary...."

"Then what ya a doing with this here stuff--this here MANNA?"

"All I know is that it's some sort of cereal. Why did you call it Manna?"

"Cause that's what it says on the side of the bag."

"Oh, that," Rustlipper said, trying to act unimpressed, and also trying to hide the fact that he could not read.

"Well, ya know what it is, don't ya?"

"Guess I don't, Ma'am."

"Well, ain't ya never read the Bible?"

"I--I never did take much to reading, ma'am, and besides, I ain't never had no Bible to read."

The old woman shook her head, feeling sorry for the boy for the first time. "Ain't your fault, boy. Ain't your fault at all." She started digging around in her wagon, and finally produced a old, worn, black book that she quickly began thumbing through. She found what she was looking for, pointed to the passage, then handed the book to Rustlipper. "Here, read it for yourself."

"I--I..."

"Go ahead, boy. It'll do ya good."

"Please, ma'am, I--I..."

Windella looked at the boy for a moment, then wiped away a tear that ran down her wrinkled cheek. "Can't read, can ya boy?" she asked, stroking Rustlipper's hair.

"No, Ma'am," said the boy, ashamed.

"Taint your fault. Not at all. But let me tell ya this one thing: iffen the Lord allows you and me ta be together fer any length uh time, you're uh gonna learn ta read, and from the Bible, too! But fer now:

When the dew that lay was gone,
behold, on the face of the wilderness
there was a fine flake like thing,
small as hoar frost on the ground.
And when the sons of Israel saw it they
said to one another, "What is it?"
And Moses said to them, "This is the bread
which the LORD hath given for you to eat."
Exodus 16:14-15

When she was through reading, Windella eyed Rustlipper as if she was seeing him for the first time. "Guess ya ain't no angel."

"Oh no, ma'am Whatever gave you that idea?"

"Cause you're uh carrying ANGEL FOOD in that bag. The same thing that the children of Israel ate, thousands of years ago and in uh desert, just like this too. So iffen you ain't no angel, and I'm beginning ta think ya ain't, then ya must be somebody special--ta the Lord--for Him ta give ya Manna ta eat. Who are ya boy? Not just your name; where'd ya come from, and all that?"

"I ain't nobody. Honest! If it's this stuff that's got you upset, then we can just dump it out--if it will make you feel better."

"Boy, don't say that! This is holy food. The Lord gave this to ya ta keep ya alive." Windella handed the small bag reverently back to Rustlipper. "Be thankful, boy. Just be thankful."

Windella again stared at the boy for a few moments. "Oh well, there's a gonna be plenty a time fer you to tell me who ya are and all that after we get a moving." Then eyeing Rustlipper carefully one last time, the old woman started repacking her wagon. "There's something strange bout all this, and I'm gonna figure it all out in good time. Just you wait and see. But fer now, we better get a cracking if we're ever gonna get to that there king." Windella took a deep breath, then ran her finger over her toothless gums; they were beginning to itch and tingle for some reason.

And the lion shall eat straw like the ox.
Isaiah 11:7

Gorbo the Great had no idea how ridiculous his name was, especially now that he was old and feeble. But that was O.K., because there probably was no one alive who remembered him, much less his name. But if there had been someone who had known him in the past, they would never have recognized him now. When he had been in the circus, years before, he had been the largest lion ever to have been captured and displayed. Bigger even than the tigers. He had been a true KING OF THE BEASTS. Now his long back sagged, his powerful muscles had atrophied, and he had lost a number of his teeth.

CHAPTER SIX

Gorbo did not feel sorry for himself, for by the grace of God, he had not enough memory or intelligence to compare the present with the past. In fact, the only thing that Gorbo knew for sure was that he was very, very tired, and thirsty on top of that. But even his instinct for thirst had been dulled somewhat, for deep within the lion something was getting him ready for death.

Gorbo slowly pulled himself along the dry earth with his great head hanging down almost touching the ground. His heavy ribs poked through his worn-out hide. He hadn't eaten anything in a very long while, and he was too weak to go much farther.

Yet something had driven the beast on, across the burning desert. Something. Someone. Gorbo stumbled on a rock he was too weak to lift his paw over, and fell heavily to the ground. So clumsy. So unlike the graceful cat he had been most of his life.

He lay quietly on the hot ground panting. Perhaps his time on earth was over. He did not think this, yet the lion knew in his own way that he would probably never move from this spot again. He tried to get as comfortable as he could. He closed his eyes, and lay still. The sun and desert would make short work of the job of putting him into a permanent sleep, where he would feel no more pain, no more thirst or hunger. Gorbo panted with his huge tongue hanging out the side of his mouth onto the dust. It would not be much longer now.

A short distance away, on Gorbo's left, was a gully about four feet deep, and as the beast lay dying, a faint trickling sound began to irritate the lion's ears. He tried to ignore it. He wanted only to sleep. It continued, seemingly louder than before. The annoyance would not go away, would not leave him alone. If the beast had had a language, he might have said something like: "Can't a lion even die in peace?" The trickling sound persisted.

Aggravated, Gorbo opened his eyes, forced himself up upon four shaky legs, and wobbled over to the gully. He would deal with the intrusion, then go to sleep for the last time. He tried to growl, but only a dry cough-like sound came from the animal. In the past, when he had growled, fear crawled down the spines of any living thing within a mile. Today, no one would have recognized the sound that came from his mouth. No one would have feared.

There it was. The source of that irritating sound, water. WATER! The beast hurriedly slid down the crumbly embankment, and landed upside down in the middle of the refreshing stream. He got water up his enormous nose, causing him to snort loudly. He righted himself, then began lapping the water as quickly as he could. Gallons and gallons of water. Finally, bloated with the liquid, he stuck his head completely under the water, then withdrew it and shook out his drenched mane.

He felt better. Gorbo began rolling in the cool water, and it seemed to have a rejuvenating effect on the tired, old lion. Finally he got to his feet, shook himself off, and let out a roar that would have done himself proud anytime in his life. He roared again, and again.

He was a wet, muddy, mess of a lion when he climbed out of the ditch, but a happy one as well. And though filthy, skinny, and still swaybacked, it almost seemed as if a lot of miles and a good many years had slipped away from the great beast since he had first stumbled into the creek. He roared once again. The ground shook. Gorbo was happy, strong and proud.

With his huge head held high, Gorbo began sniffing the air. There were several strong scents that he immediately smelled: the cool fresh scent of something vegetable, and another, one with warm blood coursing through its veins. Gorbo began trotting toward the two smells. He followed the same path that Andy and Eleea had walked less than a week before, and in the same general direction that Windella and the two children had traveled the day before.

Then Gorbo saw the vegetable he had smelled earlier. It was growing next to the water, in a wash that seemed to lead all the way to the mountains ahead. The same wash he had stumbled into earlier. He slid down the embankment, and trotted over to the grass that had sprouted from the seeds spilled from Andy's torn canvas bag. Gorbo hesitated for a moment, then took a small bite. It was delicious. The lion began filling his mouth, never wondering why he was, for the first time in his life, eating this strange green plant. He paused only long enough for a loud burp, then continued his grazing, more contented than he had ever been in his entire life.

With his belly full, Gorbo drank more of the cool water, then climbed the bank with a look on his face that was almost a smile. He smelled the air again. Yes, there it was again. That other smell. The warm blooded one. He shook out his wet mane and began trotting in the direction of that other smell.

Both Rustlipper and Windella had heard the sounds of a roaring lion hours earlier. Now they saw what had produced the sound. The creature was about a hundred yards away and moving slowly toward them. He was the largest lion either of them had ever seen. The girl, never having seen a lion, was the only one of the three who was not frightened. She smiled and clapped her chubby little hands together when she saw the big cat.

"O.K., boy, now just move slow. Let's see if we can put some distance between us and that thing." Windella said, grabbing the little girl's hand and pulling her behind the wagon. "Let's leave a little food--some bread and a apple, en maybe a pinch a that Manna. He might just be hungry."

The old woman and the boy quickly made a small pile of food, then slowly backed themselves and their wagon toward the mountains north of them. As they went they kept their eyes on the approaching lion, trying to keep the wagon between them and the creature. The wagon's rusty wheels squeaked loudly as they moved. The lion looked in the direction of the noise, and noticed the three somethings moving away from him. They seemed to be the source of the scent he was following. He yawned, licked an enormous paw, then started toward the three, letting out a tremendous roar as he closed the distance between himself and the humans. Windella stumbled, and almost screamed. Rustlipper's heart skipped several beats. The little girl smiled, giggled, and again clapped her tiny hands. She liked this new game they were playing with the big kitty.

As Gorbo came closer, Windella stopped pulling her wagon, reached into her heap of goods, and pulled out a rusty old hatchet. "It ain't much, but Samson had less then this when he killed a thousand a them heathen," she said with a quiver in her voice.

The beast continued closing the distance with powerful strides. He stopped at the small pile of food, smelled it, looked up at the three humans, then slowly ate the meal almost as if he wasn't that hungry. In the pile of manna was a single green leaf. Gorbo smelled it, then licked it up with his enormous tongue, and gulped it down without chewing it. Immediately the lion jumped up, shook his head, then alternately growled and sneezed several times, shaking his huge head as if to clear his senses. After a few moments, the lion looked at the threesome huddled behind the wagon, and started toward them again, unimpressed by their sacrifice.

Rustlipper threw one of his crutches on the ground, and grabbed the other like a club. He might get killed, but he intended to get in a lick or two before he died. The hair on the back of his neck was standing up from fright as he tried to put the wagon between himself and the beast. It was kind of strange. So many times in the past Rustlipper had wanted to die, but now that death seemed so very near, he realized how much he really wanted to live.

The lion came closer. His breath sounded like a powerful motor muffled and deep. Then he roared again. Loud. Windella almost dropped the hatchet, letting out a small scream in spite of herself. The creature seemed not to notice. He lifted his huge head, stared at the three for a moment, then dropped to the ground and rolled on his back, and laid there as if he were dead. But the giant heaving chest gave the cat away. After a few moments, he rolled back and forth with his tongue lopping out the side of his mouth, and looked more like an overgrown house cat than anything else. With his eyes only half open, the lion again watched the three somethings only a few feet away. He got up, and closed the distance reaching the wagon in but a few long strides. He began to circle around the wagon, trying to get to the three somethings that were always staying on the other side of the wagon.

Of course their defense was completely useless; the squeaking little wagon offered no real protection for the three at all. The lion could have easily leaped over the wagon and landed on top of the three humans with hardly any effort at all.

"Good Lord God, protect us. And iffen it's Your will that we be ate up, then forgive us our sins, en take us ta be with You, dear Lord," Windella whispered out loud.

The lion stopped at the old woman's voice, eyed the three, then let out an enormous burp. He plopped down on the ground and again watched the three.

Windella held the little girl's hand tightly while Rustlipper continued holding the crutch like a weapon. Long minutes went by. The humans dared not move. Finally, Gorbo got up, stretched, and roared so loudly that Rustlipper almost dropped his crutch--Windella screamed, and momentarily let go of the girl's hand. Immediately the little girl ran around the wagon to the beast.

Rustlipper dropped the crutch and went after the girl, grabbing her, and throwing her behind the wagon. Then he again picked up his crutch, and prepared to strike the lion if he came after them. But the beast simply laid down on his side, and watched the show, panting in the heat. Rustlipper pushed the girl farther behind the wagon.

Again nothing changed for many long minutes. The lion laid on the ground half asleep, and for the first time, both Windella and Rustlipper began to see the huge beast a little more like a pet and a little less like a menace.

"Why--why, I think it's some kinda tame lion," Windella said, still trembling. Both she and Rustlipper had an iron grasp on the little girl's hands this time. The beast continued looking benignly at the three.

"Here kitty, kitty, kitty."

"Lands ta Goshen, the child can talk."

The lion got up, shook his mane, then timidly came around the wagon.

CHAPTER SIX

"Here kitty, kitty, kitty...."

"Hush, child, maybe he'll go away," said the old woman still trying to keep the little girl behind her with the wagon between them and the lion.

"But I don't want the kitty to go away." The little girl said, tearing away from the old woman. She ran straight to the lion, and started petting him. The beast rolled on to his side, and laid there thoroughly enjoying the attention he was finally getting from the child.

"Why, I never..."

Windella and Rustlipper slowly approached the lion, and reluctantly touched his huge head. It was then that Rustlipper realized that he had only one crutch in his hands, and he was carrying that one. "Aaaaaahhhhhhh...." he yelled, startled.

"Hush boy, ya want ta scare the beast?"

"I--I'm walking. My leg--look!"

"Well, I'll be. Iffen this ain't uh day a miracles, I never did see one. Thank ya, Lord. Uh deaf and dumb girl talking, uh lion that thinks he's a tomcat, and uh lame boy walking. Glory be! What's the good Lord gonna do next?"

As Windella said this, her toothless gums really began bothering her. She took a calloused finger and began rubbing them. "Itching like fire, they are. Hummmmmmm. Almost feels like I'm getting a tooth over here," she said, pointing to a spot on her toothless gums. Rustlipper looked in the old lady's mouth and started laughing.

"Ha! You got more than one tooth in there. It looks like a whole mouth full is coming in." The boy started laughing; Windella blushed, and the boy's crutch went flying through the air, tossed away never to be used again by Rustlipper.

CHAPTER SEVEN

The night had passed. Maddox and Eleea looked down upon their new kingdom from the top of Holy Mountain. It seemed clear to both of them that Newland was made up of one type of land, and one type only: desert. But maybe a few things could be made to grow now that they had water. Yet they both had more doubts than they wanted the other to know.

Maddox then looked toward the southeast, toward the ever rising smoke that spewed from Hastedia Compotu. It had been ten years since that charred, burning land had been called something else: the Valley of Megiddo. Andy Maddox remembered how beautiful it had been before the tribulation, before Armageddon when the thermonuclear bombs had changed it into black ash. Nothing would ever grow there. It was a monument for others to see with their own eyes, to remember how sin can corrupt and destroy.

At the base of Holy Mountain, on the northern side, were two large sandy depressions. Andy wondered what could possibly be done with those. Maybe a few cactuses could be coaxed to grow there, he didn't know. And at the very southern tip of Newland were muddy, salt flats. Surely the only thing that would ever live there would be flies, mosquitoes, and a few poisonous snakes.

While these thoughts swam through Andy's mind, Eleea was searching vainly for a spot that she could turn into a garden. The rest of her life might be spent living in a desert, but she was determined that somewhere on Newland, in one small place, there would be an oasis where beautiful things would grow.

Eleea took a deep breath, then looked at Andy. There were times when she could almost read his thoughts, and this was one of those times. "Don't worry, dear. High King wouldn't have sent us here just to abandon us. When the time is right, we will know what to do with this land, and how to do it."

"I know, my queen, yet I often wonder why God chose me to be a king in the first place. I don't know anything about ruling. And the only things that I was ever good at in life were judo and soldiering. Surely that isn't the kind of training someone needs to be a king. And on top of that, I'm more than a little afraid that I'm going to fail, both Him and you."

"Maybe High King won't let you fail. After all, this whole thing was His idea, wasn't it? He is the One who sent us here, was He not? So it's really up to Him to help us accomplish whatever it is that He wants done, right?" Eleea scolded.

Gabriel interrupted. "Exactly, Madam. It is always our Lord Who places what is good into our hearts, then causes that good to mature. It is He Who then grants us the opportunity to put into practice the good that we have been given. And finally, it is our God Who grants us the power and strength that is needed to carry out the good thing that has been given us to do."

It was more than a little unnerving to have the two huge men appearing and disappearing without warning, but Andy made up his mind that he would try hard to get used to his two angelic friends.

CHAPTER SEVEN

Gabriel continued. "Please, Sir and Madam, come with us. We have something to show you. Come."

Gabriel walked toward the northern part of the mountain top, and met Michael there. The two then began descending. "Come, Sir and Madam, it's alright. You'll see," Gabriel said as he led the way. Eleea followed close behind the giant, followed by Andy, and last of all was Michael who shouldered the huge sack of Andy's and carried it as if it weighed nothing at all.

They were on a path that was well made, and appeared to be new. For some distance, it descended steeply, then ended at a series of switchbacks that led to a stone stairway. Next to the steps was a gleaming metal railing. The steps were made of highly polished marble, the railing appeared to be made of gold. The king and queen followed the white angel for ten minutes before they went around a sharp corner with a terrible drop-off; the view was breathtaking. As they rounded the corner, the stairs terminated at a sizable plateau, and on the plateau was the surprise: a huge circus tent complete with hundreds of flying colored flags.

"What's this?" Andy said smiling.

"Please, Sir, no questions just yet," said the white angel.

The couple glanced at each other grinning, then followed Gabriel toward the tent.

At the entrance, Michael put the sack down. "Would you, Sir and Madam, do us one special favor?"

"Sure, anything," the man and woman answered in unison.

"Then close your eyes, and keep them closed until you are inside the tent."

Both Andy and Eleea nodded, smiling broadly, and remembered the games, much like this one, that they had played in their youth. Eleea fought to keep from giggling at the two angels who were acting more like children than the fearless and holy beings they were. "O.K., let's go," Eleea said, hardly able to constrain herself. With their eyes closed, the couple felt strong hands guide them inside.

"Now you may open your eyes," Michael said, grinning broadly. Before them was a long wooden table, and on top of this table were some of the most taste tempting foods that one could have imagined. Maddox at first smiled, but then began to wear a bit of a puzzled look.

"What's wrong, sir?" Gabriel asked.

"Well, I know that we're a lot different than we used to be, and we don't need to eat--with these new bodies and all. So I was wondering: are we still supposed to eat, you know, like we used to?"

The two angels laughed loudly. "No disrespect is meant to you and the queen, sir, but you can eat IF YOU WISH to eat," the black angel said.

It took the king less than an instant to realize that he had asked a dumb question. But so much had happened to him and so quickly. Anyway he didn't mind a little humor on his account, not with friends.

"Well, in that case, I sure do wish to." he said, grinning as he grabbed a plate and began piling it high with delicious food. Eleea followed her husband around the table choosing the delicacies she had not tasted in a very long time.

Andy seated himself. "Come on you two laughing hyenas, grab a plate and dig in." Now it was the two angels whose grinning faces changed to very surprised ones, for neither had tasted more than a bit of bread, and a sip of wine in their many thousands of years of existence.

"Come on, come on. We can't eat all of this stuff by ourselves," Andy said with his mouth already stuffed with good food.

"Please, join us," Eleea added.

Michael and Gabriel looked at each other for a moment, then began loading plates of their own. They would enjoy their first real meal more than their two hosts could ever know.

Everyone was right in the middle of eating, when Andy, swallowing his mouthful of food, and without warning, bowed his head, and began giving a belated thanks for their meal. The others, caught off guard, bowed their heads, too; several were caught with their mouths stuffed with food and chewing.

"Thank you, Lord, for Your many blessings. You sure have taught me a lot of things since yesterday, when we first climbed this mountain--mostly how foolish I am, and how unworthy I am to rule anything. But anyhow, I'm here to thank you, first for putting up with me, then for seeing Eleea and I through our long trip, and finally for letting us meet these two fine angels--uh--friends. And we, Eleea and I, and--and, these two fine gentlemen here, sure do thank you for all this good food. Amen!"

The others added their "amens," then returned to their meals, but Eleea and the two angels ate with a little more caution, just in case Andy felt the need to pray again, without notice.

Thirty minutes later, each person at the table suddenly felt the necessity to finish what he or she was doing: chewing, drinking, or wiping their mouths. Each completed their task, then sat quietly waiting.

"So you liked the meal that I put before you, Andy Maddox?"

The end of the tent was ablaze with light, and at the center of the brilliance was High King. He was seated on the same wooden throne that had been in the Temple in Jerusalem several days before. The four quietly slipped out of their chairs, and prostrated themselves before their Lord.

"Arise, my children, and come close to me."

Andy and Eleea held hands, and approached the Ruler of Heaven and Earth. The two angels were right behind them.

"And what do you think of this kingdom that I have given you, Andy Maddox?"

"Well, I--uh--well...."

The High King laughed. "I admit that it's not much yet, but it shall be. You do believe me, don't you Andy?

"Yes, Lord.

"Andy, do you remember that scripture that I taught you:

> The wilderness and the solitary places
> will be glad, and the desert shall rejoice
> and blossom as the rose
> Isaiah 35:1

"Uh--yes Lord. I remember."

"And do you believe those words, Andy?"

"Lord, You know that I believe all of Your scriptures, and love them with all of my heart."

"Gabriel, go outside and bring Andy's bag to me, would you please?"

The angel hurried outside, and returned with the heavy sack.

CHAPTER SEVEN

"Andy, My servant and My king, how it grieved me to see you struggling with that bag. If only you had thought about the scriptures, and understood them." High King sighed. "But you have learned at least a little about those new bodies that I have given you, have you not?"

Andy nodded his head, embarrassed for having been so ignorant. His eyes were on the ground directly in front of his feet. "Yes, Lord."

"Please, my two servants, My king and queen, and My friends, do not consider this a time for scolding, this is a time for joy--a time for a coronation. Be happy My children! Gabriel, cut the bag open, and let us see what is in it."

The angel went to the table, got a small knife, then returned and sliced the thick canvas bag open. Countless small leather pouches spilled onto the earthen floor.

"Now, Maddox and Eleea, can either of you guess what these little bundles contain?"

Eleea gasped, then covered her mouth with her hand, as a thought entered her mind.

"What is it, daughter? Have you guessed?"

"I don't know, Lord. I was just hoping, but then, I never was very good at guessing."

"But this time you have guessed correctly. They are indeed bags filled with seeds, and seeds such as you have never seen before. They come from plants that were harvested by my servants, almost six thousand years ago, in a place called Eden. From there they went to Apartia, the home you have yet to see. They are genetically perfect. Here in Newland, they shall be impatient to sprout and grow. And Eleea, because it was you who guessed what was in the bags, it shall be you who will do the planting. And between you and Gabriel, and another that you have yet to meet, you shall turn this desert into the most beautiful of all My kingdoms on this earth."

Joy filled the woman's heart, then almost immediately she began to feel guilty for having been appointed to a job over Andy, and her concern showed clearly on her face.

"Oh, don't worry, little one, Andy is going to have plenty of things to do around Newland without worrying about planting trees and flowers. Yes, he will often be glad that you have spared him of this task. And besides, there are some things that a woman does better than a man, and bringing beauty into the world is one of them."

"Gabriel, isn't there a bigger bag in that pile, buried beneath some of the smaller ones, perhaps?"

Gabriel dug through the small bags until he found a larger, heavier bag. This he brought to High King. The Lord untied the cord around the leather package, and pulled out two very thin crowns made of gold and silver. Both were exactly alike, and studded with precious gems. The man and woman kneeled before their king.

"These two crowns in the world of men are priceless. But to Me, Who owns a thousand worlds full of gold and silver and precious stones, to Me it is your love that is priceless. Remember this when you wear these crowns, and remember also the love that I have for each of you." High King slipped the first crown onto Andy's head.

"Andy Maddox, this I have to say to you: never again doubt, for I am with you, and shall never abandon you. NEVER! No matter where you are or what you are doing. Can you believe and remember this?"

"I will try, my Lord."

"And you have wondered why I chose an athlete and a soldier for a king. The reason that you wonder is because you have forgotten that it was I who made all athletes. It was

I who ordered the strong bones and muscles, gave the quick reactions, and yes, ordered the opportunities for each one to succeed. I have done this for My own reasons, and for My own glory. And you have also wondered why I chose a soldier to be king. You have wondered this because you have forgotten that I Myself am a soldier. It is I who have fought against evil ever since the first sin was committed. It was I who fought the Evil One in the desert places when I walked the earth as a man. And finally, it was I, a soldier, who came to earth on that day of Armageddon, to fight and destroy evil and finally bring peace to this devastated world.

Andy, I have chosen you because you have a heart like unto my own. There are more reasons, but these shall remain secret to Me. Always remember this scripture:

and he that overcometh,
and he who keepeth My works until the end.
to him I will give power over the nations.
Rev. 2:26

"And now King Andrew Maddox, my special gift to you is WISDOM, because you shall surely need it. Rule well, and make Me glad that you are My king over Newland.

High King then turned His attention to Eleea. "And this is for you, My daughter." He slipped the crown onto her head. "Rule well in this land that I have given you, Queen Eleea Maddox. And as I gave Andy wisdom, I give to you, Eleea, a special heart of love. Share this love with all those who dwell in your kingdom."

Immanuel arose from His throne and embraced each of His new rulers kissing them on their foreheads. "I have given each of you an individual gift, now I give you a gift that the two of you shall share: GREATNESS. He who obeys you obeys Me, and he who serves you, serves Me." Then High

King sighed. "And if anyone sets himself against you, and it shall happen one day, it is Me he sets himself against.

"And now I give you new names. No longer are you Andrew Maddox and Eleea Maddox; You are DESERT KING, and DESERT QUEEN." The king and queen bowed before their Lord, and retreated several steps.

High King then looked at Gabriel and Michael. "Come forth my two good and faithful servants. There will be a bundle under the smaller leather bags, and in that bundle you will find two quite ordinary robes. Wear those and become as one of the offspring of Adam and Eve until the end. Serve Desert King and Desert Queen well, teach them, and love them, for in the both of you I have placed wisdom and knowledge for their benefit, and for the benefit of their subjects."

"Now, my Desert King, I have a task for you to do that is of great importance. You must journey to Hastedia Compotu, and there confront Satan, for he has escaped from the chains that were to hold him for one thousand years." At this point High King slipped a large ring from His finger and gave it to Maddox. "Here my king, wear this ring, it is a symbol of your authority. All who see it shall know that you serve under Me. So when you meet Satan, you must command him to return to his prison, and there remain for the thousand years I have determined to be his sentence."

"Lord, what if he will not obey me? And--and how do I find him in that terrible land?"

"He must obey. You are the king! You shall show him the ring that I have given you. And remember, do not doubt. As far as finding Xesduca, your tall friend, Michael, shall accompany you. He knows exactly where to take you, for it was Michael who cast him into the very pit that he is escaping from."

CHAPTER SEVEN

Desert King's face lit up at the mention of Michael's name. Because Andy was firmly convinced that there was no creature on earth who could harm him as long as he had the powerful cherub by his side.

"No, no, my king," High King said. "Michael will not be able to protect you, but rather it will be your job, as his king, to protect him. For after today, he will be fully human."

"Children, I must go, for I have many other kingdoms that need my attention. But before I leave, this I command: love one another, be strong, be wise. And be especially gracious to the first of the pilgrims that I have sent to you. For these three have known little in their lives other than misery, sickness, terror and loneliness."

High King looked at each of His servants individually, with love in His eyes. "Good-bye for a little while."

The tent was dark with the absence of High King, and it was many long moments before anyone moved or wished to speak. Finally, the man and his wife turned and faced the angels. The king and queen had become entirely different people; the unmistakable mark of YHWH was upon them. The angels bowed before their sovereigns.

Polat-Shar-Alt flew low over the dry landscape glancing back only once to the terrible land he had rescued the boy from. But now he had other things to concern himself about. There was a king and queen he would be meeting soon, whom he would serve until the Lord called him back home to Apartia. And there was still a spot of ground to be picked out for the growing of his precious little tree.

Polat-Shar-Alt had been a faithful servant to God ever since his creation. The cherub loved the Lord with all his heart, and trusted Him. It was this relationship of love and trust that the angel now leaned upon, for it was going to be very hard for him to come into the presence of humans, live with them, and even to speak to them. For Polat-Shar-Alt had never felt completely at home around men and women, and had spoken but a single word to humans in all of the thousands of years of his existence. "GO," he had said, commanding Adam and Eve to leave the Garden of Eden. And yet the Lord had told him, in the Holy Castle on Apartia, that he would learn to love the couple he was now to serve. But how could that be? How could he learn to love humans? And yet, Polat-Shar-Alt knew what the Lord said had to take place. For he had never known a single word of God's to be in error. The cherub took a deep breath and landed on the top of Holy Mountain, not far from the powerful geyser, and sat his small burden on the soil of Newland. The being then kneeled, and spoke to his Lord.

The banquet was over, the king and queen were crowned, but there were a couple of other surprises that Gabriel and Michael had in store for them. Farther down the mountain, about halfway to the valley below, was a small but elegant castle that was partially finished. The castle would be the permanent home for the royal couple for the thousand years they would rule Newland. Desert Queen was so thrilled when she saw it that she was speechless. She wiped away a single tear of joy. Desert King, on the other hand, had a hundred questions to ask Gabriel and Michael, about running water, plumbing and such. But as the day ended, there were no happier beings in God's universe than Maddox and Eleea, Desert King and Desert Queen.

CHAPTER SEVEN

"Why don't we climb to the top, and watch the sun set on our new home," Desert Queen suggested. The king and queen climbed quickly and tirelessly, marveling at the strength their new bodies possessed. As they reached the top, both saw the bright light, then discerned the creature that was the source of the light. He was obviously an angel of some sort, but very different from either Michael or Gabriel. This one was a brilliant red in color, and had thin transparent wings that constantly fluttered, helping him to maintain his balance. Additionally, the creature was very much smaller than either Michael or Gabriel.

When Polat-Shar-Alt saw the king and queen reach the top of the mountain, he approached them, then kneeled.

"Arise, and tell me who you are," Desert King said, amazed at the creature before him.

The cherub arose. "My name is Polat-Shar-Alt, Keeper of the Tree of Life. The Lord has decreed that I should serve both you and the queen in your new kingdom. I shall be human for the while that I serve you on earth." The angel watched his king and queen for a moment. "Sir, and Madam, if I may be excused, but for a moment, I have a small gift for you." The king and queen nodded. The angel flew the hundred or so feet to where the small potted plant rested, picked it up, and returned. He made a little dust cloud as he landed. He bowed from the waist, and handed the king the small tree.

"Why, thank you, Polat-Shar--ah--ah..." the king stuttered.

"Polat-Shar-Alt, Sir. And you are welcome. But sir, and madam, this is no ordinary plant. This is the tree mentioned in the very beginnings of the scriptures, the Tree of Life. The Lord has ordered that it to be placed in a garden that the queen shall plant. I am to tend and protect the tree for as long as I am here." The cherub hesitated a moment. "And if the king and queen desires, I would gladly help tend the entire royal garden, for gardening is what I do best." The being again bowed before the couple.

"Polat-Shar-Alt, I would be delighted if you would help me with a garden. But do you really think that you and I can ever get anything to grow in this soil?" the queen spoke half in jest.

"Madam, we shall have such a garden that all of the world shall marvel when they see it."

The queen smiled at the angel, stepped forward and kissed him on the forehead. It was then that Polat-Shar-Alt thought that he may have been wrong about humans after all. Maybe he really would learn to love this royal couple.

Later, on top of the mountain, the king and queen sat atop thick blankets on the ground, and just close enough to the geyser to hear the hot water hissing upward from the earth. Together, they looked at the diamond stars in the black night sky.

"Eleea, all the days that we traveled in this land, trying to get here, we never took the time to just look up at the stars. We've missed so much. You would think that after all these years, and all the Lord has taught us, and with these new bodies and all, that we would know enough to slow down, and just enjoy the blessings that are all around us."

Eleea pondered the king's words. "Maybe we're still too human in the way we think. And maybe the Lord is trying to teach us that even now, as king and queen, we still have a whole lot to learn--so we don't get too puffed up or prideful." This time it was Maddox who added the "Amen."

CHAPTER SEVEN

"Pray for me, my queen and friend, for I dread what I must do tomorrow. I know that I am king, and it is my duty, but to meet the very Prince of Darkness, face to face, and in that damnable land." He paused for a moment. "Did you know that I met him once, at Megiddo?" He took a deep breath, "but that is a long story that I shall tell you another time."

"I will pray for you, but do not let dread tarnish the mantle of authority High King has given to you. And besides, you will have Michael with you."

"You are right, my queen, but you must remember that our angel friends must live their lives on earth as mere men. Michael will be no match for the power of the Devil. It will be up to me alone to defy that terrible demon."

"Did I hear you say that you had to defy him 'alone'?"

Maddox blushed at his error, and was glad it was so dark. "Again, you are right, my love. I will not be alone. Nor shall I ever be again. For the Lord our God is with me wherever I go. It is enough."

The multicolored stars that had burned so brightly through the clean Newland air suddenly dimmed when Apartia appeared over the horizon, and began its journey across the heavens. The couple caught their breath at its beauty.

"Oh, Andy, I do hope that soon we can go up there, to the New Jerusalem, and walk the streets of gold."

"And indeed you shall, my queen." Michael had seemingly appeared out of nowhere. He looked much the same as he had before, but was now dressed in a simple brown robe that ended at his knees. On his feet were leather sandals. And though he was still powerfully built, the angel was now only slightly above average in height instead of the giant he had been only hours before.

"But first we need to establish your kingdom here in Newland," Michael said, "and plant a few million seeds, and settle the first of your new servants."

"Look!" Michael pointed down the mountain, toward the south. In the desert below, fifteen miles away, Desert King and Desert Queen saw a short boy bundled in too many layers of old, filthy clothing, jumping up and down, and yelling joyously as he pulled a toy wagon loaded with goods. Next to the wagon was an old lady who was busy rubbing away at something in her mouth, with her crooked finger. And there was a little girl riding on the back of a very large but skinny lion. Neither the distance nor the darkness hid the strange party of settlers from the powerful eyes of the king and queen.

"Who are they, Michael?" the queen asked.

"These are your first settlers, the ones that High King mentioned at your coronation. The boy is an orphan, who has been crippled most of his life, but is now healed, by the very leaves of the tree that Polat-Shar-Alt has given to you. He is jumping for the joy of having two good legs, and shall be for years to come. The old woman has been a widow most of her adult life, and without teeth until now. Her new set of teeth shall be complete in a few more days, and are also the result of the healing leaves. The girl, too, is an orphan, who has finally found someone to love her. And the lion, well, they used to call him Gorbo the Great. He was near death, but now shall live his new life in your kingdom."

Michael smiled. "Would you like to go and meet them?"

Neither the king or the queen especially felt like beginning a fifteen mile walk in the middle of the night. But the black angel read the couple's minds, and chuckled. "There are still a great many things you do not know about your new bodies."

CHAPTER SEVEN

"You mean we could get there without walking?" Eleea asked.

"Most certainly, my queen. If you wished."

The king and queen looked at each other, amazed. Then the king spoke. "No, Michael, High King brought us through all the trials of the desert, and taught us many things in the journey. Perhaps He wishes to do the same with our friends down there. Soon enough they shall be here, then we shall greet them. And then they shall have all the blessings that the queen and I can give them.

The ex-angel bowed before the couple. "A wise decision, my lord." He departed.

The evil presence seemed to grow stronger the nearer it got to the surface. It made no sound as it drifted up the long dark shaft, for it was pure spirit and soul, formless yet alive. It was the ultimate distillation of all that was evil and wicked in the universe. As it moved, it laughed, silently to itself, for it knew that it had won. Michael had chained him in the pit to serve a sentence of a thousand years, but he had escaped. And it had been so easy. Surely, even God would fear him now!

And when he did emerge from this hole, then the Kingdom of Xesduca would begin. The Kingdom of Evil. He would be the supreme master, once and for all. There would be no one who could oppose him. Michael and those who followed the angel general had shown their ineptitude by thinking they could keep him in a prison. They had been wrong.

The evil essence thought to himself: if the Bible was right, and he hated to admit that it often was, then what people were alive in the Millennial Kingdom, on the surface, should be easy pickings. They would be ripe for his influences. Instead of the innocents that they were now, they would soon become murderers, rapists and blasphemers under his tutelage.

EASY, so very easy.

The smoky substance continued its long, slow journey toward the surface that was now very, very close.

CHAPTER EIGHT

Do you not know that we shall judge angels?
I Cor. 6:3

Hastedia Compotu was directly before them. The two had been traveling since sunrise, and though it was late in the afternoon, Desert King felt no fatigue, no pain, or thirst. In fact, the only thing that slowed him down was his companion, Michael. Though still strong and powerfully built, Michael now had all the limitations that humanity owned: limited endurance, the need for sleep, and even the necessity to eat. "Shall we take a break, Michael?" The black man, covered with perspiration and breathing heavily, nodded. He stopped and drank from the water-skin he carried over his shoulder.

"Are we going in the right direction?"

"Yes, my king," Michael panted. "As you know, I've been to this land more than once. It was I who supervised the construction of the bottomless pit, and oversaw the casting of the dome."

"It's like living in the Bible itself, isn't it Michael? Satan, the bottomless pit, ruling under High King...."

"I understand how you must feel, my lord. It's hard for me to fathom, and I've been around a few thousand years longer than you have."

They rested for about ten minutes before the king spoke. "Are you about ready to get started again?"

Michael nodded, got to his feet, and led the way.

Desert King felt turmoil deep inside. On the one hand he dreaded the meeting with Satan, especially since he thought that he had made a complete fool out of himself the last time they met, at Armageddon, when he had purposefully injured himself. And on the other hand, he felt privileged knowing that he was doing the Lord's work.

As they walked, the soil beneath their feet slowly changed from the hard packed sand that covered most of Newland, to a black, cinder material. Their sandals began making loud crunching sounds as they walked. They climbed several steep, but low hills that had been formed when Megiddo had collided with the virgin soils of Newland. As they descended the last of the hills on the edge of the terrible land, they saw the first of the pits. It smoked weakly, emitting a black cloud that tumbled out of the small cone, then slid along the ground coating it with its black ooze. Beyond it were more of the pits, becoming more numerous and more active the farther into the land they occurred. A row of small conical hills was directly ahead of them and looked to Maddox exactly like overgrown anthills.

As they continued walking, Michael began to cough, and his breathing became noisy. The poison in the air was beginning to have its effect on the mortal. They stopped. The ex-angel reached into his pocket and produced a small leaf that had come from the Tree of Life, stuffed it into his mouth, and began chewing. Immediately the coughing ceased and his breathing returned to normal. The black man grinned broadly. "Polat-Shar-Alt. He gave me a couple of these," showing the king several more of the healing leaves.

The king looked at Michael, and nodded in amazement. One of the most powerful creatures that God had ever made was now subservient to him. "So be it," he mumbled out loud to himself.

CHAPTER EIGHT

"Over there, behind that tall hill, across the gully. You can see the lid shining in the sun," Michael said excitedly.

Before them was the entrance to the bottomless pit, not more than a quarter of a mile away. "Michael, let us pray before we go any farther." The two fell to their knees, and the king began: "Lord of heaven and earth, we come to this terrible land in obedience to You, and in Your Name. Give us now the strength and the wisdom to do what we must do."

"My God and Master," Michael spoke, "I thank You for this opportunity to serve. I ask for your protection and blessings upon us, Your lowly servants. Amen."

The two arose, hugged each other, then proceeded directly toward the metal cover atop the pit. When they arrived, both cautiously looked about them, but there was no one there, not yet anyway. A few feet away from the lid, they found several large boulders, flat on top, and seated themselves quietly with their eyes fixed upon the cover, waiting. Both were nervous, yet neither afraid, for both Desert King and Michael knew they were not alone. Their God was there with them.

The minutes of waiting became hours. The sun sank slowly toward the horizon. In just a few more minutes the sun would set, and darkness would begin its period of dominance upon the earth. The king remained perfectly attentive, but Michael's eyes had become heavy, and he was asleep. Desert King looked at his friend. "Take your rest, Michael, because far too soon, you and I must meet this Evil One and deal with him."

Slowly, on the metal cover, a discoloration or darkness began to creep across the lid that was not caused by the deepening shadows. The king's sharp eyes noted the slow change, and watched it carefully. The discoloration, or darkness began to separate from the metal, and became something very much like the black smoke that was all around them. It broke free from the cover and floated above it. Then it began to transform itself into an ectoplasm that slowly shaped itself into the grotesque shape of a humanoid monstrosity. A face took shape on the putrid thing of evil. As the eyes formed they fixed themselves first upon the king, then shifted their gaze to his companion. The face attempted a smile, but accomplished nothing more than a ghastly sneer.

"So I have company. A little tramp of a king and--and, HA! If it isn't my old friend, Michael."

Michael immediately awoke upon hearing his name, and stared at the perverted thing before him. He knew he should move, stand up, do something, but before he could, the ectoplasmic essence sailed through the air, and covered him; he could not breathe. Michael used all of his strength struggling to free himself, but the substance was like glue. It filled his mouth and nose with a foul tasting rubbery stuff.

"So you thought you could defeat me, and keep me chained in that hell hole," the essence said. "Now we shall see who shall be defeated and who shall live or die."

Michael continued to struggle, but without air, he would quickly lose both his strength and consciousness. The evil thing laughed as it worked to extinguish the life of his long time foe.

"Stop!" The command came from the king.

The ectoplasm quivered, lost its grip on the struggling human, then tried to reattach itself.

"I said, STOP!" The stuff immediately fell off Michael, and slid onto the black earth in a formless blob. Michael grabbed his throat and struggled to catch his breath. After a few moments, the evil thing began to reshape itself, forming a face more evil than before. It spoke through a hideous grin.

CHAPTER EIGHT

"And who is this nothing of a person who tries to command the great Lucifer?"

"I am Desert King. You trespass upon my land."

"Your land? And pray tell, who hates you enough to give you worthless land such as this."

"High King."

The grin disappeared from the monstrosity. "I know you. Yes, I remember. You are the scarecrow that loves broken noses and missing teeth." The evil thing laughed. "You are one of the biggest fools that I have ever had the experience to meet. And now you tell me that you are some kind of king, a Desert King. HA! But no, not Desert King, I call you Fool King." The ectoplasm laughed evilly.

"You tire me," Satan continued. "Begone, and I shall spare your life for a while. But not you, Michael. You, I shall kill slowly and savor your pain and your death." The ectoplasm lifted itself from the ground and began floating slowly toward Michael.

"Enough demon. Return to your hole, and come forth no more until the Lord decrees that your time of imprisonment is over!" The king arose from the boulder and faced the thing of evil.

The essense of evil stopped abruptly. "And you think that I shall obey a silly little king such as you? I, Satan?"

"Return to your hole--to your chains, and suffer as you have caused millions of others to suffer. Go. NOW!"

The thing tried to smile in defiance, but Desert King held up the ring given to him by High King. The face on the ectoplasm slowly changed to that of horror, then began to melt away.

"No. You can't make me go. No...." The ectoplasm had dissolved into a thick black smoke that was being pulled forcefully and painfully, against its will, toward the metal cover. "No. I'll do anything. Aaaaaaaiiiiiiii....." The smoke disappeared through the cover, but the evil spirit's cry could still be heard as it sunk deeper and deeper into the pit that would be its prison for a thousand years.

Desert King turned toward Michael. "Are you O.K., my friend?"

"I feel better now my king." Michael looked at Desert King with new respect.

The king put his arm around his servant. "I'm glad that's over. Let's go home. Who knows, maybe High King will have prepared us another meal, like the one yesterday. You'd like that, wouldn't you my friend."

Michael nodded. "Indeed I would, my lord." The two headed back toward Holy Mountain.

The stone steps went all the way from the top of the mountain to the valley below, stopping first at the circus tent, then farther down, at the incomplete castle, and finally ending at the rim of two large depressions that had already begun to fill with the water from the geyser. Desert Queen followed Gabriel, who was carrying the same heavy bag that her husband had carried as he descended to the valley below. The bag was neatly repaired. Behind Eleea, was Polat-Shar-Alt who carried the small Tree of Life. The seedling looked a little worse for wear; it was missing a large percentage of its tiny leaves that had been plucked off and given to the needy humans for their healing.

"Here we are, my lady," Gabriel said, setting the bag down, and helping the queen down the last of the steps. Eleea looked around for a few moments, puzzled.

CHAPTER EIGHT

"Well, I just don't know. It looks so dead. Where would you suggest I plant this garden, Gabriel?"

Of the three cherubs, Gabriel was the only one who had not as yet become human. He still had many beginnings to make in many lands and kingdoms before he would set aside his office as angel. "Ma'am, though the good Lord has given me many talents, gardening is not one of them. But behind you stands the best gardener in the entire universe. Perhaps he could advise the queen."

Polat-Shar-Alt blushed at the compliment. God's gardener looked very much different from the flaming red angel he had been only hours before. He now stood barely over five feet tall, and probably weighed less than a hundred and ten pounds. His complexion was dark, and he had thick salt and pepper hair that continued down his face and ended in a full beard. He was dressed in a short brown robe, but instead of sandals, he wore heavy work boots. His arms stuck out of the sleeveless robe displaying small, stringy muscles that had been designed for long hours of hard field work.

"Polat-Shar-Alt, I would be honored if you could help me pick out a spot for our garden," the queen said.

"Ma'am, I think you should probably call me something other than my formal name, for it means: Fire Cherub of God, and as you can see, I don't really look the part any more." He smiled not meeting the eyes of the queen.

"Then what would you have us to call you?"

"Well, how--how about just, RED?"

"Red? But--but..."

"Red is my true nature, my queen."

Desert Queen smiled broadly. "Then Red it is!"

"Thank you, my lady. Now, as far as the garden is concerned--over there. See that flat area, next to the depression? That should make a wonderful garden. It looks to be about ten acres, and will be next to the lake."

"Lake?"

"Yes, my queen," Gabriel answered. "As you can see, the spring waters have already begun to gather in the low places." He pointed to the sizable pond that had already formed in the depression. "Within a month, the lake should be completely filled."

"Oh, a lake. Thank God. It should be wondrous here in the desert. I can't wait," the queen said, looking toward heaven in thanks.

"Well, my queen, you are partially correct," Gabriel continued. "It is desert now, but by the time the lake is filled, part of Newland will no longer be desert but garden." The angel looked at the small gardener. "Right, Red?"

"Right," Red said smiling, liking his new name very much.

At this point, Gabriel began singing softly in an unknown language. His song started softly, but grew louder and stronger the longer he sang. After some minutes, Red joined in. It was the loveliest song that the queen had ever heard; it brought tears of joy to her eyes. In the distance, a small cloud appeared that seemed to be growing. It obscured both the sun and part of the sky. Soon the queen could see that it was no cloud at all, but thousands of birds headed directly for them. Gabriel stopped singing and quickly emptied the contents of the large sack on the ground, then hurriedly grabbed some of the smaller sacks and began dumping the seeds in small piles upon the earth around them. Red was doing the same thing.

In moments the birds began to arrive and to feed upon the seeds. When their bellies were filled, each took a mouthful of seeds and flew off. This continued until all of the piles of seeds were gone.

"Some to eat, and some to drop upon the earth to grow into grasses, plants, trees, and herbs. And someday, it will be necessary for you and the king to change your names to something other than Desert Queen and Desert King. You shall see, Ma'am," said a happy Gabriel.

Hundreds of empty leather bags littered the area around them, but there were twenty that remained unopened. "Those are the seeds for your garden, my queen. Tomorrow you and I shall plant them," said the gardener.

"And now," Gabriel spoke loudly, "I, Alpha, by the grace of God, create rain, which shall give birth to the seasons here at Newland." He placed his hands together, then spoke in an unknown tongue, obviously in prayer. He held his arms overhead, looked toward the heavens, and began humming the same tune that he and Red had sung before.

The queen stared at the sky. The stars that had begun to shine through the darkening sky now became obscured. Clouds formed at an amazing speed. The wind began to blow. Not the weak, dead breeze that Eleea and Maddox had experienced on their trip through Newland, this was the real thing--fresh and new, filled with strength. Streaks of lightening began to dance from cloud to cloud, ripping the darkness. A bolt of lightening struck twenty yards from the threesome with a loud crack, but none of the three was frightened. Then the rain began. Slowly at first, but before a minute was over, the drizzle had become a downpour.

"Praise the good Lord," the queen said.

The three headed back to the steps, and started the long climb toward the circus tent.

Windella hurriedly dug around in her wagon. "I know it's in here somewhere. It's got to be. Paid a feller a whole dollar and a half for it only a week ago. Ah, here it is." The old woman lifted up her prize, an old green umbrella, and though it was faded, it looked to be perfectly serviceable. "Come on, you two. We've got to find some kind of cover before that storm drenches us to the bone. I figure maybe fifteen minutes, at the most, before that there storm hits us."

The four were in the foothills at the base of Holy Mountain, and had been climbing for the better part of an hour. They had followed the grassy creek that unerringly led them to where they wanted to go, which was alright with Gorbo. He ate the luscious grass that grew next to the creek whenever the party stopped for a break.

Windella looked with apprehension at the streaks of lightening that flashed from cloud to cloud, and occasionally struck the top of the mountains. She didn't like the looks of this storm one bit, nor the idea of being caught out in the open. "Hurry up, now. We got to get us somewhere fast." She grabbed the wagon handle from Rustlipper and yanked the contraption hurriedly toward a bunch of rocks that she hoped would offer some sort of shelter.

Rustlipper and the little girl, unlike Windella, had spent most of their lives out of doors; they were not nearly as concerned about the possibility of getting wet as was Windella. "Hurry, " she said over and over. The old woman began praying.

There was a blinding flash directly ahead of them. Windella closed her eyes tightly, thinking that it had been a lightening strike. She grabbed the little girl's hand tightly. When she opened her eyes, there was a tall man in brilliant apparel standing before her. Windella gasped and began shaking uncontrollably, falling to her knees.

The man walked quickly over to the group. "Arise, madam. For I, like yourself, am but a servant of our great God."

Windella arose unsteadily. "Who are--are you?"

"My name is Gabriel. Now, please follow me. I shall lead you to shelter." He picked up the heavy wagon with one hand, balanced it on his shoulder, then led them up the path at a quick walk. Windella, the little girl, and Rustlipper had to jog to keep up. Only Gorbo followed easily, trotting happily along after the other three. The large cat liked this other thing, tall and bright, that had joined their party. It had a pleasant odor very unlike the other three somethings. Gorbo swished his tail happily.

The tall man went down a ravine, turned left around an outcropping, then seemed to disappear. As Windella rounded the same outcropping, she saw where the man had gone. Before her was an opening in the side of a hill that was filled with light. It was a cave. Windella entered with the other three close behind. The sides of the cave had old-fashioned torches attached to them, and these gave the room a warm, comfortable look. And in the very center of the cave was a rough unfinished table covered with steaming foods of every description upon it.

"Lands ta Goshen ," was all that Windella could say, and this with some difficulty because of her new teeth.

Gabriel smiled at the old lady, "The four of you should be quite comfortable in here for the night. And as for the food, it comes with the best of wishes from Desert Queen."

"Who?" Windella and Rustlipper asked in unison.

"Desert Queen. She and the king are responsible for the rule of this country. It is she and the king that you must meet when you climb the holy mountain. But for now eat and rest. I shall be back for you tomorrow, after the storm, and lead you up the mountain."

Rustlipper and the little girl wasted no time getting to the table, and piling their plates full of food. Windella looked over at the children embarrassed.

"Those little ones ain't mine. I--I love them like they was, but they ain't. But anyhow, I do thank you Mr. Gabriel."

"You may thank the queen and the king when you meet them ." He finished speaking, and immediately disappeared.

"Lands ta Goshen." It was some moments before Windella could say anything more. "And--and you two. Iffen I had a switch, I think I'd teach you both some manners." Then she saw Gorbo. He was just as bad as the children, he had already devoured more than half of a large watermelon. "And I'd switch you too, you overgrown tom-cat," she said smiling through her beautiful, new teeth. She shook her head and joined the others. "Thank the Holy Lord for His care, and--and Desert Queen, whoever she is." She couldn't say more for she was already stuffing fresh hot bread into her mouth.

Outside the winds began howling in earnest; the rains followed shortly, but inside the cave, the four Newland residents ate until they were stuffed, then three humans plopped onto the small cots, and fell soundly asleep with satisfied grins upon their faces. Only once did Windella wake up, when Gorbo loudly burped.

Peter Samtouge was a "bum" like most of the others in his group. At least that's what he insisted upon calling himself. Actually he was a farmer, or more accurately, the son of a farmer. He had been about fifteen years old living on his parent's farm when the Tribulation Period had begun. His Christian parents had been thrown in jail almost immediately, leaving Peter and his brothers and sisters to fend for themselves. Then his parents, like a lot of other Christians, mysteriously disappeared as they were shuffled from one jail to another. It was more than four years later before Peter found out that his mom and dad were dead. They had starved to death in a concentration camp.

The farm, where Peter and his brothers and sisters had lived, was quickly taken from them, and auctioned to pay for debts that had appeared out of nowhere. So with the farm gone, he and his siblings were forced to separate from one another just to survive. Now Peter wondered if any of the others were still alive.

With the farm and his family gone, Peter had drifted from city to city doing one thing and then another just to stay alive. And toward the last part of the Tribulation Period, he and a few of his friends had taken to stealing food and small items from the rich. Things were that tough. And though Peter knew that stealing was wrong, and he hated doing it, he did steal, to survive. But the authorities had caught him and a couple of his friends. Peter had been arrested, put in jail, and charged with burglary, theft (one-half pound of hamburger and a loaf of bread), carrying a concealed weapon (a small pocket knife with one blade broken off), and felony flight (Peter ran for his life when a UWO policeman started shooting at him without warning). After his arrest, Peter and twenty other "incorrigibles" had been sentenced to death on that very morning when everything changed--when High King had appeared in the sky.

After the Lord came, most of the people had been judged quickly, and had disappeared from the face of the earth. A few like Peter had been spared, he did not know why. Others, called Boeterque (Holy Ones), had been put in charge of almost everything on earth. And while a lot of things had begun to change, Peter's life had not changed that much. He was still a bum. But at least now he and those like him did not have to steal anymore. There were relief tents in every town, run by the Boeterque, and they distributed food as well as medicine and clothing to any who had need of it.

Peter, like a lot of other humans, tried to minimize his contact with the Boeterque as much as possible. They were so very different from NORMAL people like himself. In fact some said that almost all of the Boeterque had already been dead, and then had come back to life when High King appeared. And perhaps that explained why they were so very peculiar. Oh, they were kind and honest enough, but to Peter, they could never really be friends. He just felt funny around people who were, well, a lot like ghosts.

But now maybe his life would finally change for the better. At thirty-two years of age, he was getting a chance to be a farmer again, to live and work on his own piece of property. A new land was being opened up for settlement. He, his friends and their families had hurriedly formed a company and had gotten the necessary permits to settle in Newland. One of the rules for settlement was that each authorized company had to have a single type of occupation that all of its members were willing to work at after they settled. Peter's group had chosen to be farmers, and had voted Peter to be their leader.

The government had given each member of the group a dozen chickens, three pigs, one horse, mule or donkey, a small two wheeled cart to haul the belongings, two hundred pounds of seed, along with an assortment of tools, a tent, and some simple furniture. Those who had families received a bit more: a larger wagon, more furniture, and perhaps some building materials such as lumber or bricks. It was the chance of a lifetime for Peter Samtouge and the others.

But as the pilgrims entered the main part of the Newland continent, leaving the rough, narrow Ribbon Lands behind, they faced an ugly smoking land on their right, desert before them, and high mountains far ahead. And to Peter, the only one in his company who had ever really lived and worked on a real farm, the land just did not look at all promising for growing things.

Desert King and Michael retraced the path they had followed to The Land of the Dead. They climbed the small hills that bordered the black land, and immediately saw the bundles they had left behind. Michael went over to the largest one and sliced it open. Inside were a number of small leather pouches that contained seeds. Michael opened the pouches and poured them on the ground, then began looking toward the heavens above the Holy Mountain that was still miles away. The sky danced with lightening from the thick clouds that were now pouring their life giving waters on that part of Newland.

Michael smiled. "Alpha is at work."

"Who?"

"Alpha. High King has temporarily given Gabriel part of his Name: Alpha, so he can bring life to your kingdom and others like it around the world. Tonight Alpha creates rain and starts the seasons that shall march across your kingdom for a thousand years."

"And what of Omega? Is not the Lord called the Alpha and the Omega?"

"I am Omega," Michael said. "It shall be I who puts an end to all things. But I shall not use my authority for a long time. We shall speak more of my powers in the years to come. But for now, look," Michael pointed skyward. Thousands of birds were flying toward their position. As they landed, the air was filled with the loud, joyous sounds that only birds can make.

They were unafraid of the king and his servant, and many alighted upon their heads and shoulders awaiting their turn at the piles of seeds upon the ground. When there was an opening, the birds would quickly fly over to a pile of seeds, eat some, then fill their mouths, and fly off toward the Land of the Dead.

"They will drop their seeds around the borders of The Land of the Dead," Michael said. "And in a few short months, there shall be the beginnings of a great forest that shall grow around Hastedia Compotu to separate your good lands from those that are forbidden.

"May the Lord be blessed," the king said smiling.

"And so He shall be. But may I suggest that while we are here, you name the forest, my lord?"

"You may suggest, and I shall name. The forest shall be called Bird Forest."

"A fitting name, my king."

CHAPTER NINE

On Dentrosa, a small island off the northwest coast of Newland, four feet of earth covered a heavy metal lid and its attaching hydraulic hardware. The lid sat atop a large tubular shaft that reached deep into the earth. The soil above this large metal structure had been heated to hundreds of degrees Celsius at the time of Armageddon. But the shaft and its contents had not been damaged. At the bottom of the shaft, were passageways that tunneled through the earth and connected with two medium-sized rooms. In the first of these were scores of dusty technical manuals neatly lined on metal shelves. The remainder of the area was jammed with workbenches that held electronic test equipment. Everything was covered with a uniform layer of dust. There were more shelves on the northern wall. These held thousands of electronic bits and pieces, and mechanical spare parts arranged in bins and boxes, most still in their protective plastic envelopes. In fact, the room held everything that had been thought necessary for the short term maintenance of a complicated war machine.

In the other room the walls were also covered with metal shelves, but these were loaded with countless rounds of ammunition and hand grenades. The eastern wall held one hundred and fifty assault rifles stacked side by side with a strong chain locked across them. Each weapon had been thickly coated with cosmoline, then sealed in a moisture proof plastic bag to keep the weapon in good condition for a very long time. Next to the small arms were twelve disposable LAWs (Light Antitank Weapons), still in their protective aluminum cartons.

Neither of these two rooms had been entered in over fifteen years, and that was why all of the dead technicians and soldiers had been reduced to mummified skeletons littering the floor. Each of the dead had a small hole in their foreheads made by a bullet, complements of World President Earlison. All of the victims had all been involved in one way or another with maintaining and servicing the weapon that still sat in the nearby circular shaft, the Norsac IV missile.

In the castle on the northern side of Holy Mountain, Newland's first pilgrims met with Desert Queen.

"And you, young man, what is your name?" the queen asked, smiling as she spoke to the boy who continually hopped from foot to foot, and seemed to be unable to stand still.

"Rustlipper, your honor."

"Call her, 'Your Highness'," Windella whispered into the boy's ear.

"Rustlipper, Your Highness."

"Hummmm, I've never heard a name like that. And you, little one?" she asked the girl.

The little girl thought hard for several moments before answering. It had been a very long time since she had told anyone her name. "Rainey," she finally said.

"That's a beautiful name." said the queen patting the girl on the head. "And your last name, Mrs...?"

CHAPTER NINE

Windella blushed. "Oh no, your highness, these ain't mine. No indeed. I found them on the trail. Had to take care of em. You know how it is, don't you ma'am? As fer me, my name, it's Hannon, your highness. Windella Hannon."

The queen sat upon one of two identical marble thrones that Gabriel had just completed that morning. The thrones were in a large unfinished room that still had no roof over it, but was destined to become a magnificent throne room for the king and queen of Newland. Eleea arose, stepped over to the little girl and kissed her on the forehead. She would have kissed Rustlipper's forehead too, but the boy knew what was coming, so he hurriedly stuck out his hand. The queen smiled and shook the boy's hand, then approached Windella. Windella did likewise, and stuck out her hand expecting a handshake, but the queen ignored her out-stretched hand and warmly embraced her, kissing her on the cheek. It had been years since anyone had shown personal warmth toward Windella, so the queen's affection caused tears to quickly gather in Windella's eyes, then slide down her dirty face. "Scuze me, madam. Maybe it's something in the air."

"And now, let me first apologize for the absence of Desert King, but he is away on an important errand. He should be back in a few hours. Meantime, Gabriel, would you please escort Windella and Rainey to our brand new bathroom." The queen was enjoying her role as hostess. "There will be warm water, and soap, and clean clothing. Then the two of you can rest in my bedchamber and recover from your long journey until the king arrives."

Then she addressed Rustlipper. "As for you," she said with a twinkle in her eye, "we're going to get you cleaned up, too. Red, would you please take the young gentleman to the geyser on top of the mountain? And make sure he takes along plenty of soap with him--and some clean clothing, too. And one more thing; if you could trim that mop on the top of his head, I think we just might find a most handsome young man underneath all of that hair." The queen winked at the gardener, with a smile on her face.

Rustlipper wanted to say, "No thanks, Ma'am. I'm fine just the way I am." But before he could get a word out, a thin, short man with stringy muscled arms had hold of his army coat, and was leading him forcefully away. "Hey," Rustlipper protested to the man who looked vaguely like someone he had dreamed about. "Hey, not so fast..."

Though it had been less than two days since the king and Gabriel had left Holy Mountain on their journey to the Land of the Dead, the seeds watered by Newland's first rain had already begun to sprout and grow. The king paused at the first of the steps that climbed Holy Mountain, turned and looked at his kingdom in the early morning sunshine. The land that only days before had been painted by the insipid colors of brown and grey, now had areas of green to break up the monotony. He glanced back to the accursed land they had just come from. The seeds the birds had scattered around this smoking desert had also begun to sprout outlining the boundary of the deadly land with green. "It's gonna look real pretty some day, isn't it Michael?"

"Better than that, and sooner too, especially with Polat-Shar-Alt in charge of the gardening."

The king began climbing the many steps that led to the castle with Michael right behind him. After about fifteen minutes, loud screams from a boy's voice could be heard coming from somewhere above them. "Lego," the voice yelled. "Lego right now! Ouch, ouch. You're killing my ears. Please, stop. Ain't I clean enough yet?"

"What on earth is that?" The king asked looking toward the top of the mountain, toward the source of the noise.

Michael laughed. "Sounds to me like you have one very unhappy young man on your hands, my lord. Probably the same one you saw from the top of the mountain the other day. And if I was a betting man, I'd bet that either Polat-Shar-Alt or Gabriel is giving your subject his first good bath in a long time." The king laughed.

"Ow, ow! That's enough," the protesting voice continued. "I'm telling the king on you, just wait and see. Ow...."

Felix Stometz was an anthropologist, and on record, was the leader of his little group. But he had never wanted to be a leader. And that was why he had always been a better researcher than a teacher. He hated being in front of a group, speaking in public, and usually went out of his way to avoid face-to-face confrontations. When he was asked his opinion on something, he would invariably say: "Opinions are for the lawyers, and mine are probably as silly as anyone else's." Professor Stometz much preferred to stay in the background and go about his own business. If something was really important to him, he would study it, attempt to prove it with indestructible logic, then put his findings in a book or technical journal.

On the whole, Felix was fairly good looking. He had dark brown hair that had just the right amount of grey in it to make him look distinguished. He was tall, thin, and had been blessed with a beautiful smile. But Felix was a loner, he had never married, and in fact had never really formed any lasting relationship with a woman, or with anyone else for that matter. Felix always felt more at home digging around in some remote part of the world, cataloging bones and artifacts than being around people, living ones that is.

Dr. Felix Stometz had become the leader of their party of settlers only because it had been his idea to journey to Newland and there establish a small college. The others in his group were: Dr. Margaret Fenworth, a biochemist just out of graduate school, Dr. Ralph Moetta, a psychologist and author, and James Klote, an inventor and the only one of the group who did not have a doctorate.

Klote's only degree was in industrial education. And before joining this group, he had been a teacher in a high school. But his real love was tinkering and making things. The thirty-two year old had already acquired more than one hundred patents to his name, one of which had made him a whole lot of money. But the Tribulation Period had destroyed his savings as it had for so many others.

For some reason, the others in the Stometz group had gotten the idea that Klote had a doctorate in Mechanical Engineering. Klote had never lied to anyone about having such a degree, but neither did he go out of his way to correct those who thought that he had a Ph.D. He thought it was pretty neat that such highly educated people would think that he, a mere college graduate, was intelligent enough to have obtained a doctorate. So when questions concerning his education came up, he ignored them or simply changed the subject.

The group had started their journey only four days before, and were still on the thin earthen strip called the Ribbon Lands, that connected Israel to Newland. Each of the party wore the best hiking apparel that could be obtained, and carried expensive backpacks loaded with quality camping equipment and food. All except Klote that is. He was dressed in shorts and a T-shirt, and rode around inside the "Klomobile", one of his inventions, a go-cart sort of thing with large, fat tires. The roof of Klote's contraption was covered with photoelectric cells that fed power to a small high efficiency electric motor that Klote had invented some years before. And as a concession to the others, the Klomobile pulled a canvas covered two wheeled cart that was loaded with the books that would become the core of the Newland College library.

Klote was a short, fat little man. He looked ridiculous riding around in his small vehicle, especially since he filled the interior almost to overflowing. But Klote could have cared less, because while the others walked in the broiling sun, the fat little man rode around in comparative comfort in his little machine. And at night, if the photocells had stored enough extra energy in the battery, he could turn on a tiny fan mounted overhead, put the reclining seat down, and sleep soundly in the small breeze that was created, while the others suffered in or on their sleeping bags in the hot, still air.

Klote, like Dr. Stometz, was a loner. He had never had a real friend in his entire life. Not that he hadn't wanted friends. He just didn't know how to make them. And besides, people were so hard to understand. They were so much more unpredictable than the inanimate things that Klote gathered around him, the wires, the nuts and bolts, the transistors, and pipes and tools. These things he could understand. These he could control and make into things that would serve him or others. And these things also did not make fun of him for being fat, a condition he had never been able to control. So things had become Klote's only friends. They had never let him down, but they also could never eliminate the loneliness that gnawed at Klote's very soul.

On this particular night, the three doctors were sleeping much more soundly than usual, as did Klote in his little machine. The fan blew its breeze down on the inventor. He snored happily away, when a strong hand began violently shaking the Klomobile.

"Go away. It's too early to get up." Klote said turning slightly, then immediately going back to sleep. Then all of a sudden Klote's entire world was literally turned upside down as the little machine was picked up, and Klote was dumped onto the hard packed earth.

"Hey, what's happening here," he said trying to figure it out. When he could finally focus his eyes, he saw the tallest man he had ever seen in his life standing over him. The stranger had a slight smile on his face, and was staring hard at Klote.

"Hey--hey. Help, you guys. Hey...."

"They can not hear you, Mr. Klote. I have given them over to a deep sleep while I talk to you."

"Who--who are you? And what do you want? And what's the big idea of turning over my vehicle? It's private property, you know."

"You have asked many questions, but I will do my best to answer each of them one at a time. First, I am called Gabriel, and am a servant to Desert King and Desert Queen, the rulers of the land you are about to enter. As for my purpose here, I have come to destroy that machine of yours. And concerning your statement about private property, there really is no such thing. The Lord our God owns all things, and it is He Who holds all things together. Without the Lord's will, all things would cease to exist."

"Destroy the Klomobile? Why?"

CHAPTER NINE

"It is a thing of evil, and if it survived it would surely multiply and ruin all of Newland. As you know, its predecessors: the cars, and buses, and trucks, contributed as much to the destruction of the world as anything else that man ever invented. Do you not remember the junkyards, the paving of God's green earth with blacktop and concrete, the killing of the sea creatures with oil spills, the polluting of God's air with exhaust--air that He made for all of his creatures to breathe, and the killing and maiming of the thousands upon thousands of humans each year?"

"But--but the Klomobile is different; it's electric. It's not like the gas burning cars and trucks that you're talking about. It's clean."

"Look," Gabriel pointed back down the path that Klote and his machine had just traveled. There were deep, ugly ruts dug in the soil; a sea turtle had been run over and smashed as she had come ashore to lay her eggs; a patch of beautiful blue and yellow flowers had been run over and despoiled.

"But it's only a turtle, and some weeds. I'm sorry about that, but still... And the land, it's only dirt and sand. I haven't really hurt anything important, have I? And besides, who really cares? It doesn't belong to anybody, does it?"

"Again you are wrong, Mr. Klote. It belongs to God, and He cares, as does Desert King and Desert Queen, and I care. Furthermore, God has given you those for transportation." Gabriel pointed to Klote's legs and feet.

"Walk? All the way to those mountains? And in this heat?"

"Others have walked 'all the way,' and have learned much from their journey. Here, I have brought you these." Gabriel handed Klote a beautiful pair of handmade hiking boots, a backpack with everything he would need for his trip, and a lightweight sleeping bag. Gabriel then reached into his pocket, and produced four large silver coins with a picture of the king and queen upon them, and handed these to Klote.

Klote took the coins and examined them carefully. "What are these?"

"They are called Desert Crowns," Gabriel responded. "Money that will soon be used in your new country. The coins are more than full payment for your vehicle."

The angel then strode over to Klote's vehicle, detached it from the book-filled cart, and began tearing the Klomobile apart with his bare hands, as if it were made of tissue paper and cardboard. Klote watched in amazement, daring not to protest the actions of the giant. When Gabriel was finished, he took a deep breath, blew as hard as he could toward the ground, and created a sizable pit. He then pushed the scrap metal, tires, and other parts into the hole with the side of his foot and leg, and blew the soil back into the hole covering the wreckage.

When he had finished, he looked at Klote with kind eyes. "I know that you think I did you an unkindness, but you are wrong. Perhaps one day you shall understand what I have done for you. Now I say farewell until we meet on top of Holy Mountain." He disappeared.

After Klote recovered from his shock, he arose from the ground, stomped his foot in anger and almost bruised it. Finally he picked up the sleeping bag, unrolled it, and began trying to stuff his rotund body into the small opening in the contraption. When he was finally in the bag, he rolled around on the hard ground trying to get comfortable. But it turned out to be a very long night for Mr. Klote. Every time he dozed off, he dreamt of squashed turtles, and ruined flower beds, like the ones his mother had when he was a child.

CHAPTER NINE

When the others awoke in the morning, they found Klote in a sleeping bag next to them, tossing and turning.

"Where did you get the sleeping bag? And--and where's the 'Klomobile'?" Fenworth asked, noticeably confused.

Klote, with dark rings under his eyes, unzipped his bag and arose stiffly. "Don't even ask," he said. "You couldn't possibly believe the story I would have to tell you."

"And since you three--ah, four, are Newland's first true pilgrims, all of the land of Newland is open to you. What are your wishes?"

Gorbo laid before the throne wagging his huge tail in silence while the others stared at the floor before them, mute, and afraid to be the first to speak.

"Hummmm. Perhaps you wish the queen and I to make several suggestions, then you could choose from among them?"

Still nothing.

"O.K., let's see. Windella, how would you like some land next to the queen's garden? Perhaps a hundred acres or so, to farm or to do whatever you want with it? The land will be next to a lake, and should be some of the greenest and most fertile in Newland."

The old woman stood looking at the king with her mouth open. "My heavens. Not a hunnerd acres. It's too much for an old lady like me. Jest a little speck a land where I could have a garden of my own, and--and a little hut of some kind, if you please, your Highnesses. I--I could pay you back for it a little at a time by working around your castle, iffen you'll let me. I was pretty good as a housekeeper in my younger days, a--if you please, that is."

"Windella, you're a jewel," said the queen. "We would love to have you in our castle, not as a housekeeper, but as an elder sister. Because I'm going to need another woman's opinions to help me decorate, and turn this pile of stones into a home for the king and I, and for you too, Windella, if you would like to live with us."

The old lady was speechless. She tried to talk but nothing would come out of her mouth except little croaking noises. Tears ran down her face that she wiped with the sleeve of her new robe. She nodded her head. Yes--yes, she would like that very much. The queen arose from her throne, stepped down, and gave Windella a big hug, then handed her a small handkerchief.

"Good! Then that's settled. And now," the king said staring at the other three. "You," he addressed the lion, "shall be the royal guardian of our castle and property. Is that O.K. with you?" The lion arose and came over to the king and licked him in the face. The king laughed. "Enough, enough, great beast."

"And you, Russell A. Lipper. What would you wish your king and queen to grant you in this brand new country?"

The boy and girl looked at each other, then behind them to see who the king was speaking to.

"Ha," laughed the king. "So you didn't know that your real name is Russell Adam Lipper?" He stared right at the boy whose face had taken upon it a very surprised look.

"It is?" the boy asked, staring at his feet. The king handed the boy a paper that was Rustlipper's birth certificate. He took the paper, held it upside down, and stared at it unable to read what was on it.

"Yep, it sure is," said the king. "Over the years, it seems that you simply combined your first and last names, and came up with Rustlipper. How do you like your real name?"

CHAPTER NINE

The boy was silent for a moment, then: "Sir, you couldn't just call me Rustlipper, could you?"

"Ah ha, so the boy does have a request after all. What shall we do, Desert Queen? Should we call the lad Russell A. Lipper, or what he has requested, Rustlipper?"

The queen worked hard to hide her smile. "Hummmm. Let me think for a moment. Well, we could call him by a number of different names, some of which he perhaps hasn't considered. Let's see. Morgrotten, or Pentecillen, Bastillian, or, or... No, none of those seem to fit him."

The boy shuffled nervously on his feet awaiting the king and queen's decision.

"Yes," the queen said, trying to look as if she was deep in thought. "I think we could just call him Rustlipper."

"Then it is so ordered," said the king. "Russell A. Lipper is no more. The lad's name from this time forward shall be Rustlipper, at least in the Kingdom of Newland."

The boy lifted his head and looked at the king with a big smile. "Thanks, Your Highness."

"And now, Mr. Rustlipper, are there other requests that you would make of your king and queen?"

"Well--well..."

"Speak up. I promise not to bite you."

"Well, I was hoping to be able to go search for some gold or treasure. You know, look for lost fortunes, or something like that."

The king's eyes twinkled, but he did not smile. "And where would you look for such treasures, Mr. Rustlipper?"

The boy mumbled something, that no one could hear, then again began staring at the floor in front of his sandals.

"Well, I think that you have a splendid idea," the king said. The queen's mouth opened in surprise. "Yes, indeed," continued the king. "Newland needs a good prospector and explorer, and frankly, I'm glad you volunteered." The boy's entire face lit up instantly.

"Of course, you will probably first need to spend a little time learning about maps and geography, then you'll probably want to do a little study on exactly what one does when he becomes a prospector. And of course to do that, you will first have to learn to read and write." The king reached over and turned Rustlipper's birth certificate over, and handed it back to him.

Rustlipper's smile lost much of its energy by now, and he resumed his careful study of the paving stones making up the floor of the throne room.

"But it won't be too bad. You can live here with the queen and I while we arrange lessons for you." Rustlipper's countenance clearly showed disappointment by now. "However, there is one chore that you must do while you live with us: there will be a pony that needs to be taken care of and ridden every once in a while. Do you think you could handle such an important job like that?"

"Wow! A pony? You mean it?" He stared at the king hoping that it was true.

"Why, of course, I mean it, Mr. Rustlipper. A king always means what he says, doesn't he?

"And now for you, young lady," the king said looking at the girl. "First of all, I have found out that your full name is Rainey Fitsimons. Do you like your name, or do you request a different one as did Mr. Rustlipper?"

The girl smiled at the king, with her little hands held together in front of her. "I like it jes fine, Mr. King."

"Well, good. Then what would you have me grant you in your new home and country."

The little girl didn't say anything, but turned and looked at Windella.

CHAPTER NINE

"What is it, child," Desert Queen asked. "What would you like?"

"I jes wanna be with my mommy," the girl said pointing to Windella.

On May sixteenth, the tenth year of our Lord's reign, the grounds outside the Newland castle were crowded with people. All together there were over three hundred men, women, and children. The king and queen were expected to appear before the multitude momentarily to meet and bless the pilgrims, then assign to them the areas they were to live and work in.

In addition to the Stometz group and the farmers led by Peter Samtouge, there was also a group who had cuttings of grape vines, carefully potted and covered, and arranged neatly in little carts drawn by donkeys; the group hoped to grow grapes, and build a winery if the right soil and climate could be found. Another group consisted of carpenters, plumbers, and stone masons along with several other assorted skilled craftsmen. One group, fourteen fishermen and their families, had towed sizable wooden fishing boats all the way from the mainland, hoping that there would be good waters to fish either inland or off the Newland coast. There was an ex-priest, an ex-rabbi, and two ex-protestant ministers, all with much more in common, now that the second advent of Christ had brought TRUTH to the whole world.

And there were scores of other groups: the butchers, the bakers, and the machinists and factory workers. And then there were the teachers, bookkeepers, shop keepers, and numerous others. There was also one little man, clothed in a black robe with the hood pulled up that concealed most of his face. He had come to Newland alone, and no one seemed to know anything about him.

A trumpet blew. Gabriel and Michael appeared on the balcony each holding one of the double doors open for Desert King and Desert Queen. The two monarchs stepped outside and received the cheers of the crowd below. The king held up his hands for silence, then began to speak.

"Fellow travelers, brothers, sisters, and friends, I welcome you to Newland. Many of you have come a long way, through many hardships, and may now be somewhat disappointed in the country that you see around you. But let me assure you, Newland will not always be a desert. Already plant life has begun to grow on this small continent, and in the years ahead, I have been told by my gardener, that Newland shall bloom like a garden.

"So again I welcome you, each and every one of you to the land that God has given us to build into a nation. And I now call you blessed, for each one of you has been specially chosen, by the Lord, to come to Newland. It is my hope that you will learn to love your new home.

"And now, before we proceed to the business of deeds and parcels of land and such, let us bow our heads and pray to our good Lord and God who has given us the opportunities that lie just ahead."

Desert King removed his crown and bowed his head. "Our great God, we thank You for bringing each of us safely through the desert to this place You have named Newland, where together, with Your blessings and guidance, we shall build a new country. It is our prayer that each of us shall glorify You and Your Son, High King, in the work that we do here. Please help every one of us to love one another as is Your eternal will." And the people said "Amen."

CHAPTER NINE

Desert King replaced his crown, and the queen stepped forward. "I don't know quite what to say, but do wish to thank each one of you for coming to Newland. And I look forward to meeting each of you in just a few minutes. But right now, let me introduce you to Michael, who will be in charge of assigning the areas and lands to both individuals and families." Michael stepped forward and bowed, then the queen continued: "And over here is Gabriel. He shall be gone, off and on, for the next few years, before he settles here permanently. For, the Lord has given him the job of bringing life to many other places around the world like Newland." Gabriel smiled, and stepped forward. "And then there is Red. Red will be in charge of all the gardening and farming that shall take place in Newland. So if you have any problems or questions about how to grow anything, I am sure Red will be more than able to assist you, right Red?

"Right," said the small man as he stepped to the railing, dwarfed by both Michael and Gabriel.

Then the queen stepped back, and Michael began to address the crowd. "Fellow Newland citizens, please make sure that after meeting Desert King and Desert Queen, you sign our roster, so we have your legal name and a copy of your signature, for purposes of the deeds of title to the lands that shall be given to you.

"And now, if you will all go inside, through the doors on the north side, you will find food and drink prepared for you, complements of your king and queen. We, the king and queen, Gabriel, Red, and myself, will meet each of you personally downstairs.

The people cheered for their rulers, then began to make their way toward the doors that led inside the castle, to the prepared feast. Many of the travelers had not had a decent meal in weeks, so by the time many of them met their king and queen, more likely than not, they were chewing away at some food they had not eaten in a long while. But Desert King and Desert Queen did not mind. For they both remembered their own feast and how wonderful the food had tasted after their long journey across the dry and barren land.

After the royal couple had met most of the people, they noticed the small man in the black robe leaning against a wall all by himself. He had not joined the others in the prepared feast. The king and queen approached the little man. Desert King was so much taller than the hooded figure that he could see nothing of the man's face as he looked down upon him.

"And good sir, I do not think we have met," the king said, shaking hands with the stranger.

The hooded figure did not look up. "Ah, but we have met, my king. It was some years ago, in a place that is not too far from here, but then you were called something else, Sergeant Maddox, I believe." The man slowly pulled back his hood.

The king bent over to get a good look at the shorter man's face. At first there was no recognition, for the glasses were gone, and a thick black beard speckled with grey covered most of the round happy face. Then he remembered.

"Little!" The king tightly hugged the small man, then kissed him on both cheeks. "I'm so happy, I don't know what to say. Eleea, this is the soldier that I told you about, the one who helped me finally decide to accept Christ as my Lord."

The small man bowed before the queen, kissed her hand, then smiling, addressed the king. "But your majesty, I, like you have been given another name: I am now Guardian, for the Lord has given me the office of guardian of the holy scriptures. So if you have a need for such a one as I..."

CHAPTER NINE

"Then you will be staying with us--in Newland?" The king asked smiling.

"If Desert King and Queen would have me."

"Have you? Are you kidding?" The king said patting the little man on the back. "And not only are you staying in Newland, but you can live with us, in the castle. We've got over thirty bedrooms. Right, Eleea?"

"Right," said Desert Queen.

PART THREE

BEGINNINGS

CHAPTER TEN

(For God) shall comfort all her waste places,
and her wilderness, He will make like Eden.
Isaiah 51:3

Newland's initial population of three hundred settlers had grown to more than six hundred thousand people since its founding. No longer was Newland a land of deserts but a nation of towns and small cities surrounded by small fertile farms that produced tremendous amounts of foodstuffs per acre. Numerous parks and gardens filled the land with the colors and smells that only God's nature could produce.

Gabriel had long ago fulfilled his role as Alpha, and was governor of Newland. Michael was the ever present advisor, teacher and friend to Desert King and Desert Queen, but was especially close to the king.

And Windella, well, she had indeed become Rainey's mother, by adoption, and as she had promised, had become Rustlipper's reading and Bible teacher. She had also become so much of a sister to the king and queen that by decree she was made Princess Windella. And the Lord so blessed her with wisdom that in the king and queen's absence, people from all over Newland would come to Windella for her opinions and judgements.

In her former life, Windella had always had to scratch hard to eke out a living; she had never had much time for proper schooling. But during the Millennial years, Windella had had more than enough time to complete the equivalent of many college degrees. In fact, Windella's personal library was not much smaller than the one at Newland College.

And Rustlipper, well, first of all, he was adopted by the king and queen, becoming Newland's prince. And second, since he grew up in the castle, which was also the home of Windella and Rainey, he eventually fell in love with Windella's daughter, married her, and gave the king, queen and Windella four grandchildren.

But Rustlipper had never lost his love for adventure and exploration. And so no one knew more about Newland's geography than he did. In fact, on several occasions, he had even managed to get permission from the king and queen to make short trips into Hastedia Compotu, for map making and exploration. And due to his many travels, it was inevitable that Rustlipper would get to know James Klote, rescue him from the drudgery of being a college instructor, and finally become the inventor's first real friend. In fact, Rainey would sometimes complain to the king and queen that Rustlipper and Klote were inseparable.

And the two lakes in northern Newland, that had once been only sandy depressions in a desert, had became so beautiful that they were a favorite vacation place for people from all over the world. But in addition to being beautiful, they were loaded with fish, and provided thousands of Newland citizens with a good living by fishing or working in one of the nearby canneries.

The geyser, the original source for the waters that filled the lakes and the river in the south of Newland, had become periodic; it erupted once every thirty-one minutes, exactly. Little children especially loved to listen to its rumble, feel the ground shake, then watch the thousands of gallons of water catapult from the hole on top of Holy Mountain, creating the most beautiful rainbows.

Gorbo remained at the castle as a pet for many years until one day a young lioness came to Newland. Since then, Gorbo and the lioness had made their home in Bird Forest which surrounded the Land of the Dead. And the two lions had now become many hundred. But as the scriptures promised, all of the great cats were vegetarians and never harmed the nearby cattle, pets or humans.

And everywhere on earth, under the reign of Christ, peace prevailed, plenty was common, and God was constantly praised for the good He was always doing in the lives of all His peoples.

"Doesn't she look magnificent?" the queen said to her husband, as Windella approached them through Eleea's garden. Windella was wearing a blue gown trimmed in white, and a small golden necklace with a single diamond hung around her neck.

The king and queen sat on their beautiful ebony thrones that were near the middle of the garden. To their left, in the exact center of the garden, was the ancient oaken throne that was High King's. Many years before it had been moved from the temple in Israel to the garden in Newland. And to protect it from the weather, it sat under an intricately fashioned gazebo. Sixty feet or so from the king and queen was the Tree of Life. It had grown to a tremendous size, and was so loaded with fruit that it alone would supply all of the fruit for the hundreds of Boeterque who would be attending the banquet. Mortals, under law, could not eat of the holy fruit, but could use the tree's healing leaves. And of course next to the tree was its keeper: Red.

"Indeed," the king said smiling, for he was in an excellent mood. Both he and the queen were enjoying the out-of-doors on this special holiday: Nation Day. No one in Newland would work today, that was by official decree. Instead each extended family would have a feast celebrating the settlement of the Newland continent, and would give thanks to God for the many blessings He had given them all the years since the beginning of their nation. In the larger towns and cities, there would be plays and ceremonies depicting the planting of crops, the building of the towns and cities, and the perfect rule of Newland by God, through Maddox and Eleea

"Good morning, Desert King and Desert Queen," Windella said, bowing low. Windella had changed so much since she had first stepped foot on Newland's soil that no one knowing the old Windella would have recognized the new one. Not only had she gotten her third set of teeth, a perfect set, but the bent back was gone, the wrinkles barely a remembrance, and she had the strength and energy of a twenty-five year old athlete. Only her hair gave clue to her age; it had lost all of it's original color, and was a beautiful silvery white.

"And is the royal couple ready to receive the many guests that shall begin arriving shortly?" Windella asked.

It was a custom in Newland for the heads of each family, and the leaders, and teachers to come to visit their king and queen in the royal garden on this particular holiday. Each visitor would bring a gift that represented the fruit of their labors over the last year, and present it to Desert King and Desert Queen, then receive the royal couple's blessings for them and those they represented. Windella was in charge of receiving the gifts, and recording them in the royal ledger.

"I guess we're about as ready as we ever will be," said the queen, smiling at her elder sister. "But have you seen that son of ours, and his wife, and the grandkids? We haven't seen any of them in over a week," the queen asked.

"No, madam, I have not, but you know how hard the prince is to keep track of. But one thing is for sure, he loves to eat, so he'll be here in time for the banquet." Windella pointed to the large tables loaded with delicious foods and drinks. The king and queen laughed, knowing that Windella was absolutely right.

As the three talked, a shadow fell across them that was accompanied by a loud intermittent roar. The three jerked their heads back, looking skyward, toward the sound. There fifty feet above the nearby trees was a large apparatus much like a hot air balloon, only internally supported by light strong metal tubing similar to a dirigible. And inside the gondola were the two pilots, a waving Rustlipper and his good friend, Klote.

"Hello," yelled the bearded Rustlipper. "Merry Nation Day." Then in a softer voice to Klote, "Hope we can get this thing down safely."

Klote was more than nine hundred years old and just as fat as ever, but in no way was he feeble. And with a good friend like Rustlipper, he had finally learned to be content with his overweight body.

"Watch," he said. The inventor first put out the propane burner, took hold of a long rope that was attached to a small grappling hook, then threw it into a bunch of trees catching a thick branch. With the grappling hook snagged, Klote began to reel in the line with a small wench attached to the gondola, pulling them and the airship slowly toward the top of the trees.

Red looked anxiously at the contraption drawing close to earth, because in his opinion, it was way too close to his Tree of Life. "Now you two be careful," he yelled up to the pilots. "Yah, that's better. Good, just reel it in easy, yah--yah. Oh, no..."

The machine lost its lift and fell ten feet to the earth, breaking off a small branch of Red's tree in the process.

Rustlipper jumped quickly from the gondola and ran the few steps to Red, surveying the damage the balloon had done. But the broken branch was only a small one. "Gosh, Red, I'm sorry, but it doesn't look too bad, does it?"

Red was pouting, but he was not nearly as mad as he tried to act. He always had trouble staying mad at the prince. He just loved the rascal too much. "My prince, if you were younger, I think I would take this broken branch and tan your bottom with it," the little man said.

"Now, Red," Rustlipper said quickly reaching over and kissing the gardener on the forehead and embarrassing him. Red made a grab for the prince, to teach him a lesson, but Rustlipper was already out of reach and on his way toward his mom and dad.

The prince bowed low before the king and queen. "Desert King and Desert Queen, it is wonderful to see you again."

"Don't think that just by being formal, we're going to excuse your long absence from our home, Mr. Rustlipper," the king said frowning at his son. "So where have you been for the last few weeks?"

Rustlipper kissed his mom on the forehead, then hugged the king, who had arisen, and gave Windella a kiss on her cheek.

CHAPTER TEN

"Klote and I have been up to Dentrosa. Klote invented this gadget that can detect and identify mineral deposits under the ground. We were up north in Dolphin Point, and Klote's gadget kept pointing north, northwest, indicating there was a lot of iron up there somewhere. So we took the flying machine across the ocean to Dentrosa. When we got there, Klote's gadget just went crazy. It showed that there was a big mineral deposit underground, and by the readings from the gadget, it looked to be almost pure iron. In fact, it might be the biggest mineral find since Newland was founded. It sure would make the iron craftsmen happy if they didn't have to dig so much dirt to get a ton of high grade ore."

"Dentrosa isn't part of our territory, is it?" the queen asked Rustlipper.

"Humph. I guess I had always taken it for granted that it was. But now that you ask, I'm not really sure. I'll dig out some of my old maps and find out."

The king spoke. "I never did like that island, and wish you'd stay away from there, Prince Rustlipper. The soil and topography are just too much like Hastedia Compotu, and I'd just as soon not have you or any of my subjects over there. Sometimes I almost think there's something evil on that island. I can't really put my finger on the reasons, but.... Just chalk it up to the suspicions of an old and feeble king. And besides, its always been off limits to Newland's citizens."

"Sure, dad. If you don't want me over there, Klote and I can find mischief somewhere else," he said smiling. "But of course you know that Professor Stometz, Dr. Moetta and some others are over there. We flew right over their camp site that was right next to the iron deposit we located. They have about eight or ten students with them. Klote and I landed and had coffee with them. They were kind of close-mouthed about what they were doing--said it was some kind of secret. Probably for Nation's Day."

"I didn't know anyone was on Dentrosa, did you, Eleea?" asked the king.

"No. This is the first I've heard about it."

The king and queen both looked at Windella. "No, Desert King and Desert Queen. I know nothing of it," she said, sensing that they were upset over the matter.

"Well, anyway, they should both be here sometime today, then maybe we can find out what's going on," the king said.

James Klote had managed to get the flying machine secured and moved to a more open area where it could take off more easily. A bit sweaty, he now approached his king and queen, and bowed before them. "May the Lord bless both Desert King and Desert Queen on this beautiful day."

"And may the Lord bless you, too, Mr. Klote," Desert Queen said in return.

"Yes. And may He bless you abundantly, even if you do insist upon keeping our son away from his parents for weeks at a time," the king scolded jokingly.

"I--I..."

"But we'll forgive you this once, Mr. Klote," the king said with a fake frown on his face. "For you have been a good friend to this son of ours." The king winked at the inventor, then turned to Rustlipper. "And now, Mr. Prince, where are Rainey and the kids?"

"They should be here shortly. But why you insist upon calling them kids is beyond me, dad. They're more than nine hundred years old, and are great, great, great, grandparents themselves, many times over," Rustlipper said pulling on his long beard.

"I know that well, Mr. Rustlipper," the king winked at his son. "Yet the queen and I are older still. And so they shall remain kids to us."

"Can you see anything yet?" Moetta yelled down the hole to the two students who had just slid down the rope to the bottom.

"Yah--yah, we're through the concrete. Can't see too much through this little hole though. But there's some kind of room down there. Hey--hey, it looks like there's people down there. On the floor. Skeletons. Yah..." Willie yelled excitedly. "I can scc two, no three of 'em. And there's some sort of workbench right under us, with some boxes on it. That's about all I can see right now. We're gonna have to get this hole a lot bigger before we can see much more, and this concrete looks tough. It's about eighteen inches thick. Yep, it's gonna be a big job to open this baby up."

At the surface, Felix and Ralph yelled in triumph, and shook each other's hands, then they started shaking the hands of the smiling students who were with them.

"O.K., pull Gene and Willie out of there," Stometz said. "And let's get started trying to figure out a way to get that hole bigger without destroying whatever is down there."

As Nation Day quickly drew to a close, most of the visitors had already left for their homes, or for nearby lodgings. The king and queen arose from their wooden thrones and stretched. It had been a long but happy day, and behind them were stacks and stacks of presents from the happy citizens of Newland.

"What on earth are we going to do with all of this stuff?" the queen asked.

The king smiled. "You've got me. But we'll do something with it. We always do."

As the sky darkened, Apartia appeared in the sky. The king, queen and those with them stared at the jewel of the universe as it crossed God's heaven. "Andy, do you remember the first time we saw it?"

"Indeed I do, my queen. And it's still just as beautiful as it was then."

Rustlipper was also staring at Apartia. He remembered the first time he had seen it so long ago, in that terrible, terrible land, almost a lifetime ago. He looked toward the gardener. "Thank's Red."

"For what, my prince?"

"For saving my life in Hastedia Compotu, the first time we met. I don't know if I ever thanked you."

"My prince, you have thanked me a thousand times over."

"Then I thank you a thousand and one times, my little friend." Rustlipper kissed Red on the cheek.

"Now you stop that, my prince. After all, I am one of your mentors, and I am also your elder. You should show some respect."

"I know all that, Red, but to me, you're mostly my friend. But it is beautiful, isn't it?"

"Indeed it is, even to Me." The voice came from the old oaken throne that was now surrounded by light. Each of those present fell to their knees and bowed low before High King.

"Arise and approach me, My servants and friends."

CHAPTER TEN

Andy, Eleea, and the others arose and approached the Creator and King of the Universe.

"And how was the celebration today, my king and queen?"

"It was the best holiday yet, Lord," Desert King said.

"Yes." added Desert Queen with a smile.

"And Newland, how goes it?"

"Lord, Newland surely is the most blessed of Your countries." Desert King spoke happily.

"You have spoken correctly, my king, for indeed Newland is the most beautiful and prosperous of all my countries. But let Me see, wasn't there a time when you both had some doubts about this country that I gave you to rule?" High King addressed the king and queen with a twinkle in his eyes. "But no matter, for those doubts belong to the years long past, and both of you and those I have given you to rule over have brought much joy to My heart in the last hundreds of years." He arose and embraced the king and queen, then sat down again.

"But now comes the time that I spoke to you about. For you are no longer the king and queen of a desert, so I must rename you. From this day forward, you are named Bounteous."

"Thank You, Lord." the king and queen said together.

"And now, Prince Rustlipper and James Klote, come closer to me."

The two approached their King, and bowed low.

"My two adventurers, you are both a delight to My heart. For in my former days on earth, I myself often roamed about in deserts and lonely places seeking and seeing things that few but My angels took note of. And so, I now commission you both to play a great part in the days that lie ahead for

Newland. I will not tell you what part that is, but this I say: be brave and be steadfast."

Rustlipper and Klote fell to their knees before High King.

"Arise, my friends. And now Mr. Klote, I have a gift for you. Since you have long accompanied this special prince of mine, and befriended him, it is befitting that you should also have a royal title. From this day forward, you are Newland's official wizard. Be a good and wise one and not like those in the fairy stories."

"Yes, Lord," Klote said, trying hard to look as wise and as a good as a wizard should look.

"And now to you all, I shall say goodbye, for a little while. But my king and queen, this I advise: consult with Guardian, for many great and strange things are about to happen in Newland and in the world as a whole."

The light was gone.

"Over here," yelled one of the students.

Professor Stometz and Dr. Moetta came running. The pretty coed was in the three feet deep excavation. She continued carefully brushing away the dirt that was atop a large metal structure of some sort.

Stometz got into the hole, squatted down, and fingered the metal. "It looks like it's made of aluminum. Come on, some of you others. Get your brushes, and lend a hand. Let's see what we have here, but be careful."

In a little over two hours, the metal dome was completely uncovered; it was huge.

"Looks like a gigantic lid of some sort." Moetta said, wiping the grime off his face with a handkerchief.

CHAPTER TEN

"Does, doesn't it." said Stometz. "Maybe we've found an easier way to get into that room back there. Now all we've got to do is figure out how to get this thing open. Must weigh tons."

"Maybe we won't have to get it open," said one of the students, pointing to a circular disc on one side of the dome. "This might be an access cover." The circle of metal was attached to the larger dome by eight common bolts.

"You're right," Stometz said. "Johnnie, get the tool box, and hurry."

"No, madam." Windella said to the queen. "Neither Dr. Stometz nor Dr. Moetta came to Nation Day. Only Dr. Fenworth came, and she's not officially attached to the college anymore." It was the morning following Nation Day.

"Are you quite sure, Windella?"

"I've double checked, my queen. Their name does not appear on the visitors book," Windella said.

"That's strange. Not that it's law or anything like that. Yet this is the first time that I can recall any of my leaders missing the Nation Day celebration. Do you suppose it has anything to do with that business on Dentrosa?"

Gabriel was slightly behind the queen and Windella as they walked in the queen's garden. "Perhaps something has happened that made their attending the feast impossible. If the queen wishes I could check into the matter."

"Thank you, Gabriel. I would appreciate that very much." The governor of Newland bowed, and departed walking quickly across the garden.

The last rusty bolt finally gave way, and turned under the strong hands of Joel. As soon as the bolt came off, Stometz moved the student aside and pulled at the cover; it didn't budge. He pulled harder, but the thin gasket that had sealed the access cover for many hundreds of years was solidly fused to the larger structure.

"We'll have to pry it off."

Stometz was handed a large screwdriver and a small hammer. In moments, the cover began to loosen, then it broke free. Stometz gently shoved Moetta aside, then centered his head over the hole and looked down.

"Hand me a flashlight, somebody." One of the students complied. Stometz aimed the light into the hole and looked. Below him was a gigantic cylinder, topped by a badly cracked black radome. It took him only a few moments for the anthropologist to recognize what it was.

"It's--it's some kind of...." He did not finish his sentence. "Get back, all of you. Go back to the camp. Now!"

"Jimmy, go fetch that lid." Then quieter, "Ralph, I've got to talk to you alone."

The students universally protested about leaving the site, but Stometz and Moetta were the sponsors of the dig. They grudgingly gathered up the digging tools, then headed back to camp, mumbling.

When Jimmy handed the professor the access lid, Stometz carefully put it back over the hole and screwed several of the nuts down to secure it.

"Jimmy, would you please leave Dr. Moetta and I alone a few minutes." The student, frowning, obeyed.

Moments after he left: "What is it, Felix?" Moetta asked. I thought you were going to have a mutiny on your hands, a few moments ago, ordering the students away like that. They have a big stake in this dig the same as you and I."

CHAPTER TEN

Stometz whispered. "There's a missile down there."

"A what?"

"You heard me, a missile."

"What on earth is a missile doing here?"

"How should I know? But it's a missile alright. I worked with the army before Armageddon, and saw a few of these things. It's an ICBM, and a big one at that. We've got to get those students off this island, then you and I can come back and take a good look at it in secret. Because if Desert King and Desert Queen get wind of this, they're sure to make us leave."

"I don't think they would do anything like that. After all, it's not like we can do anything with it. And besides, it could tremendously increase our knowledge about the years just before the second advent."

"Knowledge or not, I can tell you, our king and queen do not have the same appreciation of science that we do. And besides, Dr. Moetta, we failed to get their permission to even come to Dentrosa in the first place, remember?"

Almost a thousand years of imprisonment had turned the demon's skin to leather. His eyeballs had atrophied, and had dropped out of their sockets. But his mind was as agile and powerful as ever. And his hate had not diminished one iota. In fact, if anything, it had grown even stronger over the millennium. He and all those like him had been imprisoned, but both he and they were still alive, and that had been a big mistake for God to make. God should have had him and his followers put to death when He had the chance. Because even though the demon hated the holy scriptures, he knew that the Bible promised he would be released from his terrible prison one day. And when he was, he would get his sweet revenge.

Then Xesduca remembered a name: Michael. The demon would pay any price to destroy the black-skinned angel.

Yes, they should have destroyed him when they had the chance, but they didn't, and his sentence could not last much longer. Soon, very soon, God would be compelled to honor His promise and release him.

"Michael," he whispered into the darkness. "Michael, I'm coming."

The king was visibly upset as he approached Rustlipper and Klote; Bounteous had Michael with him.

The prince and the wizard were preparing the flying machine for take-off. The king had not flown in any type of machine since before Armageddon, and he eyed Klote's fragile assembly with suspicion.

"It'll be O.K., dad, Klote knows what he's doing."

"I'm not anxious about myself, but for you, Wizard Klote, and Michael. Remember my son that I am not mortal, and can not die, but you three can."

"Michael? Is he coming with us?" Klote asked, looking worried.

"Of course. He's my chief advisor."

The wizard reached into his pocket, produced a handmade slide rule, and tape measure, and approached Michael. The black man stood still and allowed Klote to measure his height, waist, even his biceps. Then Klote began figuring on his slide rule. "Humph," he said looking at Michael, then going back to his calculations.

CHAPTER TEN

"Humph.... I'd say at least 265 pounds. Well, we may be able to get off the ground, and we may not. But either way, it's going to be close," Klote said, still figuring on his slide rule. "You see, this thing has only so much lift, and I figure the four of us weigh, oh, at least 835 pounds, give or take a few pounds. And my machine can only generate about 1550 pounds of lift at 75 degrees Fahrenheit, and it's hotter than that now. And then there's the weight of the machine itself."

Then the king smiled. "And my wizard, how much did you figure my weight to be?"

"Oh, I'd say, 165, maybe a bit heavier, your highness."

"Wrong, Mr. Klote. Though you may very well be the brightest wizard in the whole world, you have made an error in your assumptions. Come here, Wizard Klote."

Klote walked quickly over to the king, bowing when he was close. "Now pick me up," said the king.

Klote went behind the king, wrapped his arms around him and lifted hard. The king was effortlessly yanked off the ground.

"Aaaaagggh," yelled the startled Klote. He released the king dropping him to the earth.

"And how much would you say I weighed now, Mr. Wizard?"

"You--you didn't seem to weigh anything at all, your highness."

"Right. My resurrection body can not be weighed in pounds and ounces. And now may we get started?"

The three climbed into the metal basket, and seated themselves in a circle around the centralized propane burner. Klote lit the burner, then pulled a small handle; flame shot eight feet into the neck of the apparatus. Slowly the machine became lighter, slid slowly along the ground in the gentle breeze, then it began to ascend. When it was well above the breeze, then it began to ascend. When it was well above the trees in Eleea's garden, Klote reduced the fire, and flipped a switch turning on a powerful electric motor attached to a propeller outside the gondola. The flying machine slowly began to accelerate. It fought a mild head wind, as it began its long journey north, toward Dolphin Point, and then Dentrosa.

He was free. FREE! Blind, but free, and the fresh air felt wonderful upon his thickened hide. But now he had several things he had to do quickly. He sensed that his destination had to be northwest. He headed in that direction, crawling, for his atrophied legs had forgotten how to walk; but they would learn again. However, this would cause his journey to take a bit more time than he would have liked. But he would get there. And after that, it would start. After he got to the garden. And after he got his hands upon the healing leaves, and the special fruit from the Tree of Life.

Guardian sat across the table from the queen and Windella. He was enjoying a hot cup of strong coffee with lots of cream and sugar; it was his favorite treat.

"And Guardian, you say that Satan must shortly be released?" asked the queen.

And I saw an angel come down from heaven,
having the key of the bottomless pit
and a great chain in his hand.
And he laid hold on the dragon that old serpent,
which is the Devil, and Satan,

CHAPTER TEN

and bound him a thousand years.
And when the thousand years are expired,
Satan shall be loosed out of his prison...
Rev 20: 1,2,7

Guardian finished quoting the scriptures and took a deep gulp of coffee.

"But when shall that be, Guardian?" Windella asked.

The little man wiped his mouth on a linen napkin, thinking about an answer. "My queen, and Windella, I'm not quite sure of the exact time, because in these years of peace, record keeping seems to have deteriorated a bit. But my estimation is that Satan will be released within the next five to ten years, perhaps sooner." He gulped the last of his coffee enjoying the hot, rich liquid. Windella quickly refilled his cup, and again seated herself.

"Madam, there might be a way, to sort of narrow the time frame a bit."

"How, Guardian?"

"The Nation Day records my queen. The ones Windella keeps for the gifts. They're probably our best bet."

"Of course." Windella said arising. "If the queen wishes, I can get them, and we can begin going through them right now."

"Wonderful idea, Princess. Guardian, would you mind helping us?"

"Of course not, Queen Bounteous," Guardian said, eyeing the steaming coffee pot. "I'd be most happy to help in anyway that I can.

The woman clung hysterically to her husband, Peter Samtouge. She trembled uncontrollably. "Now just try to calm down, and tell me once again, Wilma."

"It was just like I said, Pete. I swear."

"O.K., now start from the beginning." The farmer led his wife to a chair, then took the one next to her's.

"I was in the barn when I heard the chickens kicking up a fuss. I looked outside, and there was this thing--a naked man--his black skin was wrinkled and like leather, and he must have been over seven feet tall. And--and he was eating one of the chickens alive. I swear! Blood was running down his chin as he chewed the leg off the poor critter. It was still squeaking while he ate it." She began crying again, trembling. Peter got up and put his arms around his wife.

"He knew I was there, but I don't think he could see me. His eyes, Pete--they were just sort of dried up holes, with nothing in 'em."

Peter Samtouge patted his wife on the back, then headed for the door. "I'll get to the bottom of this," he said leaving the house.

"Peter, please be careful. That thing...."

Outside, he picked up a shovel, then headed for the chicken coop that was on the other side of the barn. The sun had already set, and in the darkness, Peter at first had difficulty finding any evidence to support his wife's story. Then he saw it. Next to the door of the coop, a pile of feathers, and next to them, the dead chicken, bloody and half devoured. He stooped next to the remains, and was examining them when he heard the hoarse voice.

"Kneel, scum. Kneel before your master."

Peter stood quickly, facing the monster before him. He was indeed over seven feet tall, his eyes nonexistent, and his heavy skeleton covered with a blackened burned leather.

CHAPTER TEN

"Who are you?" Peter Samtouge demanded. "And why arc you on the land that Bounteous has given to me?"

"I will tell you who I am: I am the king, the master, your god. And I shall stand on any land that pleases me, for all of the earth shall soon be mine. Bow before me, and I shall let you keep your worthless life." The creature's voice was but a whisper. A stench left his mouth when he spoke.

"Be gone, monster, for I am master of this land, under Bounteous, and our Lord Jesus Christ. And I shall in no way bow before you; I bow only to High King and those who rule under him."

The creature came toward John.

"Stop, or I shall hit you with--with this," Peter said, threatening the monster with the shovel.

The beast was upon the farmer in a fraction of a second, picked him up and broke his back like a twig. Then with a long fingernail he carefully scooped out the unconscious farmer's left eye, and inserted it into his own dried socket.

"Ah, now I can see again," Satan said as he stood up and looked at the limp body of the human in front of him. Then he laughed. "My first victim, but not my last." The demon picked up the remains of the half-eaten chicken, and ran off, heading north, toward Holy Mountain.

"Well, it is not quite as adventurous as flying in a machine such as this, but then it is less confining. By that I mean we could fly both in and out of the atmosphere." Michael was trying to explain to the others how angels felt when they flew. "And yes, as far as I know, all of the heavenly hosts love to do it."

"I can't wait," Klote said, dreaming of getting his own wings someday.

Michael laughed at Klote. "Mr. Wizard, do not be in too big a hurry, but enjoy this part of your eternity."

Underneath the gondola was Dolphin Point. As they passed over it the land disappeared, and the waters of Newland Strait appeared. The sea was quite shallow, and the travelers could easily see large schools of fish through the clear waters. Up ahead, fifteen miles out to sea was Dentrosa. It could hardly be seen, for it was covered with a thick mist.

"How long will it take for us to get there, Mr. Wizard?" the king asked. "Well, it looks like we have about a ten mile per hour head wind, so it's gonna take us a good hour and a half."

Michael continued his previous conversation. "And then there is the matter of speed. An angel can fly considerably faster than fifteen or twenty miles per hour. Yes, quite a bit faster," he said, with a dreamy look in his eyes.

"Down. Get down before they see us," Stometz said to the others. The anthropologist had spotted the flying machine with the king's pennant streaming from the gondola. The machine was less than half a mile away. The students didn't really understand, but they obeyed their teacher. Everyone dropped to the sand and tried to be as invisible as possible, but it was no use. Klote's contraption was headed directly for them.

"All right," Stometz said angrily, getting up and brushing himself off. "Get back to whatever you were doing." The students returned to their preparations. Felix and Ralph

CHAPTER TEN

"It's the king, prince, Klote, and their body guard," Stometz growled. "When they get here, let me do the talking."

"Felix, I think you're getting upset over nothing," Moetta said.

"Moetta, you are an idiot. He's the KING! Can't you get that through your thick, stupid skull? And we are here illegally."

Dr. Moetta stared at Felix Stometz with astonishment, for this was the first truly evil thing that had been spoken on earth in a thousand years.

Queen Bounteous, Windella, Guardian, and Red poured over the hundreds of ledgers containing data on all the Nation Day celebrations from the very foundation of Newland as an official nation. It was long, hard work, for the entries were in long hand, and most of the reports were concerned with who had attended, the gifts, their problems and the counsel that the king and queen had given. But whenever anyone in the group came upon a date, a mark was made upon a parchment. Finally, after many long hours, they had finished going through all of the ledgers.

"Now we just add up the marks," the queen said.

"Allow me," Guardian said volunteering.

Ten minutes later, he had the figures. A worried look was on the face of the small saint of God.

"My queen, princess, Red, we may have a problem here."

"What is it, Guardian?" the queen asked.

"Well, if the ledgers are correct, and I have no doubt that they are, and if the first Nation Day celebration took place on May 16, the tenth year of our Lord's reign...."

"Yes, it was. I'm positive of that." Windella said.

"Then--then..."

"What, Guardian?" the queen asked, again seeing the worried look on her subject.

"Madam, I'm afraid that the time of Satan's release is upon us. In fact, he may already be free."

The two professors and their students bowed before the king as he exited the flying machine. Stometz stepped forward. "May the Lord bless Desert King," he said ceremonially.

"And may the Lord bless you, too, Professor Stometz, and your colleagues."

Stometz continued: "We don't have much here, my king, but I would like to offer you a cool drink of water, if you so desire."

"No, thank you, professor. We have had drink aplenty on our trip over here. But you could offer me an explanation about what you and those with you, are doing here."

If Felix Stometz was in any way intimidated by the king's presence, he did not show it. "Your highness, we are here on a scientific venture. As you well know, so much of Newland is covered with cities and towns, and the land that is left is privately owned farms and properties. In fact there seems to be little left in Newland that hasn't been despoiled, at least from an anthropological point of view. And most of the artifacts from our past have been destroyed. And so, enter Dentrosa. It is unpopulated, and I, and those with me, were in hopes of digging into soil that had not been ruined by civilization. Virgin land such as Dentrosa's could be quite important in providing facts about the times proceeding our Lord's second advent."

The king's voice became stern. "And did you apply for permission to dig on this island, since it is forbidden to Newland residents?"

"Why no, your highness. But we did not think anyone would care if a few scientists plied their trade here without hurting anyone."

"Prince Rustlipper, what did you find out about Dentrosa? Is it a part of Newland or is it not?" The king asked.

"No, your highness, the island is not part of Newland. In fact as far as I can determine, this island has never been claimed by any kingdom."

The king thought for a moment. "But Professor Stometz, you are a subject of Newland, and I am your king. And so, as your monarch, I am entitled to know when my subjects are journeying to an island that's off limits, am I not?"

"I--I..." The professor composed himself, then continued. "I'm sorry, my king, that I or someone from my party did not inform you of our venture. But I simply did not see the need. Anyway, what is important is that this team and I have found areas that we can study that may yield many priceless artifacts and secrets about our past. Surely that is what you will for all of your subjects: knowledge."

"Professor Stometz, you are wrong! Knowledge is not what I will for my subjects, but obedience, first to our Lord, and then to those he has appointed to rule under him. You know that before our Lord's second advent that the world was in turmoil, and much of this turmoil was the result of so called knowledge. It was with specific purpose that most of the old books and records were destroyed, so that the people in my kingdom, and those in other kingdoms as well, might not learn of the old ways--might not learn the things that were connected with evil."

"Your highness, with all due respect, I totally disagree...."

"You disagree with your king?"

Stometz was silent for a few seconds, then: "Sir, in this single instance I am convinced that you are wrong. Knowledge, true knowledge is good, and if anything it is ignorance which is the cause of evil."

The king's face flushed with anger. "Professor, this island is off limits to all Newland residents including you and those in your party. And what's more, I now proclaim Dentrosa to be part of Newland, under the rule of Queen Bounteous and myself. Please pack up your belongings and depart immediately." The king took a deep breath trying to compose himself. "And as far as your employment, as Professor and Dean of Newland College, it is hereby terminated. Your professorship too, Dr. Moetta."

The king turned and reentered the flying machine. "Oh, and one more thing, I expect a complete report about this expedition in my hands within the week."

The wizard latched the door in the side of the gondola, fired the propane burner, and in a few seconds, the machine had cleared the ground, turned, and began its journey back toward Newland.

Red hurriedly excused himself from the others, and raced down the marble stairs that dropped from the castle to the valley below, to Eleea's garden, where the Tree of Life stood. He had to protect it from Satan in case the Evil One tried to obtain some of the holy fruit.

When he reached the bottom of the steps he ran as hard as he could toward his beloved tree. But as he ran past another large tree, a leathery fist crashed into his mouth knocking him senseless. When he awoke, he had a mouthful of broken teeth and blood. He spat, and wiped his tender mouth with his sleeve, then shakily got to his feet and limped over to his tree.

It was immediately obvious that he had failed in his job as Guardian of the Tree of Life. A large limb had been ripped off the holy tree, and stripped of its healing leaves and fruit. The denuded branch had then been cast aside like so much trash. Red picked up the limb, and dragged it toward the steps. He would show the limb to the king and queen and admit his failure. His most important task, the one that he had been specifically sent to earth to do, was protect the tree, and keep anyone who was not entitled to the tree's fruit from eating it. He had failed in this task. Tears ran down the small man's face as he slowly climbed the steps to the castle above.

Moetta and two students were in the last of the boats. They waited for Stometz to get in so they, like the others, could begin their trip back to Newland.

"I'm not going," Stometz announced.

"You have to. The king ordered it," Moetta replied.

"I said that I'm not going. Just get out of here, and leave me alone." Stometz angrily pushed the boat out into the water, then turned and headed back to the diggings.

Satan gorged himself on the fruit. His leather covered stomach protruded from the stolen meal he had eaten. Now for dessert, he stuffed the healing leaves into his filthy mouth, and began chewing them with his rotted and blackened teeth. I shall now be both healed and eternal. And I shall get my revenge.

CHAPTER ELEVEN

For if after they have escaped
the pollutions of the world by
knowing the Lord and Savior Jesus Christ,
if they are again entangled in them, and overcome,
their latter state is worse than their beginning.
Peter 2:20

Stometz dug around in the supplies he had purposefully left behind, and grabbed a lightweight rope from the pile. He next drove a metal tent peg deep into the hard ground with a small hatchet, then carefully tied the rope to the peg. The rest of the rope he threw down the access hole. After he had pulled on the rope several times and had convinced himself that it would safely hold his weight, he lowered himself carefully through the opening, then repelled downward into the darkness. After what seemed an eternity to Stometz, he hit bottom. The small hole in the dome above could barely be seen from where Stometz stood. He brushed himself off, then reached into his backpack, pulled out a flashlight and aimed it at the rocket that dominated the silo.

It was hard to see much with so little light. But what he did see amazed him. Because, after more than a thousand years, aside from being covered with a light tarnish on its alloy skin, the machine looked as though it needed only the proper button to be pushed for it to take off and go wherever it was supposed to go. He devoted several minutes to giving the missile a thorough inspection, then began a search for a door that might lead to the room they had discovered earlier. There it was, sunk into the hardened concrete wall, a heavily rusted steel door. In the middle of the door was a spoked wheel much like those on board the old ships of war or submarines, that was used to make the various compartments watertight. He sat the flashlight on the concrete floor, and grabbed the wheel trying to turn it. It moved a little, with a loud squeak, then stopped. Stometz put all his strength into his next attempt, but the long years had badly rusted the mechanism. What he needed was a crowbar. He grabbed the flashlight off the floor, and began inspecting the silo walls and floor hoping that a suitable tool could be found.

After a complete circuit of the missile, he had found nothing that he could use as a lever. There were no tools, no metal rods, nothing. Stometz cursed for the first time in a thousand years. It felt good. He went over to the missile and began looking for a hatch. If he could get inside the rocket, there might be something in it that could be ripped loose to use as a lever. But it was hopeless. Every seam in the tough metal had been sealed, and he had no tools with him. He had even left the hatchet on the ground above.

He cursed again. Oh, how he hated his king. Had Desert King not come to Dentrosa and forced Moetta and the others to leave, he would have had everything he needed to open the door, and the necessary help, too. He resigned himself to depression, too tired to attempt the hard climb up the rope to the surface. Dr. Stometz sat on the floor, turned off the flashlight, and buried his head in his hands in despair.

"Hellooooo. Are you down there? Hellooooo, Felix, are you there?"

"Ralph, is that you?" Stometz yelled back, his heart beginning to beat wildly.

"Yah. You O.K. down there?"

CHAPTER ELEVEN

"I'm fine. See the rope? Come on down if you want to. Oh, you wouldn't have any tools with you, would you?"

"Yah, we brought some of em back with us. Figured we might need them. What do you want?"

"A crowbar, and anything else that you can get through that access hole. Maybe some water, too."

"O.K., I'll be right back."

Within five minutes, Ralph Moetta stood on the bottom of the silo with Stometz, and with him was Barton Steward, one of the students.

"Why did you come back?" Stometz asked, wiping his wet mouth after draining the better part of what was in the canteen.

Moetta and Steward had their flashlights on by now and were having a good look at the missile. "Couldn't let you have all the fun. And besides, anthropologists aren't the only ones interested in the past. I got the kids to turn the boat around and let me off. Bart insisted on coming with me. All the others are heading back to Dolphin Point." Then looking at the missile, "Big, isn't it?"

"Follow me," Stometz said as he circled the missile and pointed to the door. "This may lead to that other room, but it's frozen stiff with rust and age. Hand me that crowbar."

Bart handed him the tool. Stometz grabbed it and stuck it through the heavy iron spokes and tried to turn it, but the wheel would not budge.

"Give me a hand," Stometz said, but instead, Bart movod Stometz aside, and grabbed the crowbar by himself.

"Here, let me try it professor."

Barton Steward was a powerful young man, and weighed almost two hundred and fifty pounds. He had always been good at sports, especially the shot put. He now exerted his considerable strength on the crowbar. His biceps bulged; the veins stood out on his forehead and neck from his effort. The wheel moved, squeaked, squeaked again, then loosened and began turning more easily. It finally broke loose and spun free, allowing the door to be opened.

On the other side of the door was a narrow concrete corridor. The ceiling had lights every eight feet or so, but they had not worked for a thousand years. Stometz led the way through the door, ducking his head as he entered, then aiming his flashlight's beam ahead of him. The tunnel seemed to be extremely long, but this impression was amplified by its narrow width and low ceiling. Later, the three explorers found that the total length of the tunnel was only slightly more than a hundred yards long. It bent around a corner and ended at a wall. Sunk into the wall was a door much like the one they had just forced open. Bart grabbed the wheel and struggled with it for only a moment, but this one was easier than the first. The wheel protested momentarily, then turned easily allowing the door to swing open on its rusty hinges. Stometz was again the first one through.

They were in a room of moderate size, long but fairly narrow. It was filled with metal work benches, all badly rusted, and most of them collapsed upon the floor. On top of these were the remains of what had been electrical test equipment. Above them was the cement ceiling they had found earlier; the crack allowed a feeble light from the outside to enter the room allowing the three to see a little better. And littering the floor, were the bones that had once been the people who had worked on the missile, fifteen or twenty of them.

CHAPTER ELEVEN

In the Throne Room, Red kneeled before his king and queen. "Arise, Red. What happened had to be. Guardian said it would be necessary for a testing of every man and woman to take place before the end. Each would have to taste evil then choose between it and good. It has been so in every generation ever since Mother Eve and Father Adam.

"But since the Lord returned to earth the second time, Satan has been chained, and people have existed without temptation, never having to choose. In a state of innocence, so to speak. But humans do not enter into eternal life by being innocent, Red, but by choosing the Lord God and His ways. Only infants and children are permitted to enter into the Lord's presence in an innocent state."

Red arose and looked at his king and queen. "But Sir, because of me, Satan shall live forever. He has eaten the fruit from the tree."

"Nay," said the king. "He shall not live forever. He thinks he shall, but he is wrong. It is true that Satan shall EXIST forever, but there is no real life apart from God. Scriptures tell us that Satan and those who follow him shall be cast into outer darkness and separated from God. That is not life, but eternal death. No, Red, you have not surprised God with your failure. He knew exactly what would happen, and He shall yet triumph. And besides, my friend. You are totally human, and failure is an important part of being human. But you have not sinned, and that is the important thing.

"So, please, my friend, forgive yourself and partake of the leaves, and receive your healing." The king handed Red a small silver plate with several of the healing leaves upon it. Red hesitated for only a moment, then put the leaves into his swollen mouth and began to chew.

Xesduca smiled. He was healing fast. In fact he was almost back to normal, thanks to the leaves from that very special tree. He still had but one eye, but that was all he would ever need. And now kneeling before him were tens of thousands of his fallen angels who had been released from their imprisonment the same time he had. He had his army. He now had everything he needed to overthrow the Millennial Kingdom and High King. All he had to do was recruit people, flesh and blood, to do the dirty work, to be his slaves, and teach them what evil and rebellion were all about. He couldn't wait to get started. He had always been such a good teacher.

Only Abaddon and a few of Abaddon's higher ranking demons were missing from those before him. But he would have an eternity to find and deal with his rebellious general, and those who had been foolish enough to follow him.

And then there was Michael. Michael, I'm coming. And when I meet you, your life will end. The demon stared at his hands. He had just cut and filed his long fingernails, shaping them carefully into sharp claws. And at this moment he wanted nothing more than to sink these claws into the brown flesh of his worst enemy, the one who had cast him out of heaven and then chained him in the Bottomless Pit.

Michael, I'm coming.

Peter Samtouge had a bandage over the hole where his left eye had been. He laid in bed, and under him was a flat board that his neighbors had tied him to when they realized Peter's back was broken. He was semiconscious, and had not spoken since he had been found and carried inside. Guardian leaned over the farmer and anointed his forehead with olive oil, then prayed silently. Hours earlier, Guardian had tried to get Peter to chew some of the healing leaves from the Tree of Life, but Peter could not chew them. It often happened that way, when a person's life was almost over. They could not, for some reason, partake of the leaves.

"Peter, if you can hear me, blink your eye twice." Guardian spoke softly, kindly.

Peter opened his eye and looked at the small saint, then blinked once, twice.

"Peter, you know that you are dying, don't you?" Peter blinked twice. His wife whimpered in the rear of the bedroom. Queen Bounteous hugged and comforted her.

"Peter, do you love the Lord and his law with all of your heart?" Again two blinks.

"I believe you, my brother, for you have lived all of your life in Newland to the glory of God. And now you have another distinction. You are the first person to oppose Satan in a thousand years. May the Lord reward you for this and give you rest, my brother."

Peter smiled weakly, and tried without success to sit up. He did finally managed to speak: "Forgive me kind Boeterque, for I have never really understood any of you who have already been dead." Then he stiffened, and began to shake as he spoke his last words: "My--my wife. Take care of her for me, kind Boeterque. I--I love you Martha." He closed his eye. Peace was on his face.

His wife ran to his side, kneeled down, and kissed his cold cheek. Sobs shook her small frame. "If only I had not told him about that thing outside, that thing I saw eating the chicken. If only..."

The queen come to Martha's side, and embraced her. "It was your husband's duty to try and protect you. Such has been man's duty from the beginning. But take comfort in this: your husband is now in the presence of God."

In the garden, the small man raised his hands to heaven in praise to his God. Immediately the air around him began to glow. His dark complexion first became a deep pink, then took upon it a deep fiery red. He was taller by almost two feet, and in his right hand was his weapon of old.

Others like himself fell from heaven and alighted around him. It had been a long time since the man had seen these others, almost a thousand years.

Lori, one of the students in the Stometz expedition, was addressing the Mayor of Dolphin Point and his counsel. "Then he said we had to leave. No reason was given except some tripe about knowledge and the evil it could cause, or some fool thing like that. He said he didn't want knowledge but OBEDIENCE!"

Mayor Whelton shook his head. "Well, personally I am in favor of pursuing any and all knowledge. Maybe Bounteous simply did not understand. He's--he's not an educated man, you know."

"Then he should not be ruling those of us who are," Lori continued angrily.

"I will speak to him," the Mayor said. "He has simply got to be more open minded. After all, his job is to keep things running smoothly, not to cause trouble."

The demons, invisible and scattered throughout the room, smiled. Satan would be happy to hear about the beginnings of rebellion. Soon all of Newland would be just like the nations of old. Then they would spread the rebellion to the rest of the world, too.

Five demons silently slipped through Eleea's garden. Sent by Xesduca, their mission was to pick as much fruit off the Tree of Life as they could possibly carry, then get out of there fast. The fruit would be used as reward to those who followed Satan. Xesduca would give his followers eternal life that even God could not take away.

The demons knew that Michael and Gabriel were still in their human form, so there should be no one who could oppose them. Their job would be easy. Only the weakling that was supposed to protect the tree might be there, like he usually was, but their leader, Satan, had already dealt with him. If the gardener had returned, it would be their delight to dispatch him a second time, permanently this time.

Roltrex-Stein, the demon in charge, held up his hand. He thought he heard a noise. He hoped that it was the pygmy fool. If it was, he himself would deal with him. He would kill him, but not quickly. After all, he had not had the pleasure of torturing anyone in such a long time. It gave him great pleasure just thinking about having someone's warm blood running through his hands.

There it was again, the noise. Something or someone was definitely up ahead, and very close to the Tree of Life. Roltrex-Stein smiled.

Bart, using the crowbar, broke the rusty chain easily, then pulled a weapon from the rack. The wooden stock had suffered the most from the years of burial, but the metal parts seemed to be in pretty good condition, considering. The cosmoline had done its job superbly.

"I've never seen a real one--just pictures," Bart said. "Think it would work?"

By now Stometz and Moetta had gotten weapons of their own, and were inspecting them. "A little oil, and some ammunition, and I'd bet they would," Moetta said. He had once been somewhat of an expert in firearms. Collecting guns and shooting had been his hobby before Armageddon and the Second Advent.

"Hey--over here." Stometz said, pointing to piles of cartridges that had fallen from the rusted shelves, and were heaped on the concrete floor.

Moetta sat his rifle down and squatted next to the pile of ammunition, and began sorting through it. "This stuff is all useless. Look around. See if there's anymore, hopefully in a lot better shape than this stuff."

"Here. Over here." Stometz said as he pulled several rusty metal boxes from under a pile. The boxes were ammo cans. Most had rusted through and the ammunition was ruined. But there were some of the containers, underneath, near the bottom, that looked to be intact. Bart pulled a heavy screwdriver from his back pocket and attacked one of the sealed ammo cans. When the lid came off the three heads were side by side peering into it. The cartridges looked like new.

"Well I'll be," said Moetta. "Anybody got a nice little war where we can try these things out," he said smiling.

CHAPTER ELEVEN

Roltrex-Stein had been right. There had been a noise. But now that he saw the source, he was not too happy about it. For under the tree, and forming a ring around it, were five cherubim, and each had a flaming sword in his hands. In front, facing the demons was Polat-Shar-Alt, no longer the small human gardener, but a mighty angel of God.

"That is as far as you need come, unless you are prepared to be destroyed and cast into Gehenna, the lake of fire, prematurely." Polat-Shar-Alt threatened.

"So angel filth, you are healed and have painted yourself red. And look at that. He's even sprouted cute little wings. How nice."

Polat-Shar-Alt stepped closer to the five and swung his sword once. The demons jumped back, scared.

"So, you and your friends win this battle," said Roltrex-Stein, "only because we came unarmed. But this war is not over. We shall return, with Xesduca at our head." Roltrex-Stein hissed, then turned cautiously, and left Eleea's garden with his followers behind him..

The old man stood trembling before the king and queen. He was filthy dirty, and drenched in sweat; the left side of his face was swollen and had a very bad scrape on it.

"Speak, good Sir What troubles you, and what happened to your face?" asked the queen.

"Madam, Sir, I come here not to cause trouble, but to report a--well, a problem. We, myself, my wife and others near where I live, Dolphin Point, have tried to solve it, but we've failed."

"Go on, my friend. The king and I are not only your rulers but your friends."

"Madam, Sir, about ten days ago, my daughter did not come home after her job at the clothing factory. My wife and I thought nothing of it at first, since she has so many young girl friends, and sometimes stays over at their houses when she has worked late. But when she didn't come home the second night and the third, and had not sent word to us where she was, I went to look for her. So last Friday, it was, in the evening, I went into town, Dolphin Point. I looked everywhere that I thought she could be, but couldn't find her. And on top of that, nobody in town seemed to want to talk to me, to help. In fact, a few told me to go home and mind my own business. One man even hit me, here," Futhala pointed to the injury on his face.

"Finally, I gave up. It was late, and I had not eaten, so I went to a restaurant, the Fisher's Den, to get a bite before I walked the ten miles to my home. When I entered the door, I was shocked. They had a stage, and on the stage..." The man choked up, pulled a handkerchief from his back pocket and wiped away a tear, then cleared his throat.

"You may take your time. You are among friends."

"Well, Madam, and Sir, there on the stage was my daughter. She was dancing to this fast music. Loud. And the people, mostly men, were clapping and whistling. And the more she danced the more they clapped and--and... Well Madam and Sir, she was adancing up there in the lights and in front of everybody all naked. Not a stitch on her." The farmer broke down and began crying in earnest.

Gorbo the Great was so old that most of his hide was bald. And on top of that, the great lion had gained so much weight that it was only by God's grace that he ate only grass, for the beast could have never have caught another animal to eat it.

Gorbo's mate was almost as old as he was, and together they would slowly wander into the nearby villages. The people would then come out and pet the great old animals, who were legends, and make over them. And there was nothing that Gorbo liked better than being made over.

By now there were hundreds of lions all over Newland, and everyone of them was in some way kindred to Gorbo and his mate. Most of the lions made their homes in the Great Hardwood Forest that was part of the larger Bird Forest surrounding the Land of the Dead. And most of these lions were as tame as was Gorbo and his lioness.

But on this particular day, Gorbo was alone as he made his way toward the village of Serrate Major. He was almost to the outskirts of town when the children spotted him, and went running to tell their parents and older brothers and sisters. It was always an occasion when the big old lion visited them. Gorbo saw the children running home, squealing because he was there. He sat down, tired from his two mile trip, and waited for the humans to come out to him, to make over him, to pet, and feed him. He would lie in the sun and just take it easy until they all came. He loved humans.

Then Gorbo heard the roar. It was another lion, nearby. One of his great-great-great grandsons, no doubt. The lion roared again--louder. Gorbo slowly turned his obese body to face the beast that was approaching him.

This other lion had probably followed Gorbo knowing how the village people treated this old cat and wanted some of the attention himself, and some of the goodies, too.

There he stood, young, sleek, muscles rippling like Gorbo's had so many years before. He had his head down and was carefully eyeing the older lion. Then he crept cautiously toward the ancient beast. Gorbo hoped the young lion did not want to play, he was too old and fat for that.

When the young lion was ten feet away he stopped, crouched down, then in an eye blink, sprang upon Gorbo's back. Gorbo tried to defend himself, but it was only seconds before the old lion's neck was broken. The young lion roared loudly at his victory, then began to devour Gorbo the Great.

Stometz, Moetta, and Steward stood before the crudely made target. Each had a smile on his face. Behind them were six rifles that had been selected from all those below, six they thought could be made to shoot. Next to the rifles were twenty cans of ammunition that had been scrounged from below. The ammunition looked to be in good condition, but would it fire? Would the ancient primers still ignite the thousand year old gunpowder inside the brass casings? Behind the weapons and ammunition were five LAW rockets that looked like they might work too, and about fifty hand grenades.

One of the rifles sat apart from the others; it had been carefully cleaned and oiled with olive oil, the only lubricant they had on hand. The rifle's thirty round clip was loaded to the brim.

The three turned away from the target and walked the twenty-five yards to the weapons.

"Well, Ralph, you ready?" Stometz asked.

"Yep. It's about the one thing that I really missed in Newland all these years, not being able to go shooting. Hope the thing doesn't blow up in my face. All of this stuff is really, really old."

CHAPTER ELEVEN

Moetta seated himself on the sandy soil, grabbed the weapon, yanked the bolt back chambering a round, took careful aim at the target, then squeezed the trigger. The rifle jerked, emitting a deafening roar. A small hole appeared in the sign.

"Yahoooooo!" he yelled, raising his fist in victory. "Did you see that? Almost hit where I aimed." He laughed, and took aim for a second time squeezing the trigger.

The weapon kicked hard, and sent another projectile through the cardboard. The next time Moetta flipped the selector to full auto, aimed, and held the trigger back. The weapon roared loudly as it sent twenty-eight bullets ripping through the target before the bolt locked back, indicating an empty clip.

Moetta jumped up with a huge grin on his face matching the grins on the other two faces. All three were half deaf from the gun blast, but they loved it.

"Come on, you two, I'll show you how to work this thing."

Not too far from the target was a sign the three had put up earlier. "But don't hit our sign; we're gonna need it," Moetta said, again laughing.

The sign was made of cardboard and wood from the old ammo crates, and was proudly sticking out of the soil of Dentrosa. On it were four large words:

AMERICA II
A DEMOCRACY

The king and queen were at the head of the long table in the conference room. Also there were Gabriel, Michael,

Windella, Polat-Shar-Alt, Rustlipper, Guardian, and James Klote, the wizard. The mood was solemn. The king took charge of the meeting.

"So the end of God's rule in Newland draws near. Nevertheless there are some things that can be done. We as God's appointed shall not just give up, shall not simply allow Satan to have his way. We shall do everything in our power to delay his takeover. And by doing so, we shall continue to bring glory to our God as long as we are able." He looked around the table, and saw the nodding heads.

"Prince Rustlipper and Wizard Klote shall go in the flying machine to each of the larger cities, contact those in charge, and give them the proclamation Queen Bounteous and I have written. But first the wizard's flying machine shall deliver Michael, Gabriel and myself to Dolphin Point. It is there that the center of evil seems to exist. The machine will carry the five of us, will it not, Wizard Klote?"

"I'm not sure, my king. We had all better pray about it. If Gabriel and Michael weren't so doggone big, no offense meant, it wouldn't be a problem, but..."

"Then we shall indeed pray," said the king, interrupting the Wizard. He continued his instructions. "When we get to Dolphin Point, we shall take all of the children six years old and under with us. Wizard Klote, you will land the three of us well outside of town, under the cover of darkness.

"Gabriel shall then make his way to the east of town. Gabriel, we shall wait four hours for you to enter into town. The schoolhouse is quite close to that edge of town, if I'm not mistaken. As soon as the school opens, gather the children and escort them out of town the same way you entered. Hopefully the teachers will be faithful and assist you with the children. But assistance or not, I want all of the younger children out of there. Of course if some of the older ones want to come with you...

"Here," said the king, slipping off the ring High King had given him so long ago. "Show this to any who ask you by what authority you operate." Gabriel took the ring and slipped it on. His hands were so large that the ring barely fit onto his smallest finger.

"When Michael and I have met those in charge, and investigated the occurrences there, I shall call all of the faithful to ourselves. All of us shall then join you on the old road near Blue Rock Park. We will then make our way back here to the castle.

"Eleea, you shall stay at the castle with Windella, and ready all of the guest rooms, for hopefully there will be many who shall choose to accompany us from Dolphin Point. When we get back we can begin to formulate final plans to oppose the evil that has begun in Newland, and if necessary, plan for the withdrawal of all the faithful from our beloved land.

"Guardian, stay here with the queen and Windella. I place their safety within your hands.

"And so it may be that soon the nation of Newland will be at war, between those who choose the Lord and those who do not. Only God himself knows the outcome." The king's voice failed him for a moment, then he cleared his voice and continued.

"But in all of this, the Lord our God shall not be defeated. Satan and those who choose to follow him shall surely be punished, and good shall rule again. Guardian, our priest, shall lead us in prayer."

"Oh, Lord, our great God, help us in the days ahead, to withstand evil, and to continue to proclaim You and Your way. Make us strong, but give us Your kindness and patience so that many may yet choose You and not the Evil One. And dear God, just one more thing, please help the Wizard's flying machine to be able to carry its heavy load. Amen."

The king spoke again. "And now, Polat-Shar-Alt, show us what must be done."

Mayor Whelton, of Dolphin Point, had been listening to the two professors with intense interest. "So you really think we can overthrow the king and establish a democracy?"

"We've got to try," said Moetta. He had lived in Stometz's shadow for years, but was now beginning to emerge as the leader, for he alone was the expert in weapons.

Stometz had never thought much of being a leader before, but was now finding that he didn't like being second fiddle to Moetta. But there would be time enough to straighten things out after the king, queen, and those who served them were overthrown, and Newland liberated.

"How can we be victorious?" asked the mayor. "There are still so few of us that are enlightened?"

Moetta nodded to Barton Steward who stood in the corner. The tall student came over carrying something wrapped in cloth; he handed it to Moetta. Moetta carefully unwrapped it, and showed the rifle to the mayor.

"This is how we shall overthrow them."

"Where did you get that?" Whelton asked with a shock upon his face.

"Never mind that, we've got em."

The mayor's expression slowly changed--he began to grin. "With these maybe, just maybe, we can do it."

CHAPTER ELEVEN

It was a quiet and sad little party that met in Eleea's garden, and stood around the Tree of Life. It had already been cut down, sawed into pieces, and the pieces stacked high. Some distance away was a single basket of leaves that had been stripped off one of the limbs. These would be given to the king and queen for the healing of others if needed. But the fruit from the tree was holy, and could not be destroyed, so it had been picked then carefully hidden by Polat-Shar-Alt and Prince Rustlipper. This way it would not fall into the wrong hands.

Each member of the party had a torch in their hands. The king spoke: "Let it be done." One by one each of the party threw their torch onto the pile that had once been the most beautiful tree on earth, stepped back, and watched the fire as it become a huge bonfire. Tears ran from the eyes of most present.

"Please do not cry. For am I not the keeper of the trees? I have tens of thousands of these in the garden that God has given me to tend, in Apartia. So when each of you comes home, your permanent home, I shall personally plant a Tree of Life in your gardens. This is a promise that I make to each of you. But for now, my time on earth is over and I say goodby."

The queen came over and hugged the flaming angel of God, as did the king. The rest would have to wait to embrace the cherub until they received their spiritual bodies, for to touch him would have been instant death for a mortal.

"I shall miss you, Polat-Shar-Alt, for I have learned to love you as a brother." The queen said.

"I, too." said the king."

"And I have learned to love all of you, too." The angel's eyes rested just a little longer on the prince he loved so dearly. "Never in all the years of my existence did I ever think it possible for me to care about humans or those who had once been human. But the Lord our God has lessons for each of us to learn, even such as I." The angel sighed noticeably. "When we meet again remember, to you, my special friends only, just call me Red."

The cherub again looked briefly at each of the party, then his wings blurred, and he began to ascend. Apartia had just appeared in the sky. He would have to hurry to catch it. His speed increased leaving a red streak in the darkening sky, then he was out of sight.

Prince Rustlipper and Wizard Klote were having so much fun sailing through the air in Klote's flying machine that they almost forgot how serious things had become in Newland. The machine had indeed carried its heavy load to Dolphin Point where they had dropped off the king, Gabriel and Michael. The sun had arisen hours before, and the two were now on their way to carry out their part of the King's plan. "Let me steer for a while," Rustlipper said smiling at the wizard.

"O.K., my lord, but make sure that you allow for the cross wind, otherwise we'll miss Serrate Major by ten miles."

Forty minutes later, when they approached the last of the high mountain ranges between them and their destination, the wizard took over the controls and forced the machine higher, so they would safely clear Mt. St. Norris. On the very top of the mountain was a Newland flag, a picture of a lion and lamb lying at each other's feet centered on a white rectangle. Wizard Klote estimated that they would clear the peak by a good fifty to seventy feet.

CHAPTER ELEVEN

As they got closer, they saw that there was a group of men huddled on top of the peak, about a dozen of them. As they flew over the men, the prince and wizard shouted and waved to the party. But the waves and shouting were not returned. Instead three or four of the group quickly grabbed the wooden bows off their backs, put arrow to string, and began shooting at the flying machine. Two of the arrows narrowly missed, one hit the fabric of the flying machine's envelope at an angle and caused a considerable tear, and one arrow hit Wizard Klote in his right upper arm, the one he was waving. The arrow completely pierced it, and blood quickly seeped through Klote's shirt sleeve. The wizard collapsed to the bottom of the gondola in pain. The blood spread quickly over his robe indicating that a major artery had probably been severed.

The prince quickly hit the lever controlling the propane burner. It roared loudly, pumping hot air into the machine's torn envelope. The machine struggled upward. The air was filled with more arrows. Several more of these punctured the fabric, but they did cause any large tears. When the machine was high enough to be out of range, the prince turned his attention to Klote.

"How bad, Jim?"

"Bad enough to hurt like the dickens, but I think I'll live. There, in that box, there's a big pair of wire-cutters. Get em out and cut the tip off this arrow." The prince found the cutters and cut the arrow. Then Klote held his breath and painfully pulled the shaft out of his arm. Blood squirted onto the bottom of the gondola. "Aaaagggghhhh."

The prince quickly stripped off his shirt, tore it in strips, and used the material for a bandage on Klote's arm. He then used his bolt to make a tourniquet on Klote's upper arm. The wizard groaned as the prince tightened the tourniquet to slow the blood loss.

"We've got to get you back to the castle, and get some healing leaves into you."

"No, my prince--please. We've got to get these proclamations delivered. Things look like they're getting worse a lot faster than we thought. I'll, I'll be O.K."

But it was clear that he would not be O.K.. For the bandage was already soaked through and more blood was leaking onto the bottom of the gondola.

"Please, Prince Rustlipper, there are a lot of lives at stake besides mine."

The prince hesitated for a second. "You're right; we must deliver the proclamations. Maybe we can get help for you at Serrate Major." The tear in the fabric was getting worse. "We'll have to fix that tear, too."

The prince looked back at the mountain top. He could still see the men on top of it; they were tearing down the flag of Newland and putting another one in its place. The new flag was red, white, and blue, and had a single white star upon it.

Together, there were about forty craftsmen. They were assembled in the coliseum, the largest building in Dolphin Point. Actually, the building was outside the city limits, but the ground and building were owned by the city. The craftsmen roamed around looking at the contents of the boxes that filled the room. Jacob Merryfield, a master iron worker, stood next to the mayor, excited.

"I don't know how many of 'em we can fix, but there's no doubt that we can make at least some of them serviceable.

The wood's rotted away on most of them, but we can make new stocks. Fixing the metal parts will be a little harder, but I think we can do it. The real challenge will be the ammunition. We need lots of it, and we've lost almost all of our knowledge of chemistry." Then Merryfield got an idea. "Course we can always use black powder, like we make the fireworks out of. It will not be quite as efficient, but it will work."

Doctor Stometz and Doctor Moetta overheard the conversation and came over.

"Doctor Moetta has an idea." Stometz said. "That rocket on Dentrosa is a solid fuel type. We'll never get the nuclear warheads to work, but there's a lot of propellant in that thing. Moetta thinks we might be able to use the propellant as explosives, to make bombs. Can some of you craftsmen make the necessary containers, and put together something to act as detonators?"

"We sure can," said Merryfield. "This is the most exciting thing that has happened since we came to this awful country."

"You bet it is," said Moetta. "Fighting for one's freedom is always an exciting venture."

Mother Willson sat next to Klote's bed, and carefully sewed together the wizard's wound. She had been the Healer in the village of Little Star as long as she could remember. But not many people came to her anymore, since the leaves from the Tree of Life were so widely distributed in the last few years. But now there were no leaves, at least not around Little Star. So maybe the people would need her healing arts again. She hoped so. As far as Klote was concerned, he was concerned, he was feeling no pain. Mother Wiltson had given him a liquid made of some of the most horrible tasting herbs one could have imagined, and Klote had drifted quickly into a state that was more asleep than awake.

"He'll be fine in a week or ten days, faster if you can get him some of those leaves."

"I'm sorry, Mother Wiltson, but right now we can't take time out to go get the leaves."

"It's O.K., he'll heal up alright without them. He'll just need a little more time and a good deal of rest. He's lost a lot of blood. But one thing's for sure, he'll be hurting some in about three or four hours when my herbs wear off. Course, I can always give him another shot or two of my concoction."

"Thank you Mother Wiltson, but when your medicine wears off, we've got to leave. We have to be in Serrate Major as soon as possible."

The woman was startled to hear the name of the city. "My prince, you don't want to go there. There's a lot of crazy things happening in that town."

"Like what, Mother Wiltson?"

"Well, for one, do you remember that old lion, Gorbich or something like that?"

"Gorbo, sure. He came to Newland the same time that I did."

"Well, he's been killed--by another lion they say. And there's a lot of small children missing, too. Most people say the lions in the Great Hardwood Forest got 'em. So the people are forming a hunting party, they call it, and they're gonna burn down the whole forest and kill all the lions--all the animals. They're making bows and arrows, and spears, and things like that. Yep. They got killing on their minds. I wouldn't go there. That's my advice."

CHAPTER ELEVEN

The old woman looked into the prince's eyes and saw the determination there. "Here," she said reaching into the pocket in her dress and pulling out half of a small leaf that had come from the Tree of Life. It was old and dried. "I've been saving this for when my rheumatism acts up, but he needs it more than I do. It's not enough to heal him, but it might help some."

King Bounteous and Michael were met by about a hundred people just outside the main gate of Dolphin Point. In the group were the mayor, Stometz, and Moetta. The group had interposed themselves between the two and the gate to the city.

The mayor spoke for the group: "I personally have nothing against you, Bounteous, but there are some here that do, and I can't be responsible for your safety if you enter my city. So I'm asking you to leave, peacefully."

"You're asking me, the King of Newland not to enter part of own land?" The king's anger burned.

"Stometz, give the king our document," the mayor said. Doctor Stometz walked forward glaring at the king, remembering their last meeting on Dentrosa, and handed him the parchment. It read as follows:

> **On this sixteenth day of the month Savoite, the one thousandth year, We the peoples of Newland proclaim our freedom from the tyranny and rule of High King and those He has appointed: King and Queen Bounteous. And do hereby establish a new nation, a democracy, and shall call this democracy, this new nation: AMERICA II.**

This is preposterous," said the king. "This land, the whole earth--the universe, belongs to High King, and He has given rule to my queen and I under him." King Bounteous stared at the group, then tore up the parchment, and threw it on the ground.

"Barton," the mayor said to the student, "you and some of your friends escort these two intruders out of our territory."

Barton stepped forward with two of his athlete friends just behind him. Barton roughly grabbed Michael's arm, and immediately found himself on the ground with Michael's foot on his chest.

"Stay down. Do not struggle, and no additional harm will come to you," Michael said, keeping an eye on the other two, with a hand on his sword.

"So, you have nothing better to do than pick a fight with one of my puny little humans." The voice came from a grotesque, one-eyed creature, fully a foot taller than Michael. The powerful thing pushed its way through the crowd and approached the king and Michael.

Michael removed his foot and let the student up. Barton and the other two students withdrew into the crowd. Michael pulled his sword from its sheath, but knew that the weapon would be useless against the spiritual body of Satan.

"And now, my black angel friend, your time to die has come." The creature stepped quickly toward Michael, with his clawed hands outstretched before him.

"Get back, Evil One." The king leaped between Michael and the creature.

"So, it is the little Desert King. It must be that you wish to die first."

The creature sprang at Bounteous, intending to rake his claws across the king's face and blind him. But the king remembered something he had learned long before, when he had been a judo champion. He fell backward, and using Satan's own momentum, tossed him through the air. Satan landed flat on his back. The impact temporarily knocked the wind out of him. Bounteous was up quickly, grabbed Satan's arm, and turned the creature over. Then the king twisted the demon's arm tightly against his back.

"You forgot demon, that I too have a spiritual body," Bounteous said, putting more pressure on the demon's arm. The beast screamed in pain. Bounteous released some of the pressure, and standing with one foot on Satan's back spoke to the crowd. "Who else wants to try to attack me or my servant?"

No one spoke. No one stepped forward. The king still held Satan's arm tight behind the demon's back forcing his face into the dust.

"What, no taker's?"

The school teacher hurriedly readied the fifteen children. "Thank God you've come. Most of the parents have quit sending their children to school. They don't want them just reading and learning the scriptures anymore. They say there's more to life than just God, the Bible, and being blindly obedient to King and Queen Bounteous."

Gabriel shook his head in disgust, then led the teacher and children out of the school house, and through the east city gate. In an hour they would meet up with Bounteous and Michael at the park, then all would journey to the castle and to safety.

"In God's name, come," said the king. "Why do you listen to those who encourage rebellion and sin? Has not the Lord been good to all of you? Or has there been famine or war, or sickness? And is not each of you clothed and housed? And have not the queen and I loved each and every one of you? So why then do you rebel? And why do you grieve your God and Savior? Come with us!"

No one stepped forward.

Bounteous finally released the arm of Satan and allowed him to arise from the dust. "Don't try anything, demon, for you are no match for me."

Satan hissed, then eyed Michael. "You both shall be sorry that you have ever seen me. I swear this by the fires of Hell." The demon rubbed his arm, brushed himself off, then entered the city.

The people murmured among themselves. "We want nothing to do with a king or a queen. We want to be free," someone said.

Then a woman, crying and yelling hysterically came running through the city gates. "One of them has taken the children from school."

"Give us back our children," another yelled. "You have no right to take them." A tomato flew through the air that narrowly missed the king.

"You'll never make it back to your castle, not with our children," a women screamed. Another tomato flew through the air, and struck Gabriel in the middle of his chest.

The people were quickly becoming a mob. To continue to try and reason with them was hopeless. Bounteous and Michael slowly backed away, then turned and walked quickly toward Blue Rock Park. More tomatoes sailed through the air, and now rocks. But the people did not attack the king and Michael. The time was not yet ripe for that to happen.

"Give us back our children," they continued to yell.

"We're going to kill you," someone yelled.

The prince and the wizard flew the patched up flying machine into another town, but before they could even land, the people were throwing stones at them. They barely managed to escape. They now realized that it would be hopeless to try to hand deliver the proclamations. They had to find another way.

Wizard Klote's home was about fifteen miles from Holy Mountain, on the southern side, in the foothills. The structure was more of a barn than anything else, but Klote loved it, and it allowed him plenty of room to collect his inventions and antiques, and store all of the parts that he used on his many projects. Inside, except for a very nice living room where he entertained occasional guests, his home looked more like a small factory than a residence. But that was the way Wizard Klote wanted it, and it had provided the material for many conversations and jokes in Newland for hundreds of years.

The flying machine landed somewhat roughly in Klote's huge front yard. The prince jumped out, and tied a stout rope around a mooring hook that was embedded deep into the soil, then helped his friend inside. The wizard was very weak, and in a great deal of pain. But Klote knew the importance of the task the king had given them to do. So he would keep himself going the best he could until they were finished. After all, the king and queen were more like parents to him than any he had ever known, and on top of that, there was Prince Rustlipper, the first real friend he had ever known.

The proclamation read as follows:

> **Citizens of Newland are commanded to leave all lands under the rule of Bounteous, and journey to Jerusalem where they shall receive the proection and blessings from High King. Newland is to be vacated by the twenty-first day of Savorte, the thousandth year of the rule of High King. Anyone remaining in these lands will be considered to be enemies of the Lord and shall be dealt with accordingly. Bounteous**

Prince Rustlipper, with help from the wizard, entered the wording of the proclamations into a duplicating machine that was more or less, a combination typewriter, mimeograph machine, and word processor. The prince carefully typed the message into the contraption while the wizard rested on a nearby couch, and occasionally gave the prince advice on how to operate the fragile and cranky invention. Soon, if everything went well, there would be thousands of pamphlets printed and ready to go.

CHAPTER TWELVE

Woe unto them!
For they have gone in the way of Cain,
and have run greedily after the error of Balaam,
and have perished in the gainsaying of Korah.
Jude 11

Bounteous smiled when he saw Gabriel ahead. With him were fifteen children and a young school teacher, Mary Ellen Toffer. When she saw the king, she approached, then kneeled before him. "Arise, my child," Bounteous said. "But where are the rest of the children, and the teachers?"

"My king," Mary began, "these are all the children that still attend the Dolphin Point Public School. Parents have withdrawn all the rest, and have formed their own schools. Most of them said that we teach too much religion and not enough of what they call 'the essentials': math, science, history and such. And I guess I'm the only teacher left that thought the old ways were the best ways."

The king sighed, then smiled weakly. "Thank you for being faithful, Miss, Miss... I'm sorry, but I don't know your name."

"Mary Ellen Toffer, my king."

"Well, thank you very much, Miss Toffer, for helping Gabriel with the children, and for coming yourself. So far you are the only one out of the whole city that has agreed to come with us. So today, you have become someone very special to me. May God specially bless you for your obedience. And Mary Ellen Toffer, because of your faithfulness, I think that I shall call you Remnant, Saint Remnant, in fact."

"There they are," said one of the outlaws.

All of his group were armed with bows and arrows, and had black hoods over their faces. They stood directly in the middle of the roadway. Each of the men put arrow to string, then aimed his weapon toward the king and his party.

"Stop where you are!" said the leader. "If you want to live, then you better do two things: first, give us those children, and second, get out of here as fast as you can."

The king held up his hand, stopping those behind him. "And who is this that threatens the lawful king of Newland?"

"That you do not need to know. But I will tell you this: you've got ten seconds to do what I said or else everyone with you is dead meat."

"You would kill your own children?" Bounteous asked, shocked.

"Let me make myself clear! If we can't have 'em then we intend to make sure that nobody can."

Some of the children, terrified, started to cry. Mary Ellen tried to quiet and comfort them.

"Please, my lord," Michael interrupted, "you and the others stand back, Omega must now begin his work." Michael stretched out his hands and pointed to the ground in front of the bandits. "Oh, my God, Omega asks for deliverance."

Immediately the earth started rumbling, then shook violently. Deep cracks appeared in the earth, one of which became a great chasm that separated the two groups. The earth on the far side of the chasm then started crumbling and falling into the chasm. The loosened earth fell into the mile deep fissure, and carried with it all of the hooded figures.

The earth then slammed back together. All was quiet, except for the crying of the children. When the dust cleared, nothing was left of those who had opposed Bounteous except for one black hood that lay on the ground. It had slipped from the head of one of the bandits.

The prince and wizard were high over the city of New St. Petersberg. Klote was in bad shape, and was huddled on the bottom of the gondola shivering. His arm was badly swollen and infected, yet he had insisted on coming with Prince Rustlipper on this trip, for he knew that he might be called upon to help operate the flying machine.

The two, riding in the repaired flying machine, had already flown over seventeen other cities. They now approached the fairly large city of North Star.

As the prince slowed the machine, the wizard forced himself to stand, pulling the blanket tightly around himself. "Now remember, we've got--to figure--wind speed--and direction before we drop the leaflets." His teeth chattered so badly that the prince had trouble understanding him.

Rustlipper lit the torch dangling from a small parachute, and tossed it overboard. The device drifted slowly away from them toward the east at about two knots.

"Good, now take--take us just--a--little bit--that way. Slow, good. Go ahead and drop 'em."

The prince threw the copies of the proclamation overboard and watched the hundreds of papers spread out and blanket the city.

"Nice, very nice," said the wizard just before returning to the bottom of the gondola, and pulling tightly on his blanket.

Rustlipper bent over his friend. "You're going to be O.K. I'm heading for the castle."

"No--no, you can't do that. We still--have a lot of towns--cities, south of the mountains--to go yet."

"We've done our best, and anyway, we're almost out of propane gas."

"We can't be." Klote stared at the gauge, and read the meter. They were so low on fuel that it would be a miracle if they even made it back to the castle in one piece. "You're right. Guess--guess we didn't--do so good."

"We did just fine, under the circumstances. Now rest, and I'll try to get us back to safety."

The wizard needed no coaxing. He huddled under his blanket and drifted off into a troubled sleep. Prince Rustlipper consulted his map for a moment, then turned the airship around and pointed it toward home.

They had been flying for about an hour before Prince Rustlipper smelled the smoke. He hurriedly checked the airship, but found nothing amiss. The smell was not coming from the flying machine.

The smoke was stronger now. Thicker. The airship was surrounded by it. Rustlipper began to cough and his eyes teared badly. He looked below them, on the ground. There it was, a little toward the east, the source of the dense smoke they were flying through. The orange and red flames were less than five miles away, and leapt high into the dark sky. The Great Hardwood Forest was engulfed in fire.

The king was sitting on the balcony of their castle speaking with the queen, Windella, and Guardian relating the occurrences at Dolphin Point, when they saw the flying machine approaching from the east. It looked very unstable as it approached Eleea's garden. The four jumped up, and ran through the castle, then down the many flights of stairs that descended the mountain and terminated at the garden. Poor Windella could not keep up with the Boeterque, and fell far behind.

The king, queen, and Guardian reached the last of the steps, and ran through the garden staring up at Klote's machine . It was coming down far too quickly. Then they saw that there was no fire being emitted from the propane burner; it had run out of fuel. As the heated air in the envelope cooled, the airship descended faster and faster, finally falling out of control the last few feet. It hit the ground hard, caving in one side of the gondola, and tumbling the two occupants roughly to the ground. The prince was up in a second, yelling for the others to come over and help with the comatose Klote.

"What happened to him?" the queen asked, looking into the wizard's face.

"He's been shot. I'll tell you the whole story in a few minutes, but I've got to get this machine tied down before it blows into the trees."

The gondola was made of light gauge metal that was reinforced with plywood bulkheads. One side was badly damaged and would require repairs before the machine could be flown again. But the rest of the airship appeared to have survived the fall from the sky fairly well, with only a few small punctures occurring in the envelope from nearby branches.

The king gently picked up the wizard and headed toward the steps. "Let's get him up to the castle, and in bed as quickly as we can," Bounteous said, as he quickly climbed the steps, carrying the heavy Klote easily.

On the way up the steps, the party met the breathless Windella still coming down. She just shook her head, turned around, and started back up. "Guess I'm heading the wrong way." Then she saw Klote. "My king, what has happened to the wizard?"

"Prince Rustlipper will tell us shortly."

In the few short weeks since the discovery of the missile silo complex, Dolphin Point had become a busy center for making black powder weapons, and for repairing the old ones found underground. Tents housing the workmen were everywhere, and a huge Quonset hut had been erected to serve as the factory.

At Dentrosa was another prefabricated building. Inside it were two teachers from the Newland College; one was the head of the mathematics department, and the younger, an instructor of science. The two had somehow managed to be given the nuclear warheads from the missile for study. As they carefully disassembled the hydrogen bombs, they wrote down everything that they did, making drawings where applicable. The warheads were so old that the two scientists had no hopes of being able to repair them so that they could detonate, but whatever they could learn from the weapons would surely be invaluable in the future, after America II had been liberated and had its own nuclear weapons program.

Professor Kerety, the older of the two, spoke to his assistant: "Too bad these things are in such bad shape, because whoever owned one of these things--if it worked--would rule the world."

Kerety's assistant smiled. "Yah!"

"We did our best, father, but there are a lot of towns and cities we missed in the southern part of Newland. The wizard and I were hoping that since the rebellion hasn't spread south of the mountains, that the faithful will spread the word as they make their way to the Ribbon Lands on their way to Jerusalem.

"But the wizard does have two bottles of propane stored on the far side of Eleea's garden. If you want me to, I can refuel the airship and make another trip to drop the leaflets in the other cities that we missed. But I'll have to repair the gondola first."

"No, no--it's too dangerous," the king said.

"Lord--lord and lady," Windella interrupted, leading an elderly man into the conference room. "This is Rammon, and I think he has something to tell us that we all need to know."

"My king and queen," the man said kneeling before Bounteous.

"Good sir, arise. And what is this important news?" asked the king.

"King Bounteous, I am a fisherman in the village of Ferbane, about five miles west of Dolphin Point. Two days ago, some men wanted to rent my boat if I would make a trip with them off the eastern coast, down to the Ribbon Lands. They offered me more than a year's wages. I asked them why they were offering so much money for a single trip. They wouldn't tell me at first, then one finally said that it was a TOP SECRET mission. I declined, and found out later that some of the men, led by Stometz and Moetta, had gone to Dentrosa, and had found a rocket there...."

"A what?" The king asked.

"A rocket. Like they used to have before the Lord came back. Anyway, a bunch of the men dug all of this rocket's propellant out of the motor--said it was the same as high explosives, and--and sir, they're going down to the Ribbon Lands to blow a hunk of it away, so there won't be any way for the faithful to get to the mainland. They want Newland to be an island. Said it would be easier to defend. And lord, and lady, they also said that if there was no Ribbon Lands connecting America II with the mainland, it would be easy for them to get the children back." The fisherman paused giving the king and queen a chance to digest what he had said, then added: "And one more thing: they got guns."

Five small fishing boats skirted the coast heading in a southward direction. Stometz was in the front of the lead boat. It was nighttime and overcast, so the small armada would have been invisible to anyone on shore, but there was no one on that particular shore, for it belonged to Hastedia Compotu. Stometz stared at the sail above his head, it made a loud popping sound as it alternately filled with air and then went slack. The sound seemed to do something to his soul--invigorate it.

His boat's crew, consisting of two fishermen and a helper, were working hard to keep the small craft close to land, but the gusting wind made that difficult, for when it did blow, it tried to force them out to sea, and the tiny sailing craft had never been designed for that. In the bottom of the small boat were fourteen heavy canvas sacks stuffed with cargo that pushed the boat deep into the water, making it especially hard to maneuver. But the money had been so good that the fishermen, owning the craft, had willingly overloaded their little boat. Fishing six days a week was hard work. Now in a few hours they would make more than a year's wages. And besides that, they had the chance to become patriots and heroes. They had a chance to really be SOMEBODY.

A wave splashed into the boat. "Watch what you're doing, you idiots." Stometz growled. "We've got to keep those sacks dry. That stuff is worth a lot more than gold. Just remember, it took a lot of hard work to tear that rocket apart and scrape all of that solid propellant out of it."

Moetta was in the second boat, a short way behind. His boat should have been the first one, he told himself. After all, it was he who was the foremost expert in weapons, maybe in the whole world, and not Felix Stometz. But the anthropologist had insisted on being first, and so Moetta had given in. Now he was almost angry enough to kill his ex-colleague.

Moetta fiddled with his rifle, picked it up and yanked the bolt back chambering a round, then flipped the safety off and pointed the weapon toward the lead boat. It would be so easy to kill him. But he might still need Stometz. So for the time being he would do nothing. He flipped on the safety, and put the rifle, butt first, in the bottom of the boat. But there might be a time when he would not need Stometz, and then there could simply be an accident. Moetta wondered what it would feel like to kill another human being. It would probably feel pretty good, he thought to himself.

Inside the castle, in one of the many bedrooms, Wizard Klote rested in bed. Standing next to him were the king and his son. "Please rest a while longer, my good wizard, for you have had a hard time of it. Give the leaves a chance to complete their special healing."

"But Sir, I feel fine, and--and there's so much to do."

"I can think of nothing to do right now. Newland will soon be cut off from the mainland. There will be no way for the pilgrims to get to Jerusalem. And worse still, the children must remain on Newland where there is so much evil about. In fact, I can sense the presence of the evil ones closing in even now. And I fear that the innocent hearts of the children may yet be ruined.

"It would be easy for Michael, Gabriel, and I to fight the rebels, but Guardian thinks that we should not use Omega's power, at least not yet. He thinks that we must simply let the events unfold by themselves, and let the people choose who they wish to believe and follow."

The wizard sat up. "Sir, I have an idea."

"Go ahead, Wizard Klote. For I have surely learned to trust your intelligence, if not your judgement, over these many hundreds of years." He smiled at his son's friend.

"Sir, the prince can lead the children and some of the others through the Land of the Dead...."

CHAPTER TWELVE

"But my wizard, that would be suicide. Have you forgotten what happened to Prince Rustlipper many years ago?"

"No, my king, I have not forgotten. But this time he could take some of the healing leaves with him. He could lead them through Hastedia Compotu to the coast. No one would ever think to look for the children in that terrible land, and meanwhile I could fly the airship to the mainland, and there get a sailing ship to come and pick up the prince and the children off the coast."

The king pondered the wizard's plan for a moment. "My good wizard, you certainly have earned your title. I think you have hit upon the beginnings of an excellent plan."

It should never have happened. After all, the warheads were over a thousand years old. The wiring circuits had been eaten away with time. Even the radioactivity of the elements should have decreased over the millennium. But it did happen. One moment there were over one hundred men and women working on Dentrosa, and the next, a tremendous flash, brighter than the sun, and Dentrosa was gone. The phenomenal power that had been packaged into the warheads produced a fireball ten miles in diameter, completely vaporizing the small island, the people, and millions of gallons of sea water all at the same time.

This began a series of events that would create a gigantic tidal wave that would decimate Dolphin Point and the other fishing villages on the northern shore of Newland. And after the tidal wave had done its work, the horror of radioactive fallout would begin.

Abaddon smiled in the midst of the fireball. He and the few that still followed him had succeeded. They had caused the stupid humans to commit a series of fatal errors as they worked on the hydrogen bombs, errors that had caused the warheads to detonate. Abaddon laughed aloud. No, he was not finished with his rebellion against God or Satan just yet. In fact, he had really just started. For he would be the king of the earth or no one would. No, he was not finished, not by a long shot.

King Bounteous, the prince, and the wizard made their way down the steps leading from the castle to Eleea's garden. The prince and wizard held torches to light the path. Then in a split second, a brilliant flash of light from the north drove the darkness away. The intense light slowly shaped itself into a mushroom shaped fireball. By the grace of God, the prince and wizard were facing away from the blinding flash when it appeared, but the king saw it in its entirety. He had seen something exactly like this a thousand years before, over the Valley of Megiddo.

"Down!" the king ordered.

"What was that?" the prince asked lying face down on the hard soil.

The wizard didn't have to ask. There was only one thing that could turn the night into day. "It was a hydrogen bomb," said the wizard. "Had to be."

Seventy miles south of Dolphin Point, Moetta cursed, when he saw the intense light in the distance. The fools had blown themselves up. He told Stometz not to give the warheads to anyone. But Stometz had insisted that the warheads were too old to be any kind of a threat. So he had allowed the bumbling fools to play with the bombs. But Stometz had been wrong again, and he had been right. He wanted to say "good riddance," but Moetta knew that the explosion had done more than just kill people. It had destroyed all of the weapons and ammunition, those being repaired and the new black powder ones too. Why couldn't people just listen to him once in a while? He cursed loudly.

Wizard Klote lit the propane burner, and smiled at the king and his best friend, the prince. "Then I will see you, my prince, and the others at Point Death, just north of the river of pitch in two days."

"Be careful," said the king. "No telling how far this rebellion has spread. Just make sure you deal with one of High King's men. He should be able to get you a boat. And may God speed."

The wizard bowed, then hit the lever controlling the burner. Fire leaped high into the opening of the aircraft's envelope causing the craft to skid across the ground for a few feet, then climb into the air.

Thirty men had come by boat. They landed as near to Susan's Pond as they could get. It was the narrowest part of the Ribbon Lands, less than a hundred yards wide. Four of the party, Stometz, Moetta, Steward, and one of the fishermen stood just north of the others. They were to act as guards. Each had a rifle in his hands, and several clips of extra ammo. Each of the men had told the others that they really didn't want to shoot anybody, just wanted to stop them from leaving Newland. But each of the four secretly hoped that he would get the chance to use his weapon, and to see what it could really do to a living person.

The other men were split into teams. Some dug the holes, others poured the mixture of rocket propellant and black powder into metal containers or stuck in the detonators. Several of the men strung wire between the charges, and connected them to a battery that would be used for triggering the explosives.

All the preparations were almost finished when a group of twenty-five pilgrims, heading for Jerusalem, approached the four gunmen from the north.

"Peace," yelled the old man leading the group. Because of the dark, the leader was still too far away to see the weapons in the four men's hands. "We come obeying the king's law, to go to Jerusalem."

"Get back," yelled Moetta at the top of his voice. "No one is leaving America II--not for a long time."

The old man drew closer until he was close enough to see the weapons pointed at him and the others. "What is the meaning of this? We come by the lawful decree of King and Queen Bounteous."

"You are cowards and traitors. Go back to your homes immediately," Moetta yelled, pulling the bolt back and chambering a round in his rifle.

"The others that have come with me must decide for themselves what to do, to obey you or to obey the king. But I myself chose to obey my king, and High King over him."

The old man stepped forward and began to go around the four when Moetta's rifle roared, sending half a clip full of bullets through the old man, and almost cutting him in two. Moetta stared at the mess that had once been a human being, and smiled.

"You idiot. You didn't have to do that." Stometz yelled. "He wasn't a threat to us."

Moetta pointed his gun at Stometz. "You have called me an idiot one time too many."

He pulled the trigger, and watched as the professor dissolved into bloody pieces before him. He then jammed a new clip into his weapon and began firing into the crowd of pilgrims. Steward and the fishermen, hesitated for only a moment, then following Moetta's example, and began firing their guns into the crowd. When all of the guns were empty, the three stared at the dead, bloodied and piled haphazardly before them in the dirt. They smiled at each other.

"That should teach everybody what happens to deserters and traitors," said Moetta.

The airship was descending. It had been as high as eight thousand feet when it was over Hastedia Compotu, to avoid as much of the poisonous smoke and polluted atmosphere as possible. But now the wizard allowed his machine to descend to a lower altitude as it left the terrible black lands. He was making good time, the Ribbon Lands were just below him. He would play it safe and follow them back to the mainland. After all, he did not want to have to ditch the airship on the open sea if something went wrong. It was a little longer, but he should still be able to make the mainland by noon. That would give him all afternoon to find and arrange for the needed boat.

And there was a second reason he had decided to follow the Ribbon Lands. He wanted to see what the rebels were up to. But he would have to stay plenty high and out of the effective range of their bows and arrows, and their rifles, too, if they had them. The wizard looked at his altimeter; it read just a little over forty five hundred feet. Plenty high enough. He checked the backpack that he had brought with him, and pulled out a pair of binoculars. It was still dark but getting lighter by the minute. He would have a good view of the ground below in just a few minutes.

Klote knew that evil had been loosed in Newland, and right now it seemed that everything good was being ruined, but he also had a lot of confidence in his king, and was convinced that Bounteous, with the help of High King, would certainly win the war. And besides, he was kind of enjoying the adventuresome side of things right now. In fact he had almost forgotten he had just recuperated from being wounded by an arrow, and that he had almost died.

Prince Rustlipper, Princess Windella, and Mary Ellen Toffer led the fifteen children on a little known trail that the prince had discovered years before, when he had first mapped Newland. The trail was actually more of a wash than anything else, but would lead them right to the edge of Hastedia Compotu. In the prince's backpack were the last of the leaves from the Tree of Life. Behind him was Windella. She carried a small cage that contained two snow white homing pigeons that could be used to ferry messages to the king if needed.

The group had with them three small donkeys that were burdened with heavy packs containing the group's food and water as well as blankets and some incidentals. The animals would accompany the group only as far as the border of the

Land of the Dead. There they would be set free, for there were not enough leaves for all of the group and the donkeys, too.

They had made good time considering the young age of the children, but to the prince they never seemed to be going quite fast enough. "Now let's try to hurry," he would say from time to time. But the children, already tired, wanted nothing but to sit down and rest and maybe take a nap. After all, it was still dark.

But they did not have that much farther to go. Ahead of them, over some rolling hills would be the Great Hardwood Forest. Rustlipper knew a special trail that cut straight through. And when the forest ended, there would be the low mountains that marked the edge of Hastedia Compotu, and finally the dead lands themselves. He wondered how the children would do walking across that accursed land.

The smell of smoke awakened the prince from his thoughts. He had forgotten all about the fire in the Great Hardwood Forest. He now hoped that the fire hadn't gotten this far north yet. But if it had, what would he do? He would just have to find another way to get to Hastedia Compotu, that's all. But it had been so many years since he had been in this area, and now he had an enormous responsibility. "Please help us, Dear God," he whispered. "Please help Your lowly servants, and the children, too.

"Mary Ellen, here are some healing leaves. Please give everybody one of them. There's gonna be a lot of smoke for us to breathe pretty soon."

They were about a mile to the south of him when he first spotted the men. Wizard Klote began trying to count them, but they were still a little too far away for that, but not so far away that he could not see the pile of dead bodies on the ground. "My dear God, what have they done?" the wizard whispered to himself. He hit the lever that controlled the burner, to put a few more hundred feet between him and the ground below, just in case. It was beginning to dawn upon the wizard that war was something quite different from an adventure.

"There--look, it's that airship the prince and his fat friend enjoy flying around in," Moetta yelled to the others. Instantly Barton Steward swung his rifle to his shoulder, took aim at the flying machine and began shooting. The fisherman did the same.

"Cease fire! It's out of range. And besides, the ammunition that we have with us is all that there is, since those fools blew themselves up and all of Dentrosa, too."

Besides, Moetta knew a better way to bag the airship. They had brought two of the LAWs with them. "Barton, get me those LAWs, fast." The student dropped his rifle and ran to the pile of supplies, picked up the two metal containers, then ran back to Moetta.

The weapons were disposable, one shot rockets, originally designed to give ground soldiers a lightweight, anti-tank weapon to use in close combat. Moetta grabbed the launch tube out of its container, shouldered the weapon, and yelled for everybody to stand clear as he took aim at the airship. He pulled the trigger. The small rocket that exited the tube did not ignite properly. It trailed a weak stream of smoke, went about one hundred feet, then fell harmlessly to the earth.

CHAPTER TWELVE

Moetta screamed, cursing wildly. He grabbed the second LAW, aimed it at the airship and pulled the trigger. This one worked perfectly. The rocket left the disposable tube with authority, headed straight for the envelope of the airship, hit one of the light metal girders supporting the fabric, and exploded, ripping open a huge hole, and weakening the superstructure.

The men with Moetta cheered loudly as they watched the airship spin toward the earth out of control. The gondola crumpled like cardboard upon impact. Then the heavy envelope crashed down on top of it. The men ran over to the wreckage and began ripping pieces away, but it was almost a half an hour before they finally got to the gondola and its occupant. The wizard was very seriously injured, and would probably not survive.

In the center of a large pentagram drawn on the warehouse floor were six black robed figures, five of them stood around the leader, Cody Santar, the High Priest. Cody, bared his left wrist, then drew the blade of the ceremonial knife across his flesh, and watched the blood flow out of the wound and drip onto the floor. The knife was then passed on from convert to convert, each cutting his left wrist, until all present had been initiated into the secret coven. The six then kneeled on the red, sticky floor, and bowed their heads. The high priest said but a single word: "Enter". Satan and the five demons standing at his side smiled, then leaped toward the human followers, and entered them.

Immediately the six humans convulsed and writhed on the ground in their own blood, then were still. Cody was the first to awake. He arose, walked over to the nearby table, opened the first aid kit that was there, and bandaged his wrist. Next to the kit was a large bowl full of small leaves. He put one of these into his mouth and chewed it, then put several more into his pocket. When the others awoke, they did likewise. They were now prepared for their unholy mission, to locate someone who knew the whereabouts of the fruit from the Tree of life. Surely Prince Rustlipper would know where the fruit was if anyone did. Or perhaps the fool, Klote. They would find these two, and when they did, they WOULD convince them to tell of their secret hiding place. The convincing would be the fun part.

Moetta hurriedly glanced through the papers they found in a pouch next to the unconscious wizard. He came upon a small parchment with the king's seal upon it. He stopped and read it:

> **Greetings from Bounteous, ruler of Newland: My faithful servant, the Wizard Klote, is directed to procure a sailing ship and crew that will be used for royal business. Please assist him in every way that is available to you. Any expenses that result form this project are guaranteed to be paid by King and Queen Bounteous. And since this is a most urgent project, may God abundantly bless any and all who help my servant complete his important task.**

Attached to the parchment with a paper clip was a map of Newland with a thick red line indicating a route that began at the royal castle, went east along the foothills south of the Holy Mountain, then made its way to the Great Hardwood Forest. The red line then became dotted until it exited the forest and entered the Land of the Dead. There was a question mark next to the dotted line seemingly indicating some doubt as to the actual route. But once the line entered Hastedia Compotu, it was solid red again, and made straight for the coast where it ended at a "X" next to the sea. Under the "X" was a note that said: Prince Rustlipper and party.

"May I see that," asked a tall figure in a black hooded robe. Behind him were five other strangers. Moetta noticed that the leader's left wrist was bandaged when he reached for the map.

Moetta quickly pulled the map and parchment out of reach. "And who, may I ask, are you?"

"My name is Cody Santar. I, and my followers are patriots like yourself, dedicated to the overthrow of Bounteous and his entire system. But we are on another mission quite different from yours. Let me explain. Shortly after you and your men left Dolphin Point and headed here, the king and some others took the kidnapped children out of the castle. We are quite sure that they will try to get the children out of America II as quickly as possible. Our mission consists of liberating the children from our enemies, and disposing of the kidnappers."

"Well, you don't have to worry about them getting the children off America II," Moetta said. "Because my men and I aren't letting anybody past us. In fact, if everything works out right, America Two will soon be an island, totally isolated from the mainland."

The tall figure tried to smile, an act that looked strangely unnatural. "What you and your men have done and are doing is quite commendable, and will surely be remembered once a democracy has replaced our present dictatorship. But this I say as advice, my comrade, do not underestimate your enemy, for unless I am mistaken, I believe that the wizard was on his way to Jerusalem to get help, possibly a boat or ship of some sort, to get the children back to the mainland." The figure stared at Moetta expecting a response.

"Well, again you don't have to worry, because the wizard is over there, and it looks like he's not going anywhere soon. So if he was the one going for help, that help will never arrive." Moetta pointed to the wreckage.

The stranger quickly ran over to the gondola, and made his way through the wreckage to the wizard. Klote was covered with blood; his skin was a deathly white, and his breathing shallow. Cody grabbed the wizard's hair and slapped Klote's bloody face. "Wake up, fool." Nothing happened. Cody slapped the wizard again. Klote opened his eyes slowly. He was in great pain, and groaned weakly.

"Where is the fruit from the Tree of Life," Cody demanded.

"I--I shall not tell." Klote closed his eyes, but another slap from Cody brought the wizard's eyes wide open again.

Cody reached into his pocket and pulled out some of the healing leaves, and waved them in front of Klote's face. "Tell me where the fruit is and you may have some of these."

"Ah--ah--No..."

"Fool, do you want to die like this, far away from all your friends, and surrounded by enemies?"

"Not--not by myself...."

"You ARE by yourself. Look around you. You will die here in pain and among your enemies. Is that what you want."

"Not by self--God is Friend--He's here..." The wizard was dead.

Cody returned to Moetta and those next to him. "Let me see the papers." Satan tried to smile through Cody's flesh. "As I said before, you and your men are doing a superb job.

But we still need to rescue the children and punish those who abducted them."

"Well, I guess it's O.K. Anybody who's against the king and dictatorship is on our side. Here let me show you what we found in the gondola." Moetta handed the hooded figure the parchment and the map.

The tall stranger quickly read the parchment, then stared intensely at the map as if he were memorizing it. When he was finished, he handed it back to Moetta, and walked toward the five others with him. He spoke softly to them: "You all know what to do." Without another word the five headed northeast, toward Hastedia Compotu. Cody returned to Moetta. "Now, my comrade, I beg the use of one of your boats, for I have something quite important that must be done at Jerusalem."

The king sat silently on the balcony that was outside a small room in the castle. Next to him was Michael; both were in a meditative mood. Queen Bounteous, Guardian, Gabriel, as well as his daughter-in law, Princess Rainey, and all of his grandchildren, and great-grandchildren, were gone from Newland. All had been summoned by High King days before to stay with him in Jerusalem and await the outcome of events in Newland. So the castle was deserted except for the two.

Finally the king spoke. "It almost feels like we're all alone in the whole world, my friend--abandoned. I know, I know, before you say it: the Lord is still with us. But without Eleea and Gabriel here, and the others..."

"I know, my king. But it is not as strange as it may seem, for you and I have much in common. We were--no, are warriors, and right now, Newland is at war--a perfect place for such as you and I to be."

The king reached over and patted his muscular friend on the shoulder. "Perhaps you're right, Michael, but I sure don't feel like a warrior just sitting here. And on top of that, warriors need information about what's going on around them. Sure wish we knew how Rustlipper, the wizard, and all the others are doing."

"Rest assured, my king, when we need to know something, High King will make sure we get all the information necessary to do our job. I have found this out in the many thousands of years that I have fought for him." He smiled at Bounteous knowing how hard it was for his friend to wait.

Prince Rustlipper urged the group on. He, Princess Windella, and Mary Ellen each carried one of the smaller children on their shoulders. They were all nearing exhaustion. The children could not go much farther without rest. But the fire in Hardwood Forest was less than a mile away, and blowing in their direction. They had to get through the forest before the fire surrounded them or cut them off. And besides, they had to be near Hastedia Compotu, if this was indeed the trail he thought it was--the one that led directly through the forest. Doubt entered the mind of the prince, for it had been such a long time since he had tramped through this forest. He looked around him carefully, but could not see a single landmark he recognized.

The prince stopped and put the little girl that was riding on his shoulders lightly on the ground. "Let's rest for a few minutes. Give the children a quick drink, then let's be on our way again."

CHAPTER TWELVE

"I pray the trail is true, for the smoke is getting thick," said Windella. "The fire cannot be very far away from us."

"I know," said the prince. "If this smoke gets much thicker we may have to give the children more of the leaves, and we have so few of them left."

Windella smiled at the prince. "My prince, do you remember the danger that you and I faced together, long ago, or at least perceived danger?"

Prince Rustlipper had not smiled in hours, but now he did. "I remember. And if my recall is correct, it wasn't too far from this very spot. But by the grace of God we survived back then, and now may our God be gracious to us once again."

He got up, put the child back onto his shoulders. "Guess we better get moving," he said, already heading east, down the trail through the thick forest around them.

"Everybody take cover," yelled Moetta.

He waited ten seconds, then touched the two wires to the battery. The ground bounced under him, and he was deafened by the tremendous concussion of the explosions. Rocks and dirt fell all around the group for some time.

Finally the professor yelled, "All clear." The men stood up cautiously, and looked around them. "Everybody O.K.?" Moetta asked.

They were. And what was even better was the fact that their hard work had been a success. They no longer stood on a continent connected to the mainland by a narrow ribbon of land. They were on an island. The explosives had done their job, and had blasted a channel seventy feet wide through the narrowest part of the Ribbon Lands. The men watched the

Mediterranean Sea swirl through the gap and fill it. The men, filthy from sweat and the falling dust, first smiled, then cheered, and began pounding each other on the back. They liked the taste of victory.

"Good job, men!" yelled Moetta. "Nobody's gonna get to the mainland now," he said smiling, his white teeth contrasting strongly with his filthy face.

The majority of Newland had arisen from the sea when the tremendous pressures created by thermonuclear explosions had forced the earth to buckle. This new land was then joined by the part called Hastedia Compotu, also the product of thermonuclear explosions. So it was fitting that the death of Newland should be initiated by the same forces that had brought her into existence.

Dentrosa was gone, vaporized. But the blast had done much more than simply eliminate a small island, it had weakened the very foundations of the Newland continent itself. Most of the people near the northern shores had been killed by the tidal wave created by the explosion on Dentrosa, so there were few who saw the land itself slowly crumbling into the sea, meter by meter. Already more than twenty miles of what had once been Newland lay under the Mediterranean sea, and the process was speeding up. Newland's death was at the most only weeks away.

They were more than five miles inside Hastedia Compotu. Prince Rustlipper left the group behind to rest while he climbed one of the small conical hills to have a good look around. When he reached the top, he sat down and looked at the land ahead of him. It was as ugly as he remembered it. Colorless, burnt, and blackened earth, smoking pits, and deep gullies filled with stinking pitch. Lifeless ponds emptied their poisonous, yellow water into some of the gullies with pitch producing a strong acidic steam that was blinding if one was too close.

The prince pulled out a small collapsible telescope that had been a birthday present from the wizard, and looked through the instrument. There it was, fifteen miles ahead, maybe a little farther, the sea, the place where he and the others would be rescued. And for the first time, he began to think that they might just make it. He might really be able to save the children, and get everybody safely out of Newland. Prince Rustlipper smiled.

He swung the telescope toward the west to look at the fire behind them. The smoke from the trees climbed high into the sky, polluting it almost as badly as the smoking pits polluted the land around him. The forest had been one of the most beautiful on earth. Soon only the skeletons of trees and white ashes would remain on a burned, dead ground.

Then he saw something move. There, about two miles behind his group. He focused the telescope. Men. Three, no, five men, moving swiftly across the blackened soil of Hastedia Compotu. They were almost invisible because of their black robes. The icy chill that ran down the prince's spine told him they were evil. He jumped up, and ran down the hill toward the others. Somehow he had to get the children to safety. Somehow.

CHAPTER THIRTEEN

But the day of the Lord will come like a thief
in the night; in which the heavens shall pass
away with a roar, and the elements shall melt
with fervent heat, and the earth also
and the works therein shall be burned up.
2 Peter 3:10

Prince Rustlipper sat on a boulder near the entrance of the cave and finished the note:

Father, we are being followed. Please help us. We will wait for you in the cave of the hill with twin peaks, almost due west of the castle, and just north of the great ravine. You will recognize the place by the pile of animal bones outside. So far all of us are safe, but we fear that the evil ones may find us at any time. Please hurry. Your son, Rustlipper

Windella brought one of the pigeons to the prince. He carefully folded the note and slipped it into the small container on the bird's leg, then tore off a small portion of a healing leaf and put it into the pigeon's mouth before releasing it. He watched the bird take off, climb for altitude, then circle to get its bearing before heading straight for the castle. "May God give you speed and a safe journey my little friend," Rustlipper whispered in hope.

The king and Michael stood on the balcony. Below them, filling the courtyard, were thousands of his subjects. The king held up his hands trying to silence the yelling crowd. But it was hopeless. The people were near riot, some shouting one thing, some another, but almost all shaking fists at the king. A few began throwing fruit, then rocks. They began chanting in unison: "Down with the king. Long live liberty. Down with the king. Long live liberty." Over and over again until the king finally lowered his hands and shook his head sadly. Tears ran down his thin face.

More rocks sailed through the air. One struck the king in the jaw, but material things could not harm the king's spiritual body. Michael, on the other hand, had to duck several times to protect himself.

"Come, my king. We must go to Jerusalem. They have chosen the path they wish to follow."

"But we'll have to go through that crowd to leave the castle. They'll tear you to pieces, Michael."

"When High King gave Gabriel and I the plans for this castle, it included a secret passageway. Come, I will show you."

They started slowly backing toward the doorway behind them to leave when they spotted the white pigeon. It circled high overhead, then dropped quickly toward the king and Michael, landing on the king's finger. Bounteous quickly retreated to the room behind them, pulled the note from its container, and read the note from Rustlipper before showing it to Michael. "We've got help them," said the king.

Michael motioned the king to follow him. The huge man lead the way moving through the hallways and down the stairs with the grace of a cheetah. He headed for the basement, went directly to a stone wall, and looked for a particular stone. He pushed hard on it when he found the right one.

CHAPTER THIRTEEN

Immediately a section of the wall slid away revealing a passageway filled with cobwebs. Michael grabbed a torch off the wall and lit it, then burned away the cobwebs before stepping through the opening. They heard a series of loud crashes upstairs as the crowd broke through the heavy wooden doors at the front of the castle.

"We've got to hurry, sir. It would not do for them to find our secret." As soon as the king stepped through the doorway, Michael pulled the false wall back into place, then led the king quickly down the passageway.

Over two hundred thousand people encircled the city of Jerusalem waiting for their black robed leader to give them the signal. Finally, Cody spoke. "Let us destroy everything in our path," he cried. "Let us show High King that it is we who are in charge and not Him." Satan smiled through Cody's flesh then yelled the command: "BEGIN!"

The hordes cheered, then began their advance through the streets of the holy city, burning, and destroying. Occasionally the mobs would find a human being in hiding, these were quickly killed as sacrifice to their leader. Slowly, from all sides, the mob worked their way toward the center of the city, toward the holy temple and its grounds.

Eleea, Gabriel, and Guardian waited expectantly, watching the doorway to the temple, waiting for High King to appear. Around them were five or six thousand other people who had chosen to put their trust in High King. Eleea was happy for those around her, but there were so few compared with those who had chosen to rebel.

Guardian seemed to knew her thoughts. "A remnant has chosen God, my queen. It has always been so."

The secret passage had taken the king and Michael to the top of Holy Mountain. Omega now unsheathed his sword, and aimed it north, over Newland. A series of brilliant flashes of lightening lit the evening skies, dancing across the northern part of Newland. When it ended, everything north of Holy Mountain was on fire. Every living thing, human, animal or plant was dead. Only the lands south and west of the holy mountain range were yet untouched. "Come my king. Let us go quickly and find our prince and the others."

Abaddon smiled as Satan's followers worked their way through Jerusalem toward his little surprise. Buried just outside the temple wall was one of the Norsac's warheads. He and his followers had stolen one of the devices from Dentrosa before the explosion, had repaired it, and planted it where it would do the most harm. When it detonated, the temple, and all of the faithful in the courtyard as well as the thousands storming the temple would be obliterated. He laughed to himself. He would wait until the very last second, when all of the rebels were within sight of their goal, when they could taste victory, then blow them all to atoms, and the eternity they deserved.

CHAPTER THIRTEEN

The smoke from the pits was all around them, as they walked toward the south, toward the Ribbon Lands, leaving Hastedia Compotu. The king and Michael had found the prince and his party. All were dead. Michael had buried them, and God had restored Michael's office of Archangel to him. The king was dwarfed by the mighty angel next to him. After about an hour, the king quoted a scripture:

He who believes in Me,
though he were dead yet shall he live.

"Do you believe this scripture, Michael?"

"Indeed I do, my lord."

"I too. So then, somewhere my son and the others live."

The two continued to talk as they walked across Hastedia Compotu. Finally Michael stopped and faced his king. "My king, the time has come for me, as Omega, to put an end to all of your lands and subjects. High King awaits you at Jerusalem. Go to him my king and friend, and I shall join you shortly.

The king looked at the angel with love in his eyes. "Michael, do what you must. I shall be waiting for you inside the Temple courtyard." The king disappeared.

Michael pulled out his great, silver sword, pointed it before him, then turned in a complete circle. Lightening exploded from the skies. All of Newland was in flames. When the fires died out, the land would be as dead as it had been when Maddox and Eleea had first stepped foot upon its barren soil. He took one last look at the country where he and his friends had lived for the last thousand years, then departed. There was one last thing to do before he joined his friends in Jerusalem.

And the devil who deceived them was cast
into the lake of fire and brimstone,
where the beast and the false prophet are also,
and shall be tormented day and night forever and ever.
Rev. 20:10

Michael found Satan outside Jerusalem in his hideous spiritual body. Satan had discarded Cody's body. It had been too confining for the things he now wanted to do. The two spiritual giants faced each other. Satan had his great sword in his hand. "So, black angel filth. We finally meet, and there is no one to save you this time."

Satan had been powerful throughout his existence, but he had never really understood that his might and strength had came from the Lord. And on this day, there was no strength left to him. Michael walked over to the demon, yanked the sword out of the demon's hand, and cast it away. Then he grabbed the evil one securely and pulled him high into the heavens, toward the spot that had been reserved for him and those like him, and cast him into the eternal Lake of Fire.

With his task finished, Michael turned, and headed back to earth, toward the holy city of Jerusalem.

And they went up on the breadth of the earth
and surrounded the camp of the saints
and the beloved city, and fire came down from God
out of heaven and devoured them.
Rev. 20:9

Michael was greeted with smiles from the king and queen and the others with them. Immediately there was a commotion among the crowd of saints--High King had come out of the temple. Every knee bowed before Him.

"So, My beloved, we are all here. And now time, as you know it, draws to a close."

Abaddon watched as the thousands of Satan's followers reached the temple wall. He smiled, then detonated the warhead, and watched as everything within miles was vaporized. But he had not counted on two events which quickly took place. First, the fire from the nuclear device continued to spread until the entire earth, and then the heavens were consumed with it. And second, two strong hands, belonging to an angel of God, yanked him high into the air, then farther away, to the darkest part of the heavens, and cast him into the place of eternal torments.

All those who had been in the temple's courtyard stood together on Apartia. Their eyes were glued upon the Lord. Michael whispered to the king and queen "Now comes the good part."

"What do you mean?" whispered the queen.

"Watch," said the angel.

"Behold, I am making all things new "
Rev. 21:5
And I saw a new heaven and a new earth,
for the first heaven and the first earth had passed away
Rev. 21.1

THE BEGINNING

About the Author:

J.E. Kirk spent most of his childhood moving from place to place: St. Louis Missouri, Little Rock Arkansas, then Florissant Missouri. After graduation from Hazelwood High School, he served for four years in the United States Air Force as an airborn radar technician. After his discharge, he has had a varied work history that has included positions as an electronic technician, probation and parole officer, motorcycle salesman, social worker, and non-denominational chaplain in a county jail.

Jim completed a B.S. in Psychology from Southwest Missouri State University in 1970, and a B.A. in Biblical Studies from Grand Canyon University in 1985. His hobbies include painting in oil, watercolor and acrylics.

Presently the author lives in Glendale, Arizona with his wife, Ann, and his dog, Uboo.

At your local Christian book store or use this handy page for ordering:

Apogee Arts Press

Box 238
5126 W. Olive Ave.
Glendale Az. 85302

Please send me _______ copies of
The Last Shall Be First. I am inclosing $8.95
plus $2.50 per book for handling and postage.
Enclosed is ________.

Ms/Mr/Mrs:______________________________
Address:________________________________
City/State:_______________Zip___________
Telephone: (   )_____________________

Please allow 4 to 6 weeks for delivery.